BARBARA SPENCER

TIME
BREAKING

Matador
9 Priory Business Park
Kibworth Beauchamp
Leicester LE8 0RX, UK
Tel: (+44) 116 279 2299
Email: books@troubador.co.uk
Web: www.troubador.co.uk/matador

ISBN 978 1848767 331

British Library Cataloguing in Publication Data.
A catalogue record for this book is available from the British Library.

Typeset in 12pt Sabon MT by Troubador Publishing Ltd, Leicester, UK
Printed and bound in the UK by TJ International, Padstow, Cornwall

Matador is an imprint of Troubador Publishing Ltd

On the wall above my bed is a picture of a graveyard that I took on my mobile. It's a bit blurred, I was crying when I took it; but in my mind's eye I can still see daffodils swaying in the breeze and read the words engraved on the polished granite headstone. I've seen the graveyard twice now and may never go back. So why do I keep it? Perhaps as a reminder of how things might have been.

ONE

I glared at Mum and Dad, my face buried in my cereal. Why *do* they have to start getting at me when I'm not even awake? I took a giant-sized spoonful of cornflakes, knowing it would divert the dreaded lecture.

'Oh, for goodness sake, Molly,' snapped Mum, 'at least try to eat like a well brought-up girl.'

'I'm late,' I gurgled, spitting milk and chewed flakes onto the table.

Dad rustled his newspaper loudly, adding to the glares whizzing round the kitchen walls – like a merry-go-round – although merry isn't the word I'd use, shitty-go-round, perhaps.

I stuffed in another mouthful, anything to stop me having to reply to the dreaded words: *And have you made up your mind yet?*

'Molly, this *is* your future we're talking about.'

So – I know it's my future. I knew that two million years ago when you started talking about it.

I glared – properly this time. Well, I'd done my best to avoid an argument but if that's what they want – okay! I know who'll win. After behaving like an orang-utan, I'll exit at speed, slamming the door, and go to school leaving Dad frustrated, rustling his newspaper loudly, and Mum crying.

Then I remembered. 'Not now, Mum, I'm late,' I said, trying to delay the inevitable.

And without awarding any prizes, I knew, one hundred percent positive, what the next two words were going to be.

'*But Molly – you never* sit down to talk about your options. Every time we bring it up, you avoid the issue. It's as if you don't care about your future and it's *so* important. Besides, you owe it to us to do well, after all the years we've slaved and done without just to give you the chance of a good future.'

No! I'm not having that – it's so *unfair. What about Meg? You know – my* **sister!** *At least half those years of slavery belong to her. And what about the years before we were born? Who were you slaving for then? So don't give me that crap, it wasn't only for me. Anyway, just so you'd like to know, my future's on hold for at least two years – so stuff it.*

I didn't say it, but I wanted to.

'Bye, Mum; bye, Dad.' And leaving my half-eaten breakfast – yet again – I grabbed an apple and a banana from the fruit bowl and scarpered, the traditional wail of, 'But Moll-ee ...' following me down the path.

Why do parents start the moment they see you in the morning? I have this picture buzzing round my head of trillions of motor neurons, all lined up and ready to go into battle the moment Mum – invigorated and refreshed after a good night's sleep – opens her eyes. Now, take my motor neurons. If they're feeling especially optimistic, they might manage to crawl out of bed by fourth period – usually maths – to which they drag themselves, match sticks propping up their eyelids because, yet again, I have had to go to school without breakfast to avoid a row.

I must have still been glaring when I fell into my seat in the bus, because the year-sevens up at the front shifted nervously in their seats. But I'm not into shrimp baiting, so I gave them a quick reassuring smile and tuned into my Ipod, still chunnering.

The word *chunnering* belongs to Grandma. She was brought up in the north – Cheshire or some such place – which is where the word comes from. She says, 'It's better than brooding, Molly, and sulking, and pulling a long face, so even if you're really upset with your mum and dad, stay unique and chunner.'

Grandma's like that and I wish she was my mum because she listens and understands, something Mum never does. And when I ask her why, which I've done hundreds of times, she replies: 'Don't forget, Molly, I've been through all of this, and worse, with your mother and look how she's turned out.' At which point we collapse into giggles and reach for the biscuit tin, because Mum's a genuine, gold-plated geek. Worse, she works for a Merchant Bank and is the world's greatest snob. Of course, she has to be great looking although Grandma says it's a wonder.

'But why can't she be ordinary, like other mums?' I whined, after running away and ending up at Grandma's for the third time in six months.

'My God, Molly, you surely can't want her to be ordinary, after all I've gone through,' she teased. 'When she was a child she was fat with crooked teeth, wild hair, *and* short-sighted. It cost me a fortune to get her straightened out. Of course that's part of her problem, she still cannot believe she's actually good looking.'

I wondered what the other part was, but Grandma refused to tell me. Instead, she gave me a hug, telling me how sorry she was I had a mother who was as blind as a bat when it came to her kids.

'I so hate my life, Gran. Why can't I be somebody else?'

'Like who?'

'*Anybody!* Anything would be better than what I go through every week.'

'By that I suppose you mean starving in Africa.'

My glare brushed off Gran like a biscuit crumb. 'Course I don't.'

'Then what do you mean, Molly?'

'A family; a real family with brothers and sisters who do things together. And a dad and mum that actually *like* being in the same room as you and don't spend all their time shut away working. I could advertise through the Internet – *new family wanted, apply in writing.*'

'But if you had a different family, you wouldn't have me,' she said, giving me another hug.

She's right there, but I still wish I had different parents.

I was still munching my way through my apple when I strolled through the school gates.

'MOLL-EE,' a chorus of frantic, hand-waving voices, 'OVER HERE.'

Over here's a sort of corner outside the science lab where two walls meet; sheltering us from wind, footballs, and annoying year-sevens. It's also the regular meeting place for the Misfits.

'What's up?' I said, quickening my pace just a tad.

'What's up with you more like?' Blue, my best and only real friend, peered into my face. 'No mascara.'

My faced flared.

'Parents?' she asked. 'Row?'

'No!' I laughed triumphantly, shaking my head. 'You'll not win that easily.'

'Win what?' said Jan, leaning both shoulders against the wall to do her back-straightening exercises. She started the Misfits, which is a club for loners and there's plenty of them – if you're too clever, too tall or too fat, weird or foreign. And although, at first glance, it looks a technical impossibility for Jan not to make friends, because she's got everything – right height, great teeth, fabulous figure and a skin without spots – once you know her, it's easy to see why.

4

She's totally self-centred and obsessed with boys – boys she likes, boys she hates, all boys – and she's not the slightest bit interested in anything else.

We don't do much and members don't stay long, except for the hard-core like Blue, me and Jan. Once members get accepted mainstream, they move on. But that's the point of the club. I mean, who wants to remain a misfit all their life? I know I don't. *I'd give anything to move on.* But when they go, they go with thanks for making it possible to survive. As Blue says in her lofty manner, 'Surviving the hostile environment of the school playground is a worthy life-choice.'

'Molly's been having pare-probs,' explained Blue, 'so I told her to walk away.'

By rights, Blue shouldn't be a misfit she's far too nice; her problem is she's too clever. Took half her GCSE's early, plays the violin like a dream and absolutely refuses to listen to pop music, which sort of rules her out for the club scene. Of course, Blue's not her real name – it's Annabel.

'And that didn't work,' I broke in, 'until we put five quid on it.'

'What is pare-probs?' asked Serena looking puzzled.

She's the latest to join the group and so far has only two expressions: puzzled and worried. We don't even know how she ticks yet because her English is still a non-event. I mean you can't be funny or witty in another language unless you can speak it fluently. She came from Estonia hidden in a truck. She'll only say it was horrible and sometimes she cries about it, especially the detention centre bit. But her dad's an electrician so now they can stay. Her family's still pretty poor and she hasn't any smart gear, which is a sin at most schools – ours included – but she's okay.

'Pare-probs,' I said, 'are problems with your parents.'

'So Mol here,' continued Blue, ignoring the interruption, 'is bloody determined to win the bet – you know what a tight git she is.'

'Awesome!'

That's Peter, who loves screwy words. He's another long-standing member and it doesn't take a genius to see why.

'You going to become a shrink, Blue?' he said, checking his immaculate-looking nails. He can't help it, poor guy, obsessed with his appearance. He had a hell of a time too – nicknamed Penelope by the losers in the schoolyard until Jan rescued him. Now he's her devoted slave and won't hear a word against her – which is good, 'cos we slag her off at regular intervals. But he's a good friend – hangs round with us for protection and gives brotherly advice, when needed.

She shook her head. She's got this sort of brown hair that stays tidy, and is never moved, like her. 'No, but I got sent to one.'

'Psychiatrist,' I said, automatically explaining the word for Serena's benefit.

'You didn't,' gasped Jan really interested now, her own news on hold.

All agog, Peter beckoned encouragingly. 'Go on, tell, there's a good girl.'

'Nothing to tell,' Blue said, her voice totally matter-of-fact. 'She said the issue problems Mum and I were having were due to my dad. I ask you, *how stupid can you get*, since I never knew him. And now he's responsible for Mum and me shouting.'

'So what happened?' Jan's eyes were open so wide her eyebrows had merged into her flowing fringe.

Blue shrugged. 'Didn't go again. The woman was a moron. She did say one sensible thing though, walk away and never start a fight. Anyhow, to cut a long story short, that's what we do – one of us walks out of the room.'

'Oh, is that all,' pouted Jan disappointed. 'So let me tell you my news. There's a new boy – totally fit – just arrived in the lower sixth. Hands off, and that includes you, Peter. I saw him first, so he's mine.'

When Jan becomes unbearable, spouting off about her latest catch, I make myself remember she was the one who rescued me from non-stop crying in the girls' toilets.

Fortunately, when I got home from school the house was empty, Mum and Dad both at work. It doesn't bother me; I'm quite used to it. I guess I've been an official latchkey-kid for two years ever since Meg, my sister, left for uni but we had the run of the house for years before that. I remember quite clearly my first day at school – it was Meg that walked me home, not Mum.

I was starving, so I quickly stuck some chilli in the microwave, making a beeline for the brown bread. It was only four-thirty and if I ate now I'd be okay to go training at seven.

I did my maths homework while I was eating – glad of the peace and quiet. To be honest, I keep my maths books as far from my parents as possible. I think I'd die of shame if they discovered I'm actually quite good at the subject and doing some pretty advanced work, 'cos that would start their generators running for yet another row. Anyhow, I got finished and, promptly at six-forty, I was waiting at the corner for my lift to the pool, where I go four nights a week to train.

I learned to swim when I was five and loved the feel of the water even then, so I begged to be allowed to join the local swimming club. Mum and Dad, who were in favour of anything that kept their kids busy and out of their hair, positively leapt at the chance. I got good and swam for the team which was better still, because now my parents didn't have to concern themselves about me on Saturday nights either – only long enough to arrange for someone to drop me off at the pool and collect me again.

It was only when they discovered, "*my little hobby to keep fit,*" as they called it, had just produced a County

Champion that it suddenly became a problem. That was when Mum decided sport was for dropouts, those who couldn't make it in the academic world. She didn't exactly talk about footballers, but she was glaring at my poster of Christiano Ronaldo when she said it. And she wasn't having a daughter who was a failure. I mean – *God! How low can you get!* But, to be truthful, it was more than that. She was scared my swimming might possibly demand some sort of commitment – you know like taking me places – which would interfere with their lifestyle of work and the pursuit of success.

I strolled out on to the poolside and there, right in front of me, was the new boy from school – Ben. For a second, the old scared feeling swept over me and I wanted to hide, which is pretty stupid. Here, it doesn't matter what you look like, only how you swim.

Still, even looking like a Neanderthal didn't stop me from checking him out and he looked pretty cool in swim gear. Visions of Jan, jealously wanting to scratch my eyes out, made me giggle. She wouldn't half be mad if I stole her new bloke. My float slipped and, trying to grab it, I staggered and fell over him. Me, in my three cozies – all baggy and holey – my hair confined under a passion-killer swim-cap, cluttered up with pull-buoys, float, water bottle and spare goggles; I almost felt sorry for him.

'Hello,' I gasped, pretending to be surprised.

'Er...'

'From school?' I said helpfully. 'I'm a friend of Jan's,' I added cheekily, interested in his reaction.

Right on cue, he blushes. 'Oh *yes*, hi,' he said, with a lot of emphasis on the yes.

I turned away, defeated – but only temporarily. No doubt about it, he hasn't a clue who I am. I comforted myself with the thought that he'd know all right, once he'd seen me swim.

It's not often anyone gets the chance to turn the tables on Jan. Don't get me wrong, we all love her to bits because she'll help anyone out at school, but that doesn't stop us hating her most of the time. And she's such a nympho. We excuse her behaviour by saying it's a disease – like acne – she can't help it. Still, it's pretty gross watching years-ten and eleven drooping about after her, wearing silly grins and goggle-eyed. So when you're presented with a golden opportunity to cut out one of the boys from the pack – and a sixth former at that – you don't hesitate.

I'm kidding, right! No way can a geek like me pull off a stunt like that in a million years. We might be sharing the same space four nights a week, five if there's a gala, but it won't make a jot of difference; I'm simply not girlfriend material.

Still, it's some comfort to know that even Jan hasn't a fan club, like me. Come the relays at the end of a gala, our lane is crowded with boys, even if they are only sprogs – nine and ten year-olds swimming galas for the first time – they are still there to cheer me on. I'm not proud of much in my life, but my dive is really something. A grab start, my body flung into overdrive, straight out over the water, totally horizontal as the water comes rushing towards me; then a length of the pool – not even stopping for unimportant things like breathing – arms and legs flying to get us into first place. I'm not conceited or anything but I really can swim. I sighed loudly, knowing I'd even give up swimming if I could be pretty and attract boys like Jan could.

'Molly?' It was one of the eleven-year-old hopefuls.

'Mm.'

'Can I talk to you?'

I plonked myself down on the bench pretending to be engrossed in the widths swimming. These are little kids that have their lessons before the seniors take to the pool. By the time it's finished they're so exhausted, the moment the air hits them they start shivering. But that's not the end to it. Their route to the changing rooms involves hacking a path through a jungle of madly chattering, semi-naked giants. Now, this would be a challenge even if you'd just climbed Everest; but if you're still struggling to swim a width and have just swallowed a gallon of water, it's impossible. The poor kids get completely stuck and stand there frozen to the spot, their arms hugging their little pigeon chests, shivering helplessly. They're such a pathetic sight you're forced to take pity on them, convinced they're about to succumb to pneumonia – even though it's eighty degrees on poolside. So I wade into the chattering swimmers and, using my elbows as a battering ram, make a space for them to get through.

'Mm,' I murmured again, hoping she'd take the hint.

'It's about school.'

'No, Hannah, *absolutely not*. I don't do school when I'm swimming – you know that.'

'I *know* but I *really* need your help.' The young kid's round face, under her close-fitting cap, gazed up at me as if I was the greatest thing since sliced bread.

'Go on – *but make it quick*.'

'Well, it's one of the girls in my class – she's being bullied.'

I glanced up from watching the weenies trying to get across the pool on their backs, without putting their feet down.

'Tell her to speak to her teacher.'

'She did but that's made it worse.'

'What do they do?'

'It started with her books – in the mud, you know …'

I fixed my eyes on a little kid who seemed in distinct danger of drowning as he struggled across the pool. I knew quite well that if he did go under I'd have to go get him because the lifeguard wasn't even looking, too busy chatting up one of the girls.

'Her mother says she's got to stand up for herself,' Hannah ended her woeful tale. No different from others I'd heard, but it still angered me.

'Okay,' I groaned, 'just this once but don't dare try it again, Hannah, I don't care how well you swim.' Hannah gave me a hero-worshipping half-smile. 'At swimming, I think of swimming, *got it?*'

She nodded enthusiastically, her whole face – eyebrows and all – bobbing up and down.

The little kids were climbing out of the pool, including the drowner, so I gathered my five-foot-eleven-inch length – all one hundred and eighty-one centimetres – together and strode off to help the boys get the lane ropes in.

Five minutes later I dived in, my body cutting its own symmetrical shape through the water, butterfly kicking to the surface, my left arm ready to curve through the air re-entering the water again to pull me forward. This was my joyous freedom, two hours of pushing my body to the limit, my brain switched off, a miniscule part focussing on the black line which told me how far I was from the wall. I counted my strokes, as length after length fell behind me in the warm-up. Emerging after the set to drink water and check my pulse, I fluffed water at Nick. He was supposed to swim behind me but usually spent his entire time trying to buffet my toes or pull on my flippers, so he could overtake me. I laughed at the sheer joy of doing something I loved.

I wasn't swimming in the same lane as Ben; he was in with the real fast boys. Girls are slower – fact of life. Still, I'm in the second fastest lane, next to it. But that's cool, because it made it easier to check him out. We always start training on front crawl but once we got on to main stroke he showed himself to be a flyer. Butterfly is the second fastest stroke, and the most difficult. He was poetry in motion. I looked up after the main set, in which I led our lane swimming breaststroke, and he winked at me across the lane ropes.

***

'Mum home?' I said as I opened the car door and slid in, my wet hair steaming in the cold air.

'Molly, for goodness sake, where's your hat?'

I fished it out of my bag.

'Yes. Mum's home. Homework done?'

I nodded not wanting to talk and sometimes Dad understands that, although understand isn't quite the right word. Accepts is a better word, because neither of them really understands how I feel. And that isn't rebellious teenager stuff. They haven't an inkling what it's like to climb out of that pool, after two hours of laughing and joking and serious stuff, full of energy; your body feeling a mile high without a single problem in the world. And you have to hold on to that feeling for as long as you can, because you know the moment you set foot indoors it'll vanish and you're stuck with those terrible spikes of anger that you want to hurl at your parents.

TWO

I cuddled my mobile to my ear. 'Gran?' You're not asleep are you?'

'Even if I was, Molly, I most certainly wouldn't be now. What's happened?'

'Well, nothing really,' I replied darkly, 'except that *they* want to come and watch me swim.'

'And you woke me up for that,' laughed Grandma, her voice sounding tinny at the other end of the line.

'But it's tragic, Gran. *Mum and Dad among my friends – I'll die!* I'll never be able to show my face at swimming again, especially if she's wearing her Jimmy Choos.'

'And your dad in jeans.'

Grandma broke into giggles and I couldn't help but join in. It's like we both think exactly the same things. Mum and Dad should not – ever – absolutely *never* – wear modern street gear. Dad, a learn-ed lecturer and writer about dead people, could *not* wear jeans; they made him look like a prisoner on death row. Mum was fine, except everything cost a million bucks *and* looked it. And Mum in trainers! I shuddered.

'Did this idea come from you, Gran?'

'You might say that. I actually think it's a good idea for them to find out exactly how good you are and why you want to be involved in sport.'

'But Gran,' I squeaked. 'How can I get my national times with them watching?'

'Don't be stupid, Molly, if you let a little thing like your parents stop you, you might as well give up now. You'll never be good enough to make it to the Olympics, where there'll be twenty-five thousand watching. Do you hear me?'

I sighed. 'Yes – I'm sorry.'

'And so you should be! When do you go?'

'There's worse.'

Grandma laughed. 'There always is.'

'We're staying in a religious retreat.'

'You're doing *what!*'

'*Yeah*,' I said, knowing Gran always knows exactly what I mean by the tone of my voice.

'Oh, Molly, this is *so* exciting. *Where?*'

'Dad says it's a seventeenth-century manor house. Belonged to a cavalier of all people. Anyway, it was bought by a Jesuit order, light years ago. They built rooms and stuff, and people go there to escape the world. Dad thinks the peace and quiet are just what I need.'

'*Quiet!* You're fifteen, for God's sake, Molly.'

I giggled, and we chanted simultaneously, 'I know it, you know it, but do *they* know it.'

Grandma sighed. 'Take loads of books. Sleep well.'

I clicked the switch and her matter-of-fact voice vanished, except that it was still in my head as was her face, kind and interested, so sometimes I forget she's no longer young.

Dad's newspaper has been temporarily replaced by a car map – or in his case several car maps – so he can plot the most historically interesting route to Millfield in Somerset, where the Championships are to be held.

Mum isn't going on at me either for a change, although I recognise this particular ploy from way back. She starts out convinced that if she leaves a subject alone, I'll come round. But after a few days, when nothing happens, she'll start having a go at me again.

As a result, though, I managed a humongous breakfast. Mum did cast an eye at my plate, after I finished a second bowl of cereal and was busily spreading peanut butter onto slices of wholemeal toast, and sigh vocally. But since my frame is slight – the complete opposite of her teenage years – she can't say much.

Still, she's said plenty in the past. For as long as I can remember she's been apologising for my height.

'I'm *so* sorry my daughter's *so* tall, it would be so much easier all round if she was normal, but she *has to* stop growing soon.'

She'd actually feel better about it if she knew where my height came from. I once joked that even the milkman was short but Dad got all peppery at that, so the subject of my genes is left well alone.

Meg, my sister, is quite properly five feet six inches tall – one hundred and sixty-eight centimetres – which she arrived at shortly after her sixteenth birthday, and I've never known Mum say one nasty word about her. Despite such good fortune, she still got the hell out the moment she could. She's nearly twenty now, never comes home, and still resents me. She was the one that had to look after me when we were growing up – Mum and Dad were never there.

I arrived at school to find the same groups gossiping, exactly like yesterday, with one exception. Ben was talking to Jan by the bus stop. As I got off surrounded by year-sevens – like the BFG – he actually left her and, giving me a grin, came my way. In a state of total panic I took a step backwards. My height, dressed in a school skirt, white shirt and tie, is not a particularly pleasant sight at the best of times, even with mascara. I tower over the rest of the year-eleven girls, who always look as if they've stepped out of *Just Seventeen* magazine where everyone is dressed to kill. Grotesque is generally the politest word I can think of to describe my appearance.

'You swim great. Doing Western Counties?'

I nodded. 'Friday and Monday, if I make finals.'

'You will. I'm there Friday and Saturday, fly and free. I hear you're an out-of-this-world sprinter. You can count on me to cheer you on.'

I shifted uneasily from one hip to the other, wishing this conversation was taking place on poolside where I wouldn't have felt so awkward, not here at the school gates with Jan throwing steel barbs into my back as if it were a dartboard.

'Er … by the way, I don't mention swimming at school.'

Ben laughed. I could feel the deluge of barbs between my shoulder blades increase. 'You mean swimming isn't cool.'

Thank God, swimmers understand. Blue knows what my hobby is, and the Misfits, but they don't blab. If I'm having a real bad day, I convince myself they only keep it secret because they'd be too ashamed to be seen with me if it got out.

I grinned back, beginning to relax. 'Well, you know what it's like. Someone once told me …' I mimicked a high-class voice with long vowels. 'You don't *seriously* expect me to believe you do nothing for two hours, except swim up and down with your face in the water. How boring. What do you do, count tiles?'

Ben screwed his face up in pain.

'I crept away and for two weeks pretended I was ill so I didn't have to train. That's when I made up my mind to keep it quiet.'

'You mean the plebs think it's akin to train-spotting – a dork sport.'

I laughed, a sarcastic tinge colouring my voice, 'Until you make the Olympics – then you suddenly become the greatest.' I sighed enviously – *if only*. 'Do *you* keep it quiet?'

Ben shook his head. 'They all know,' he said casually. 'At my old school, I made sure I won all the swimming races and the cross-country, which kept everyone off my back until the next year.'

'I don't even go in for them,' I replied gloomily. 'Our lot would think I was showing off.'

'Let 'em. Okay, zipped it'll be. See you tonight,' he called loudly, before disappearing through the gates. I watched him saunter across the yard with a couple of mates. Obviously at home, even if he had only changed schools a few days before. How I wished I could be like him.

Hannah was waiting just inside the school gates, nervously kicking the gravel. 'That's Gemma.'

Clutching the door handle, waiting for the bell to ring as if her life depended on it, was a miserable-looking object. If you're being bullied your life *does* depend on it. No one can possibly understand what it's like, your world reduced to a tiny space in which – if you're extra-specially careful – you might be safe.

'I hear you got problems.'

She nodded, big eyes looking up at me as if I was the Good Shepherd.

'Which ones?' I said.

She pointed to the group strung out along the railings in the nonchalant pose of know-it-alls. None of them were any bigger than Gemma; in fact two were smaller. And I bet the only way they escaped being bullied was by becoming a hanger-on or acolyte, whose sole purpose in life is to fawn and flatter. Pointed iron bars had been cemented into a deep brick step and they were perched on top of it, their arms outstretched and laced round the spikes. They leered down at the milling school kids, seeking likely targets. It's funny, but if you've been a target you never forget that look homing in on you, it sends shivers down your spine.

The Misfits are world experts on bullying we spend so much time talking about it. Blue insists that girls are worse than boys because they're sneaky. I told her she only thought that because girls should be above that sort of thing. Though she's right in a way, girls don't need to descend to physical violence. They use slow torture – drip, drip, drip – until you have an ego the size of an ant, and are terrified of your own shadow. And you can't tell anyone because they don't actually *do anything;* only keep on at you.

'Okay, so Hannah and her friends are on escort duty – to and from your house *and* in the schoolyard – until you feel okay again. I'll deal with the boys.'

'You will? Aren't you scared?'

I gave her my special look, my eyes opening wide as if *scared* was a word I'd never heard before.

I thought about it during double English. Macbeth remained unread and, as far I was concerned, he could stay unread. I can never understand what the bloke is babbling on about. No one talks like that any more – so it's not relevant. It's no good calling someone the *greatest playwright of all time* if he's writing in a foreign language

There's two ways to deal with bullying in my school; the official way – which means you go to the head, who tries to persuade you that you're imagining it. Even if they do act, the bully only gets suspended for a week. It solves nothing and the bully generally returns to school seeking revenge. Then there's the unofficial way – which a few of us prefer, since it saves embarrassment all round and scares the shit out of the bully.

I was waiting after school, carefully blocking the boy's path with my size nines as he came out of the schoolyard.

'Want a word.' I smiled.

'What about?' His face wore that superior smirk which made me long to choke the life out of the little toad.

'A little bird tells me you're a bully. And – *I* – don't like bullies.'

That got him. He looked up startled and his two mates took a step back. *Great* – that's what I needed to see – that precious gap, telling the world they weren't really a party to it.

'And – *I* – particularly don't like bullies that carry knives and cut up girls' skirts, making them walk home in their knickers.'

'Piss off!' He took a step towards me and his hand reached aggressively for his pocket.

Big mistake.

Next second his knees crashed to the ground as I grabbed a large hunk of hair, while his arm began to scratch an itch in the centre of his back. I fished in his pocket, pulling out an unopened switchblade.

'You said?'

'So-rr-ee,' he mumbled.

'What was that? I have a hearing problem.'

'I said *sorry*.'

'That's better. Now, you see here, brat, I'm giving you a choice, which is real nice of me since you didn't give that kid a choice. We go right now to the head and show him your nice little knife or I take it for safe-keeping and you stop your little games – forever.'

'Not the head!'

His pals took another step back – this time reclaiming their freedom – as I released my adversary. *Some adversary.*

'No more Mr Nasty.'

'OK! I've said okay, haven't I,' he growled, rubbing his head furiously.

'Now, as to punishment ...'

His eyes flashed up. 'What do you mean *punishment?*'

'Well, the way I see it,' I said sweetly, 'there's three naughty little boys wandering around with too little to do. *So, I'm going to make you an offer you can't refuse.* You have to join one of the after-school clubs until the end of the summer term.'

'Us too!' exclaimed one of his followers. 'We didn't do it.'

'No, but you little worms went along with it – which in my book is worse. So come and see me tomorrow and tell me which club. And, don't think you can trick me; *I* – wrote the book, remember. I'll be checking up on you, and every time you don't attend I'll add a week to your sentence in the autumn term. *Capiche?*'

With a bit of luck, by the time they'd finished their sentence, they'd be so used to spending two evenings a week doing something interesting for a change, they'd actually like it and stay on – and stay out of trouble. If I stumbled across the head-boy I might mention it but I honestly didn't think they'd try to double-cross me. Blue calls me the BSG – the bloody soft giant – but the bullies don't know that.

One by one they slunk off, taking care to stay on their own until they were out of sight of the half-dozen year-elevens, who'd been propping up the railings at a polite distance – backup provided, no charge.

***

The truce lasted four days – which was the best we'd ever done – then Mum decided it was time she donned the *good parent* role for half an hour, which meant showing an interest in my schoolwork.

I don't know whether she tried it on with Meg, because Meg was extraordinarily devious and carefully buried information so Mum never saw it, leaving her with the impression that Meg got straight A's in everything.

But for me, it's always been different. She hates everything about me, my size, the way I dress, what I eat, how I talk, my swearing, my music. I'm convinced she believes she gave birth to a direct descent of the missing link. Whenever she gets the chance she's on my case, until I scream at her like a two-year-old – at which point she stops, delighted to think she'd been right all along.

So she looked in my school bag, which I carelessly left in the sitting room when I went off to train. I could have kicked myself for being so bird-brained. When I got back from swimming, all wrapped up in my nice little cocoon, she took a pneumatic drill and shattered it into pieces.

'I see you got a D for your last essay. I have to say your English marks this term are appalling; most of them appear to be C minus, which I sincerely hope isn't an indication of your GCSE results. It might be a good time to remind you they are less than two months away.'

'As if you ever let me forget,' I retorted angrily. In a few days I was swimming the most important race of my life. *Why couldn't she have waited to have a go at me? Surely, that's not too much to ask?* Any decent parent would have saved up the lecture for the beginning of next term or, at the very least, until after my race – but not her.

'Well, what are you going to do about it?' came the question I dreaded.

What could I do about it? If we tried to have a sensible conversation, I only had to mention the word swim and end of sensible conversation – because swim, swim, swim isn't exactly my parents' idea of a career choice. They want a daughter they can boast about to their friends; a gold-plated geek, who's a whiz at languages and swans off to study European Law or Merchant Banking. Sports Therapy, which I want to study so I can swim, doesn't exactly fit the bill.

'*What the hell do you want me to do about it?* I can't help it if I hate English.'

'Molly, you're not to speak to your mother like that,' said Dad. He shut the front door behind us, following me into the sitting room. 'It's so impolite. And how can you ignore English? It's the backbone of civilisation; without it we'd still be in caves trying to invent the wheel.'

Why the hell couldn't Dad get off the fence for once and have an independent view. He might be dull, but he wasn't seriously evil – like Mum.

I remember this programme on telly about a comic;

Tommy Cooper, his name was. One of his jokes reminded me of Dad.

"Stop letting your wife boss you around. Stand up to her. What are you, a man or a mouse?

Answer: I can't be a mouse, my wife's afraid of them."

That's Dad.

I glared and made to go upstairs.

'Haven't you anything to say for yourself?' Mum said.

I shook my head, remembering Blue.

'Well, unless we see some serious changes in your attitude towards your exams, you leave us no option but to stop you swimming until they are finished.'

'Jesus Christ, Mum! If you want to go snooping, why couldn't you have snooped in my maths book – I get sodding A's for that!'

'Don't you dare swear in this house, Molly,' said Mum, the sanctimonious bitch.

'THEN I'LL BLOODY LEAVE IT,' I screamed slamming the sitting room door as hard as I could. I stamped upstairs. *Bloody parents. I'd lost my bet, behaved like an orang-utan and –* I listened – *Mum was crying!*

So that's how we set off for Somerset – me sulking – Dad and Mum giving me the stranger treatment; scrupulously polite.

THREE

The journey from Exeter, where I live, wasn't too bad and, by taking a determined interest in Dad's route, by the time we got to Street normal relations had been resumed. But my penance, to explore as many old houses as Dad could squeeze in, was a tough one.

Then, because we were going to stay in a building which was so old it had once belonged to a Cavalier, Dad lectured me about the Civil War. He explained that only parts of England were involved. Most people went on about their own lives and stayed well clear of the fighting.

I gazed out of the window; the words, *if people in history can stay out of it, why can't I*, on the tip of my tongue. I stopped myself in time, remembering the truce. Instead I asked, 'Where do all the soldiers come from then?' A question which guaranteed a half-hour explanation as to why men, tied as vassals to a nobleman, were expected to fight if their Lord and master wanted them too – only Dad said *required them to*.

With an entry time of 1min19 for my hundred, I knew I'd probably be in the final heat of the Age Sixteen Breaststroke, so I had no need to hurry. I changed slowly, stopping to gossip with fellow competitors, finding out who was swimming, who was missing, and who was going out with whom, taking particular note of any new faces.

Competitive swimmers meet up regularly at Open Galas

and we pretty much know who'll make it through. In my case, though, my latest growth spurt has knocked a couple of seconds off my times which no one knows about yet. Quite simply it comes down to this; if I find myself neck and neck at the flags there's no way I'm going to lose – my arms are too long.

I was right, I am in the final heat. I dived in, reacting immediately to the buzzer. The two girls to my left, in lanes four and five, disappeared into the water already two metres ahead of me.

I began to settle, building my strokes as I'd been taught, watching the shoulders in front of me power through the water. I felt the acceleration before I saw it the fifty-metre wall rushing towards me, the shoulders of the girl on my left vanishing behind my eye line as I hit it, my feet planted firmly to thrust me back out into the choppy water of the turn.

On the return length, I could see the clock on the left of the scoreboard. I glanced up; I was okay – well on target. Now I could feel the fatigue creeping into my arms and realised I had slowed slightly. This is why we train so hard, so we can ignore the build-up of lactic acid. I reacted the only way I know – go faster. There was no one in sight, the water clear and flat in front of me, the lane ropes swallowing any turbulence. I slammed into the wall and stopped, turning to watch lanes three and four come in behind me, lane five trailing – out of push. The scoreboard stopped, as the last of the eight hit the wall, and the magic number appeared – 1:17:12. I'd done it – my trip to the nationals was booked.

I snatched off my cap and goggles, disappearing into the waves for my own private second of joy; then arms reached over to pat my shoulders and the referee's whistle sounded to release us. We dived over and under the lane ropes climbing out at the side; eight kids with the same ambition – to be the best.

I glanced back over my shoulder as I left poolside. Mum was sitting wreathed in smiles – disappointed that she didn't know any of the spectators so she could accept their homage.

It was a good championship for me, with all my heats scheduled for the first day. Ben was there and kept a seat for me while I raced. You can't hear people cheering – only a wall of sound. I reckon you'd hear Ben though; he nearly split my eardrums cheering his mates on. However, despite the fact that I drank gallons and gallons of juice and water, ate bananas and sandwiches, and was in the water for less than twelve minutes, I was knackered by the time I finished – but it was worth it. I was through to three finals and had three national qualifying times under my belt. Now, I had two days off before the finals on Monday.

After I'd changed, I met Mum and Dad by the car. It was about four o'clock and we'd been there since eight that morning.

'Hi, Molly!' Mum waved her hand gaily, as I made my way through the cars. 'Such a pity you couldn't have won *all* of your races, dear, but I'm sure you did your best. Still, you're going to have to watch that girl from Bournemouth, who beat you in the two hundred. She was in front of you in the hundred too, you know. You really will have to practise getting off the blocks more quickly. Never mind, I asked Dad to time your race. He's got your splits and will go over them with you.'

He has my what! Bloody cheek! They only learned the word that morning and here they are taking over – world-renowned experts. The savage pain of disillusionment swept over me yet again.

My Mum and Dad are the type of people who, if you get one hundred percent ask why you didn't get one hundred and one, before saying a grudging, *well done.* Today, so far, I hadn't even got that.

'That's okay, Dad, you didn't need to bother, coach has already gone over the splits with me.'

'And did she notice you slowed down in that fourth length on the two hundred?'

'Yes, she did, but it's quite normal.'

'I don't think so, dear, because that's when you were overtaken,' Mum interrupted quickly.

'I ... *oh, it doesn't matter.* Let's go.' It wasn't any use explaining that I was only interested in qualifying for the two hundred, cruising in to a comfortable third place, confident that the two in front had been pushed to their limit.

We were heading southeast into Dorset where the Retreat, our lodging for the next two days, was located. I felt sleepy and took little notice of the countryside as we trundled at thirty miles an hour – Dad vigorously observing the speed limits – towards Sherborne. From there, we dived into a maze of country lanes, through villages that seemed old even without Dad telling me they were.

We stopped.

'Dad?' I said.

'Molly, come and look. It's the most *superb* example of a sixteenth-century house.' Dad actually sounded excited, an event he usually kept strictly for his work. At home, he's so calm he never ever uses superlatives.

He got out and I trailed miserably after him. Our truce was proving itself to be extremely hard work. A quick glance through the car window was all I needed.

He had pulled to a halt in the main village street; a seemingly endless row of houses that curved round a narrow track of road, scarcely wide enough for two cars to pass. Some were thatched and most were old, like a collage made from scraps of material. The house, he was drooling over, was tall with stout beams running up and down and from side to side; the squares of wash between the wooden beams dark brown in colour. Casement windows peered out below the eaves, tiny checkered replicas of the walls. It looked dreary and I couldn't imagine why anyone would want to live there, coping with ancient floorboards that creaked in the night and woke you up, making you believe in ghosts. I preferred the modern bungalow opposite with its square plainness; it would be cosy and snug in the winter.

'This is the village of Lingthorpe, Molly. I imagine the Retreat is probably quite near.'

Thank goodness.

'See,' Dad continued, enthusiastically patting a wooden beam on the side of the house as if it was his best friend. 'Even in Elizabethan times they used stone foundations to stop damp seeping up from the ground. These uprights are called studs and you can calculate the age of the house by their distance apart.' Dad lectured on, almost forgetting it was me, Molly, who hated history, in his delight at having a captive audience. 'Of course, everything was done by hand. They had only a few tools, not like today. Mostly they used a two-handed saw and a wonderful little gadget called an Adze …'

'*An Adze*! Dad, you can't be serious – how can you call something an Adze?'

'Of course it's called an Adze, Molly,' Dad's voice instantly sounded defensive. 'It resembles a garden hoe with a long blade. Craftsmen in Elizabethan times were very skilful, you know. Think about it; an ordinary house built by ordinary workmen, none of whom could read or write. Yet it has survived intact for five hundred years. Can you imagine anything modern lasting that long?'

I gazed at the patchwork pattern of wooden beams, like squares on a chessboard.

'See, Molly,' Dad repeated.

Bored already, I tuned out while Dad prattled on about floor joists and horizontal timber, listening again in time to hear him say, 'Elizabethans were smart, Molly, much smarter than the Stuarts who followed them. For instance, they used local materials because of the problem of transport.'

He pointed towards a dense line of trees, high-up on a hill in the distance, their silhouettes just visible over the rooftops. 'I expect if we visited that wood, we would find oak trees there which are direct descendents of this house.' He patted the wood lovingly. 'When the framework is finished, the open spaces in the walls are filled with wattle and daub, which to a layman are wooden sticks and mud. Now, look at the one next door.'

I swung round staring at the thatched cottage with its great fringe, every hair in place under a neat hairnet of wire. Some sort of greenery covered the whitewashed walls; a modern kitchen partially visible through bright sparkling windows. Beyond it, I caught a glimpse of a tailored lawn.

'Originally, there would have been a ground floor with a ladder up to the loft ...'

'Where the people slept, while the ground floor housed the animals in the winter. I do know something, Dad,' I moaned.

He smiled. 'But it's so interesting, Molly.' It wasn't, but my opinion doesn't count. 'Imagine a dozen people and animals living in one room.'

'I bet it ponged,' I said.

Before setting off again we strolled round the immaculately-kept houses; even I – ignoramus of all ignoramuses – aware that only posh people could afford to live here. Even the flippin' grass verges looked as if they'd been cut with nail scissors. I could just imagine the storm of letters to the local newspaper if someone found a pile of dog poo in their garden – God help the dog, that's all I can say.

Leaving the village the road forked, the wider of the two signposted: *Blandford Forum 8 miles*. The other, no more than a country lane, doubled back on itself shadowing a high brick wall that formed the boundary to some great mansion, its chimneys clearly visible above rusty-coloured copingstones.

Dad slowed, the narrow track twisting in front of us like a corkscrew. Long threads of grass brushed noisily against the side panels of the car as it crawled along; the meadow on our right falling away towards a river. Beyond it, the ground rose steeply in folds, like a pleated skirt, into a dense thicket of trees from where the oak had come to build the Elizabethan house.

The sunshine was still hanging on, although it was gone six o'clock. Around me were the first signs of spring; delicate fingers of light green tiptoeing along branches, patches of grass scattered with white daisies like polka dots. Dad stopped so Mum could drool over the countryside. I was drawn to the water, walking down through the flower meadow towards the stone bridge. The river flowed fast and deep, and so clear that banks of amber-coloured shale were visible on the riverbed, the current too strong for weed to grow.

'This might have been be the villagers' only source of water, Molly,' Dad said, joining me by the bridge.

I glanced up. 'No wonder they all got typhoid and died,' I replied cheerfully.

'I do wish you could break yourself of this silly habit of making childish statements.' Dad's voice was tight. He hates my sarcastic side-swiping at his beloved history. For him it's the truth, the whole truth, and nothing but the truth, whereas I like to mix it up a bit – it's more interesting that way. 'If that had been the case, the population in the countryside would have died out centuries ago.'

Leaving the lane, we swung into a drive guarded by an ancient stone gateway, cracked and leaning. On either side giant trees sprang from a wide-expanse of lawn, their trunks so vast it would take at least three kids – fingertip to fingertip – to span them and so high, they dwarfed the house, their canopy of leaves casting a deep shadow.

The house was built of stone and appeared rather battered, like an old granny who has seen better days but still stretches out welcoming arms to greet you. Its central section was long and narrow, while the wings at either end appeared shorn off, stubby, as if the builders had run out of stone before finishing the job. And, unlike the village, where houses had sparkling new glass in them, the tiny diamond-shaped panes were encased between narrow stone uprights, linked with strips of black lead. Mould had settled in the cracks and hundreds of years of weather had left a filmy residue on the glass. Dad called them *mullion windows* when I asked.

No one was about, so Dad went looking and returned with the manager. He could easily have been one of the original Jesuits – except for his modern clothes – the weight of sin giving him a lifeless, hangdog expression. He explained about meal times and the rules: no smoking, no telly, no loud voices – peace and quiet at all times. We had to make our own beds and clear the table after meals.

He wasn't exactly forthcoming though. 'It used to be a stable,' was all the comment Dad got out of him when he showed us to our rooms. In a separate block tucked behind the house, all you could say was they were clean; the furniture that awful bright brown colour that you buy in flat-packs – utilitarian – is the word I'm thinking of. With a miniscule shower room, it was a place to sleep in – nothing more.

The dining room was equally spartan and, even though electricity had been installed, remained gloomy and cold; its floor laid with flagstones and uncarpeted. Panelled in dark wood, the only feature of any interest was an elaborate staircase, so wide you could get lost in the shadows beneath. There was no furniture, except for a serving trolley on wheels and a vast rectangular table, which guests were expected to share. Through the serving hatch I caught sight of the kitchen; modern and cheerful with fridges and cookers, and one of those blue, fly-killer thingies buzzing away on the wall. Apart from the kitchen and the shower rooms, very little had been done to drag the building into the twenty-first century and I pitied the generations of children who had grown up in such forlorn surroundings.

As we sat down to eat, Dad tapped the table. 'This is an original,' he said approvingly. I hadn't even noticed it, so used to dumping myself down at one of the long melamine tables in our school canteen. This one had been built from the same dark wood as the walls panels, then polished and polished for hundreds of years until you could see your face in it. There were matching chairs and, when full, the table could have seated at least twenty people. We were at one end, a group of five at the other; so far away you needed a telephone to speak to them.

Dishes of food had already been placed on the table in front of us and I was stretching out my arm, to help myself from the enticing bowl of chicken, when a voice cut in.

'We will now say Grace.' The manager stood there frowning.

I froze, feeling my face dissolve into a furnace of fire, and I hastily pulled my hand back.

A party of four appeared in the doorway muttering their apologies and, embarrassed like hell, sat down next to us.

And why was I not surprised when Mum swooped down them, dazzling them with her wit, her beauty, her successes; all of which left them drowning them in a sea of negativism. She topped their stories, dropped names, and totally dominated the conversation. By the end of the meal she was Queen Bee, her adoring subjects hanging on to her every word – exactly as she does with my schoolmates, until they're driven to envying me such an amazing mother.

If only they knew.

***

I slept well, my bed quite comfy. I had wondered if we'd find hair-mattresses or even a bed of nails waiting for us, but since the food had been great I guessed we would probably be okay on that score.

Admittedly, I had gone to bed early for me. An hour of Mum telling her stories is enough for anyone and, by the end, even bed sounded attractive – although, to be fair, I was tired.

I took my place at the breakfast table, remembering to wait for Grace – but the amount of food more than made up for this slight inconvenience. Mum's subjects kept a respectful silence further down the table, speaking in low voices, waiting for her to drop pearls of wisdom in their direction.

I hate what she does to them. Why can't she leave people alone? They're all quite content living their little lives until *she* blasts onto the scene, and I bet they're never happy again.

'I thought …' I began hopefully, between mouthfuls.

'I'm going to work, darling.'

'But, Mum, *it's Easter Saturday*,' I protested.

'Someone, darling, has to earn the money to pay for your swimming.'

I wouldn't object to her saying it if it was true. But she's got pots of money and Dad's okay for cash, too. She doesn't need to work, she *wants* to work. And the way she says it – loud enough for everyone to hear – gives everyone the impression that she's forced to scrub floors for a living. It's embarrassing like hell. And the bloody *darlings* are out in force too; they never see the light of day at home. Visions of a day trip to Paris or Jersey or Weymouth or the local pub faded, and I angrily buried my face in my toast.

'Molly and I will explore the house and village,' said Dad. 'There is so much history in this small area of Dorset it will keep us occupied until at least dinner. Did you know, Molly, that during the Civil War this manor was owned by Sir Richard Blaisdale, a Royalist? He maintained his loyalty to the king until the bitter end, although the villagers were Puritans, loyal to parliament.'

'Did they fight?' I said, intrigued despite it being boring.

'No, they didn't. Sir Richard refused to get involved. He told the villagers that war would set father against son, and neighbour against neighbour, and he wouldn't have that.'

'He sounds sensible.'

'He was. You go and work, Margaret, we'll be fine.'

Oh no, we won't, I thought gloomily as I helped clear the breakfast table. My only hope lay in the tour being cut short by earthquake or tempest so I could escape back to my room for a book.

Dad, his notebook and pen at the ready, set the pace eagerly lecturing me on the history of the building. It was a nice bright morning and the other guests had already gone out for the day – somewhere interesting.

After what seemed like forever – with me disguising yawns galore – we moved into what, Dad said, used to be called the parlour. It was a really big room with windows at either end and all stone except for its beamed ceiling. Dad called it sombre. I thought it dreary, but nothing would have made it any better unless you covered the stone with reams of posters or wallpaper.

Sunlight was drifting through the arch-shaped windows. I stared longingly down the drive. I could have gone walking for the day, I'd got my music with me.

'Not particularly efficient as a source of overall heat, Molly.' Dad, seeing me linger by the vast stone fireplace, thought I was actually admiring it.

'Central heating is far more conducive to comfort, where radiators are sited under the windows and warm the cold air as it passes over them. Of course, Romans had under-floor central heating but, sadly, that particular skill died with them and did not resurface until modern times.'

I groaned silently, wishing for the millionth time he could stop using long words like *conducive* and choose words I could actually understand.

'You must have seen those tacky Christmas cards depicting Georgian or Victorian family groups, with the master of the house warming his posterior in front of the fire. It used to be exactly like that. In winter, these open fires burned your face and left your back frozen.' Dad pointed to a carved wooden fire screen. 'The heat was so fierce ladies had fire screens to protect their complexions.'

Me, being me of course, had to spoil everything. 'Did they sit on the ground then?' I asked naively. 'This one only comes up to my thigh.'

'Really, Molly, can't you ever be serious,' snapped Dad, walking off in a huff. 'When you can control your levity, come and find me.'

As if I could be serious – *as if ever!* I thought about escaping then, because if he meant it I was off the hook for the rest of the day.

Once he'd gone I bent down to have a closer look. It was only a rectangular piece of wood on legs, the wood a bright chestnut colour, but it had been elaborately carved into a picture of an old-fashioned family, with long hair and long dresses. It crossed my mind that it might be a real family. The mother was seated with a baby on her lap, while the eldest son stood by his father at the back of the group. I couldn't make out their faces, they were too small. I felt sorry then that Dad had stormed off in a strop – if he'd been here I could have borrowed his magnifying glass. Still, it was really lifelike, even to the delicate folds on the lady's dress. I caught a glimpse of something peeping round the edge of her skirt and took a step forward into a patch of dusty sunlight to look more closely.

It was gorgeously warm in the sun but unexpectedly I felt cold, as if I was about to faint. I glanced down at my hands. They were fading and I could barely see them, my head spinning into a black hole – with the fireplace, which had been right in front of me, heading away down a long tunnel.

I must have fainted, although I've never done that before, because I found myself on the floor. Dazed, I shook my head, blinking rapidly in an attempt to focus my eyes. Thank goodness, I could see my hands quite clearly again.

I pushed myself up onto my feet, stretching cautiously like someone testing his limbs after a bad fall. It was then I noticed I was wearing a long skirt and shoes with heavy wooden soles, like clogs. Bewildered, I gazed around me. Nothing else had changed; it was all exactly the same.

No, it wasn't.

The fire screen had been moved to the side of the fireplace and its picture was gone, and the table held an embroidery frame. When I passed by a moment ago, it had been covered with religious pamphlets.

'What are you doing in here, girl? You know perfectly well to wait in the hall.' A loud voice broke the silence.

I jumped, startled. Behind me appeared an old woman, shapeless in a long grey dress, with a white apron and cap.

'Be off with you and don't let me catch you in the parlour again or I'll speak to your father.' The old woman flapped her apron at me, shooing me down a passage and out of the door. 'Go on now, you baggage, get yourself home,' she said, and shut the door in my face.

I leaned against it, wondering if Dad had run off without paying the bill or if Mum had, at last, overstepped the mark. *But why was I wearing a dress? And who was the old woman? And what about the embroidery frame?*

I stared down the silent pathway towards the walled garden and on to the lane beyond. That hadn't changed. But something very weird had happened and, until I found out what, I had better watch my step.

FOUR

I stood quite still, leaning back against the heavy wooden door, knowing, for the first time in my life, that screaming and shouting, running round in circles scattering all before me like a tree-climbing primate, couldn't help me here. Was this the standard Jesuit joke played on all non-believers? If so, it was pretty cruel. But it meant that Dad was in the house and he'd rescue me, or Mum would. She was in her room in the stable block. Eagerly, I headed across the lawn to find her and stopped dead. I stared about me, overcome by the feeling that I'd just been parachuted into a child's puzzle.

Here are two identical pictures, spot eight things which are different:

A horse's head gazed at me over a stable door.

I whirled round.

A young man gardening, his wheelbarrow made of chunky wood with a wooden wheel; a scythe, its blade wickedly curved lying in the barrow; the man wearing a sort of jerkin with funny trousers that ended just below his knees.

Other differences came hurtling into recognition, like being on fast-forward.

The trees were quite small and there were no daffodils; the paths were of ash and mud. I swung round in panic. The garden wall was bare and free from ivy and I could see gates at the entrance but no signs to the car park – *and no cars.*

In a daze I reached the tall gates and walked through, shutting them carefully behind me. I don't know how I felt. Yes, I do. There's this huge block of ice and I'm trapped inside, unable to think or move or scream.

'Molly,' shouted a voice. 'Oh, Molly dear, I've been looking everywhere.'

Mum! I spun round eagerly to see a woman walking up the lane waving a white cotton bonnet. She was tall like me and wearing a grey dress with a bunched-up skirt over the top. She had a shawl round her shoulders and a white cap on her head. As she came nearer, I noticed that she was pretty in a gentle sort of way, her eyes a deep grey with clear, clear whites. She looked kind.

'Child, I've been so worried, and you without your cap. Quickly, tie up your hair.'

I did as I was told, too stunned not to. Next second a cap was being put on my head, its strings tied under my chin.

'That is the best we can do.' The woman sighed, turning back the way she had come. 'We must pray to God that your father does not learn of this. Come along, dear, let us go home.'

I went with her. What else was I to do? Somehow I'd gone back to another century, but which century? All I know is that my name is still Molly and somewhere I have a dad who hates me going out without a cap.

The lady tucked her arm through mine leading the way towards the village. She was chattering merrily but I heard nothing, the words lost in the layers of ice encasing my brain. My feet functioned; I could walk in a straight line – my eyes too. I swivelled them from side to side, trying to spot differences between yesterday and today, hoping they might provide some sort of clue as to where I was – when – and why.

We stopped halfway down the street in front of the same timber house Dad had showed me – was that yesterday? It didn't feel like yesterday. It was more like revisiting somewhere you'd spent a holiday as a child. It was the same but different … smaller somehow and not as vivid as your memory of it.

The village hadn't changed either, a clutter of houses on each side through which the road ran. But it couldn't be the same, could it? Then I noticed that the village shop, where we'd parked the car, had vanished. The building with its thatched roof still existed, as did the duck pond where some children were playing, but the shop with its *Walls Ice Cream* sign was no longer there. The lady pushed open a door at the front of the house and we went in.

It was gloomy inside. As we entered a child, dressed exactly like me, came flying down the wooden staircase. She stopped as she saw the lady, hastily curtsying.

'Margaret, child, you run as if the house had caught on fire. Be more careful, you will trip,' the lady said.

'We are playing seek, Mother, and Edward is …'

A child's voice floated downstairs and a younger version of the girl came pattering down, wearing a long tunic-style dress in beige.

'Mama,' the child shouted and ran to the lady, calling, 'Good day, sister,' to me over its shoulder.

By now I was thoroughly confused and must have looked it.

'Shush, Edward,' said the lady, 'Molly has a headache and should go and rest. Go along, dear, I will send Margaret to wake you before your father returns home. Come along, we will go into the kitchen and see whether Beth can find some cake.'

The trio disappeared through a door, leaving me alone at the foot of the stairs with a serious problem. How to find my bedroom?

I walked in slow motion up the stairs, focussing my attention on the carved wooden panels running up the wall, as if they really mattered.

The stairs were broad with wide treads, wide enough for me to place my ice-bound feet down safely. I counted carefully. On the seventh step they swung at right angles, continuing up another seven. I stopped, my foot poised to take its last step, and inspected the panels of dark wood lining the walls of the square landing, in the hope they might provide a clue as to where I should go next.

Light was trickling into the landing space through an open doorway. I tiptoed into the corridor-like room, a second doorway at the far end, and peered through the window pressing my nose against the glass. Below me was the village street. Eagerly, I craned my neck to see down the road, somehow still expecting cars to drive past.

The room was empty except for a long table against the wall and two chairs, a silhouette of the window frame reflected in its polished surface. I glanced back towards the landing. As I did, a beam of light from the window fastened on an iron latch hidden among the panels. Retracing my steps, I opened the door and found myself in a small bedroom.

That has to be for Edward. I stared across at the small four-poster measuring the height of the child, whom I had just seen, against the bed. Next to it stood a cot on rockers, its framework of heavy bars covered with white padded cloth that felt coarse and scratchy.

Another doorway, on the far side of the room, drew me into a second bedroom. I started to feel even more peculiar – if that was possible – as if each doorway represented the threshold to another dimension. Like an alien, I lacked any sense of belonging to this world; the sound of my feet on bare boards an intrusion into someone else's life.

Again I saw two beds, slightly bigger, the posts at each

corner of the flat box-like shape rigid and unbending. Trancelike, I floated across the room towards yet another doorway, colliding with a young woman carrying sheets.

'Oh, Miss Molly!' she exclaimed, giving me a half-curtsy. 'The mistress has asked me to see to you.' She pointed to one of two four-poster beds – larger again – in a third room.

'Thank you,' I whispered.

She smiled, dropped me another curtsy, and left.

I needed my bed.

***

'Mother said not to disturb you.'

Startled, I opened my eyes. A girl had entered the room; again dressed identically to me. She flung herself on the other bed, her thin face miserable looking.

'Molly, where have you been? I was so anxious when you did not come home for dinner. Never mind, your chores are done.'

I glanced up catching sight of her hands. They were red, the skin soft and spongy as if it had been immersed in hot water.

'What …'

'You know very well the meat had to be salted today.'

'I'm sorry,' I said automatically.

The girl sighed and inspected me closely. 'We have all been so worried that Father would return before you,' she repeated. 'Was it because you can't see Richard?'

I lay back down staring at the embroidered canopy above my head, its curtains tied back against the carved corner posts. It was covered with wild flowers and great handfuls had been scattered on the dark fabric, as if carelessly tossed – golden buttercups, white daisies, the greenish-yellow of the dandelion, pinpricks of intense blue from forget-menots, celandines, hyacinths, violets and daffodils – each one drawn with amazingly delicate stitches.

One flower in particular appeared everywhere as if it was special – a mauve bell – not purple or lilac but a soft mauve with delicate green stems. The lines of embroidery were so fine, I found myself tracing them with my finger as they wove in and out of the tangled mass of flowers – the soft green stalks with their mauve bells drooping sadly over the happy colours of spring.

'Is that where you went today, Molly?'

I lifted my head. 'Are you going to tell – er – Father?'

'*No!*' The girl sounded quite shocked by the suggestion. 'I would never do that, Molly; I would never break our pact.'

'But I still don't see why I can't see Richard?' I kept my tone purposely innocent. If I was correct this girl was the right age to enjoy the importance of telling me stuff, I simply needed to ask the right questions.

She didn't disappoint. 'Because Sir Richard declared for the King. You know that.'

Well I didn't actually, I thought, casting my mind back to what Dad had said. 'But I understood Sir Richard doesn't want people to take sides.' I repeated Dad's words parrot fashion, hoping I was at least in the right century.

'Who told you that?' She heaved a loud sigh. 'I suppose it was Richard. Well, whatever you do, Molly, don't say that to Father you're in enough trouble. Your hands must be burning.'

'Ears,' I corrected automatically. Hastily, I sat bolt upright, the unmistakeable footsteps of the girl, Margaret, flying up the heavy stairs.

'It's ...' I began and stopped.

'Father,' the girl finished for me. 'Quickly, Molly ... Smooth your skirts and tie your cap on straight.'

'*Agnes – Molly!*' panted Margaret from the doorway.

'We know, Margaret,' I replied. 'Do I look tidy?' I took my cap off to retie it and my hair came bounding down round my shoulders.

Little Margaret squealed, putting her fingers to her mouth.

'Keep quiet, Margaret,' hissed Agnes. 'Get the brush and hurry.'

Quickly and expertly, Agnes grabbed my hair, brushing it and winding it round her fingers into a knot, hastily pinning it at the nape of my neck. I was trembling. I don't really know why, unless it was the look of absolute terror on the little girl's face as she implored us to hurry. Agnes snatched at the ribbons of my cap, tying them neatly under my chin.

'Come on,' she whispered, her eyes sick-looking.

She ran out of the room like a bee out of a bottle, pelting down the stairs closely followed by Margaret and me.

In the hallway was the lady I now knew to be the mother; the child, Edward, and a nursemaid with a baby. We joined the line just in time. A loud voice cut the silence and a man appeared.

I gazed down at a pair of black buckled shoes as the entire line, me included, sank into a curtsy. I glanced sideways at Agnes demurely gazing at the floor and followed suit.

'Well, Agnes?'

'Very well, Father, thanking you.'

Her voice quavered slightly and I wondered why.

'And Margaret?'

'Yes, Father, thanking you.'

'Wife?'

'Yes, husband, all is well, as you see.' The mother spoke in a firm, reassuring sort of voice and I felt the girl beside me relax.

He didn't speak to me for which I was glad. I couldn't have spoken anyway, fear adding to the dense fog paralysing my brain.

'I am early. We will go immediately to prayer.'

In single file, we followed the forbidding figure through a large hall, empty except for a long refectory table, more imposing than its upstairs sibling. A small room led off where three servants were already waiting, one of them the girl I'd met in the bedroom. The room was dark, lit only by a branch of candles, their flickering light tinting the walls dark ochre; and it was empty, except for an ornately carved chair and a small table with a Bible on it. I copied the two sisters, taking a cushion to kneel on. The prayers lasted an absolute age and my legs started to kill with kneeling for so long. I muttered my way through them, hoping not to be heard, sometimes recognising words from our school assembly. I had no idea of the time, I hadn't seen a clock anywhere about and when my clothes had vanished, so had my watch. Had clocks even been invented? I didn't know. But now, my urgent need – and very soon – was the loo and, as far as I knew, those definitely hadn't been invented.

At last it was over. I watched the mother getting slowly to her feet, noticing she was pregnant. The servants left first, then the nurse with the baby, who had not uttered a single cry during the prayers. Everyone waited.

'Molly...' The man had remained standing throughout. He appeared to me as a beige blob, with beige hair and eyes. Even his white collar merged into the general beigeness, while his jacket and trousers made him look like a Cossack. He stared at me as if I was a cockroach he was about to step on, his voice harsh without a scrap of warmth in it – exactly like Mum's when she's having a go at me. He beckoned and I stepped forward.

'It appears that your voyage along the road to perdition continues unabated, for you are determined on your own way. Is there nothing I can say or do that will make you take heed.'

It wasn't a question and I kept silent.

'If that is so, the Almighty has indeed forsaken you and left you to the mercy of the Devil. I expressly forbad you to see Richard Blaisdale.'

'But I didn't,' I burst out.

'Hold your tongue.' His voice lashed at me. I caught the agonised expression on the face of the mother, imploring me to be silent.

'I beg your pardon, sir,' I murmured, hiding my face so he couldn't see how bloody mad I was. How dare he speak to me like that; I'd done nothing wrong.

He bent down to pick up the Bible, a massively heavy book bound in leather with iron hinges. It was obviously well used, the book falling open of its own accord. He found his place and began to read.

'"*And the Lord said unto Moses, Whosoever hath sinned against me, him will I blot out of my book.*" It pains me to chastise you, Molly, but I would be failing in my duty as a Christian if I didn't pursue the fight to bring you back to the path of righteousness. Hold out your hand.'

Without giving it a moment's thought, I did as I was told. Next second I was doubled-up in agony, as a leather thong cut viciously through the air landing on my open palm – *thwack!*

'Your other hand.'

'NO!' I shouted.

'Molly!' implored the lady.

I glared; I couldn't stop myself, my fingers clutched together in a tight fist.

The thong whistled again, and a second time, landing on my clenched knuckles. It hurt so bad I had to push my feet hard into the ground to stop myself falling, the pain soaring through me like a speeding arrow.

'Go to your room, and pray to the Almighty to forgive your lying, for is it not told in Revelations: "*And all liars shall have their part in the lake which burneth with fire and brimstone: which is the second death.*"'

I left, my shoulders hunched up, clutching my hands together against my chest to protect them. I wouldn't have stayed there anyway, not even if he'd begged me on bended knees. Tomorrow, I was off back to the manor house to get back to my real life.

I crept blindly upstairs, my hands burning and stinging, understanding now what Agnes had meant. *Bloody hellfire!* Is there something in me that attracts bullies? Like a sign saying, *Bullies step this way.* I can't even get away from them in another century. Once again, I was a target. Last time I had Grandma; this time I had no one. I gulped back my tears, determined not to cry.

A candle was burning, lifting the friendless shadows with a small circle of warmth, and highlighting the face of the servant girl I'd met before. She was waiting for me. She glanced up as I stumbled in, her fingers on her lips. Without saying a word, she pushed me down on the bed and, taking one of my hands in hers, wrapped strips of white cloth round it soaked in something cool. My knuckles were bleeding badly. I looked down, as she skilfully wound the cloth around them, seeing something white like bone, and guessed they would scar from the savagery of the beating. Still without saying anything, she helped me take off my bonnet and dress. I let her – too wiped-out to argue. She got up, collecting the bowl and cloth, and pointed to a covered plate with food on it. I nearly burst into tears then. Somewhere I had a good angel that cared. Next second she was gone, leaving the candle, her slippers disappearing silently into the darkness.

I was desperate for the loo and crawled under the bed, knowing there had to be a chamber pot. There was. I hated the thought but knew, as long as I was in this house, I'd probably end up emptying it anyway.

I'd lost my appetite but I still gulped down the bread and meat, food – any food – a great source of comfort when I'm in trouble. Then I climbed on to the hard bed and, drawing the curtains, lay down. My hands hurt like hell, but as long as I kept them still the pain was okay, I could bear it.

Some hours later, I heard Edward and the baby being put to bed by the nurse and then the footsteps of Margaret who ran everywhere.

I heard the girl, Agnes, whisper, 'Shush you'll wake Molly.' There was a sort of soft giggling and the sound of clothes being hung in a cupboard.

'Are you asleep, Molly?' Agnes's piercing whisper broke the darkness. I ignored it – lost in my little cocoon of pain and humiliation.

**

I lay there a long time and must have fallen into a doze, when a silent footfall woke me. I froze as the bed curtains were drawn back. Then I recognised the tall shape of the mother. It was dark but I could still see her smile.

'Are your hands less painful now, Molly?'

I nodded, tears springing to my eyes as I realised I wasn't alone. She climbed into my bed and put her arms round me.

'There, my brave girl, everything will be all right, you will see.'

I cried then, and she rocked me until I fell asleep.

FIVE

The next morning, it was Agnes who woke me.

'How… What time is it?' I asked. 'It's not even light.'

It wasn't inside my bed, the thick curtains keeping out every scrap of light. I glanced out of the window. Outside it was grey, an early morning mist obscuring the dawn, with no clue as to whether the sun will shine that day or not.

'Molly, can you carry water?' she asked, gazing at the bloodstained bandages on my hands.

I glanced down. 'If I have to.'

She nodded and left the room. I followed her blindly, feeling my way down a narrow flight of steep steps. We emerged into a square hallway at the back of the house, a door between us and the garden. I didn't ask. I knew from the smell we were off to the privy; not much more than a wooden seat over a large hole, closed in by a shed-like construction for privacy.

Automatically, I washed my hands at the pump in the washhouse. It was cold outside and I shivered, my bandages wet.

'Don't you …' I began and stopped. *No, they didn't wash their hands; that's why disease spread.*

I watched the metal cans slowly filling, carefully lifting the full ones out of the way. They looked heavy and they were, my fingers beginning to throb even as I thought about carrying them. But I had to. I looped them over my wrists, the only place that didn't actually hurt, and followed Agnes back up the stairs.

I walked slowly, trying not to let the water slop over the rim, but already I could feel the cut in my left palm opening up under the strain. I ignored it, determined to get the cans up the stairs or die in the attempt, because HE wasn't going to get the better of me. I did it, one step at a time. Agnes waited patiently, her foot poised on the next step, her face a picture of concern like she was wishing it was her that was hurt. At the top of the stairs, she vanished through the open doorway overlooking the street, only to reappear a second later empty-handed.

So the parents slept on that side. That was good; at least my enemy was as far away from me as possible.

Still without saying a word she took up my burden, leaving me the job of holding open the bedroom door. One can for the kids and one between us two.

Like the rest of the house, the bedroom possessed only the most basic furniture. A small carpet lay between the two four-posters, to protect our feet from the cold wooden floorboards, with a tall cupboard for clothes. Next to the window was a wooden washstand with two bowls on it, and a single chair. The room didn't even have curtains at the window but I guess that's the role of bed curtains, to stop draughts. I thought about my bedroom at home; its walls plastered with posters and piles of toys, books and CD's; my swimming medals hung in rows against the wall. This resembled a house on moving day waiting for the furniture removers to arrive.

The water was freezing, even the thought of it touching my bare skin made me shiver violently. Appalled, I saw Agnes giving herself a good wash.

'I can't,' and held up my hands, comforting myself with the thought that since I showered twice most days, I was well in credit.

Agnes frowned and, to my horror, seized the cloth from the stand in front of me. Dipping it in the freezing water, she proceeded to wash my face and neck, handing me a piece of rough cloth to dry myself with. I watched, unbelieving, as she cleaned her teeth on what resembled a twig from the hedgerow which had sprouted bristles – even re-using her washing water. I flinched and followed suit. The soapy water tasted vile.

I had slept in my petticoat. Now I opened the cupboard putting on a second layer and taking out the clothes I had worn the day before; a bodice in white, like a vest with long sleeves, the beige dress worn over it. The fabric was stiff and heavy, similar to the brocade used in curtains, and I wondered if they wore lighter clothes in summer as these would be roasting. Naturally, there was nothing labour saving like zips; a long row of buttons stretched all the way down the back of the dress. Seeing them, I came to my first conclusion that no one could exist in this century without a maid, relative or close friend, unless they were double-jointed.

Agnes stared at me in horror.

'Molly, it's Sunday. Had you forgotten? Do hurry.'

She reached into the cupboard and pulled out an identical outfit in black. Okay, so Sundays I wear black and the rest of the week, beige – *yuck*. If I get out of here, these are two colours on my banned list for evermore. I shivered at the word *if*, hastily substituting *when*, as Agnes quickly fastened the buttons on the back of my dress.

We got Margaret up then. The nurse dressed and fed the baby, and then helped Edward. While this was going on, Agnes carefully re-bandaged my hands, leaving Margaret to struggle with the buttons on her dress. Agnes didn't ask me; she knew I couldn't help, my hands in plain view in front of her, blood and a yellowish sort of goo oozing from the cuts.

She was quick and skilful, her little face – its dark hair

confined under a cap – worried and intent-looking, concentrating on the job in hand. She reminded me in a strange way of Hannah, the same earnest air about her unformed face, and I guessed her to be eleven or twelve; although, from where I'm standing, she could have been much older. As far I can see there's nothing she can't do, whereas Molly obviously needs looking after. I didn't ask how often she had to do this particular job. I had my suspicions it was a pretty regular occurrence, by the speed with which she worked, handing me a pair of fingerless gloves to wear.

Shortly afterwards I found myself once again, my eyes fixed on the ground, following the parents in single file. This time not to the room used as a chapel but a large room at the back of the house, overlooking the garden, where breakfast had been laid.

Darkly furnished, its walls swept clear of any pictures, it reminded me of Dutch paintings in which browns and blacks predominate; a lamp or fruit bowl providing a solitary unit of colour. Here, it was long curtains. Patterned red and green, they hung stiffly against a small window breaking the dark heaviness of the table and chairs; their legs carved in an ornate pattern. A matching dresser stood against the near wall, a handful of coloured plates leaning against its solitary shelf; its polished surface reflecting beams of light from the fire burning in the grate, its warmth very welcome after washing in freezing-cold water.

I hung back watching the rest of the family take their places at the table, before sitting down in the empty space. Again, HE had spoken to everyone except me, but I'm not about to argue.

I was starved, although it was way earlier than I usually get up; the plate of bread and meat, I had consumed last evening, a distant memory. I expected Grace to be said and got it.

We stood silently, heads bent and hands clasped, waiting while he turned the pages of the Bible. I stared at its iron hinges, their rigid shape reminding me of him; not exactly appropriate for a book that is meant to convey messages of love and forgiveness – but perhaps he hadn't got to that bit yet. He started to read, his voice cold and forbidding.

'"Remember the Sabbath day, to keep it holy. Six days shalt thou labour, and do all thy work. But the seventh day is the Sabbath of the Lord thy God: in it thou shalt not do any work, thou, nor thy son, nor thy daughter, thy manservant, nor thy maidservant, nor thy cattle, nor thy stranger that is within thy gates."'

He stopped and closed the Bible. No one moved and I didn't either, guessing there was more to come; I was right.

'We have laboured in Thy service for six days, Oh Lord God, Creator of all Things on this earth. It is now the seventh day on which, according to the Scriptures, you have commanded us to rest. Bless now the food of our rest and grant us the strength and courage to stay on the path of righteousness always.'

Exactly on the word *righteousness* he lifted his head. Heat from his glare penetrated right across the table. I glanced down at the polished table top somehow expecting to find scorch marks.

We sat down. My hands were bent like claws and so painful I couldn't reach for food, like I usually do at home. That was my first lucky break, because no one else moved a muscle either until both parents had served themselves.

'Children, you may eat,' said the mother.

In front of me was a knife, a plate, and a silver-coloured mug made from pewter. The plate reminded me of those bowls, you can buy at *The Pound Shop,* with a Japanese pattern on them. Here the pattern was smudged, while the plate in front of Margaret was a different blue and not quite round.

I wish I'd listened when Dad talked. If you have to go back in history, at least you should know when things – like pottery – were invented. At this precise moment knowledge would be like wearing a bullet-proof vest in war.

The table was heaped so I wasn't going to starve; a loaf of freshly-baked, mouth-watering bread hugging the centre of a large wooden platter. But I wished someone would say something. Still I hesitated. Agnes, catching my eye, picked up the loaf and holding it against her bodice cut slices off, handing them round as if she was performing some sort of weird ritual. First to Margaret, who was sitting next to her; she handed them across the table to me, leaving me to pass them on to Edward. We did it all again, first with the butter, then the honey and milk. No one helped themselves. There were slices of beef, too, and a type of paste in a brown pottery jar. I heard HIM use the word *brawn,* but I hadn't a clue what that was and it smelt horrid.

While this was going on, HE, ignoring his family completely, concentrated on his own meal, all the while talking to his wife who responded with a half-smile or a gentle nod. No one else made a sound.

I hated him passionately for what he had done but still felt consumed with a need to watch him. I don't know why, his table manners were sickening – like kids at school who behave as if they're straight out of the trees. Leaning across the table, he speared slices of meat with his knife, using his teeth to tear chunks off; all the time taking great swigs of something that smelled like a watered-down beer, its sour yeasty odour wafting across the table. I might not have been so hung-up on his table manners if they hadn't stood out from the rest of the family. The three children ate silently, small mouthfuls invisibly chewed, as if scared that the slightest sound would earn them a telling-off. Suddenly, I remembered Grandma: *children must be seen and not heard,* she'd tease me when I got too noisy. Thanks, Gran.

It was now light and, by the time we left the table, the sun was beginning to send a few feeble rays over the horizon. I stayed silent, trying to watch and learn. I had to, and fast, if I was to carry on this masquerade long enough to get back to the manor house. No one took any notice though, which made me suspect this was Molly's usual behaviour. So, when Agnes and Margaret, chattering merrily, went to the privy – I followed. They went upstairs and I followed again, collecting my cloak to join the silent group in the hallway.

We left the house and, in procession, walked down the village street. On either side doors were opening and sombre clad families, dressed identically to us, appeared. It reminded me of those unending reflections in a hall of mirrors; the adults greeting Molly's parents, children curtsying or bowing. Occasionally, a horse and cart trotted past heading in the same direction, its occupants wearing black too; a great black and white plague – only the hedgerows having colour in them.

Edward walked sturdily by my side. Thankfully, he *was* a boy in a dress not a girl with a weird name, something I'd discovered when asked to take him to the privy. He kept glancing up at me through long sandy lashes, as if he wanted to say something but daren't. I gave him a smile and saw relief sweep over his small face. *Was even he, a little kid, worried about Molly?*

Like a grieving cortège following a hearse, we walked the length of the village street, along the route Dad had driven the previous day heading in the direction of the river. As I passed the closed gates of the manor house, I heard this screaming noise from inside my iceberg, *make a run for it, Molly, go on, go for it.* But my feet continued to walk forwards, as if my movements were being controlled by some powerful force outside myself.

It must have rained heavily in the night, the surface of

the lane pitted with potholes now full of water. A game of *follow my leader* started. Wanting to keep their Sunday shoes dry and free from mud, the procession waited in an orderly fashion to cross the next puddle. At any other time, I might have found lines of people, cautiously skirting puddles, hilariously funny but I'd left my sense of humour in the manor parlour. Instead, I worried about the likely punishment for getting mud on your Sunday skirt, copying Agnes and Margaret who were carefully lifting theirs over the soggy ground.

That's when I looked up and saw the church on the far side of the river. A stone-clad building, with a steep roof and bell tower, it stood near the small bridge where Dad and I had stopped to look at the water, its doors open. My brain crashed into overdrive. On a scale of one to ten, this was definitely the weirdest. It was like trying to get your head round the Big Bang theory. Yesterday, there'd been no trace of it. So how between yesterday, today, and sometime in the future – it did not exist – it did exist – then had fallen into ruin and been pulled down?

Molly's father made his way directly to the top of the room, its walls covered with scroll-like carvings on which verses from the scriptures had been engraved. Dad had often dragged me into cathedrals and old churches – elegant buildings immersed in an aura of piety. This, by comparison, was a box filled with seats. He took his time, stopping to greet families as he passed, before joining a group of men seated sideways-on to the congregation. The mother led us into a row of bench-seats halfway down, she at one end, me at the other clutching my Bible. My eyes flicked curiously, eagerly drinking in the sea of black bobbing and bowing shapes; the box-like room beginning to bulge at the seams as it filled to capacity and overflowed.

A big man, his white face partially obscured by a black wide-brimmed hat, got to his feet. Dressed identically to the rest of the congregation, there was nothing to mark him down as a preacher. He remained silent waiting for the noise to die down before speaking; his voice weary-sounding as though exhausted from reaching into dusty corners.

'Good people of Lingthorpe, let us remember those who have gone before us, who have fought and died for the freedoms we enjoy today, to worship in safety and peace. Let us pray.'

I heard shuffling as the congregation rearranged themselves. No one could kneel; we were so tightly packed my knees were pressed painfully against the bench in front. I watched hands folded piously against foreheads and eyes shut tight. After a resounding Amen, there was more shuffling as people struggled upright again. The Preacher began to speak.

Without thinking, I slipped on my special face, a mask of eager concentration and the result of years of boring lessons, guaranteed to fool anyone. Once firmly in place, I can drift off into my own thoughts and, today, I badly needed time to think. Suddenly, I heard this warning voice in my head: *What if HE asks questions afterwards?* Instantly, my hands started to throb and, scared, I came out of my quiet place and listened, hoping I hadn't missed much.

It wouldn't have made a jot of difference, I still couldn't make head or tail of what he was saying, his sentences so long and convoluted they were mind-boggling – full of words like *heretofore, henceforth, hereafter*. By the time I'd worked out what one sentence meant I'd missed the next – there was even a *forsooth*. The only bit I really got was his opening sentence, '*Puritans have been placed on this earth to restore the church to its original purity in doctrine, worship and government.*' It sounded great, but after the unchristian-like behaviour of Molly's dad, I wasn't sure I believed it.

I inched myself up in my seat and sneaked a look at the mother, surreptitiously yanking at my petticoat which had managed to bunch itself up with my shuffling, wondering how she could stand the smell and the boredom, week after week. She was listening intently, a dried orange stuck with cloves held to her nose. I smiled at that, pleased that even here she was my ally, hating the smell of unwashed bodies in that confined space as much as I did.

Finally, the preacher stopped and took a deep breath. A barrage of coughing broke out. I was almost on my feet when I realized this was only the interval. No one else was standing, except for kids who wanted to see if their friends were there. After a minute or two another man got to his feet and called for quiet.

'Your pastor has kindly permitted me to address you,' he boomed, bowing towards the man who had taken the service. 'Will the sufferings of the good people of England never cease?'

He spoke slowly and clearly, pausing as if expecting an answer.

'It is indeed a dark time in which we are living, our very religion – the foundation of our belief, tossed about by King and Parliament as if *they* – not God – were the creators of mankind. General Cromwell speaks of a crossroads. He is not alone. Many believe the road to peace can exist only if the King is replaced.'

There were gasps from the congregation and a general stirring, as if the people previously asleep had woken up. I tried not to fidget but the bench was hard and narrow and, after years of slouching, my spine wasn't the right shape to sit upright naturally. Instantly, Margaret leant forward to give me a look, her sandy eyes reminding me of HIM. If any kid from school had done that I would have been right mad. Then I remembered her fear of the day before and understood she was warning me to sit still. I glanced across at Agnes, her back ramrod straight, her feet set neatly side by side, her hands primly crossed in her lap. On her far side

Edward hadn't moved either; his head bent quietly studying his hands. Clutched in each fist was a toy soldier. His mother met my gaze and smiled. How kind and sensible she was, recognising that little boys find it impossible to sit still, and making sure he didn't get into trouble.

'There is worse, my good people,' the speaker waited for the muttering to die away before continuing. 'Once again support for the King's Majesty is growing; the city of London demands his restoration. And rumours abound that General Cromwell has thrown in his lot with the King, upon a promise of aggrandisement when the monarch is once more upon his throne.'

'Not Cromwell, he would never betray us,' a voice called from the back of the room.

There was a jumble of noise, people shouting and talking among themselves. In the midst of it all the pastor suddenly leapt to his feet and, diving from the platform, descended on the women and children of the congregation like the wrath of God himself. I flinched, wondering about his intended victim. He strode past me. Next second, I heard the sound of a sharp slap and, unable to stop myself, swivelled round in my seat to look. The mother leant across touching my knee. I swung round reluctantly, but not before I had seen the victim clutching a scarlet ear and silently howling.

'I tell you only what is said,' the speaker replied. 'General Cromwell is charged with an alteration of his beliefs, appearing indifferent to the principles that government hold important. They believe that a republic means freedom; a monarchy – bondage. Whereas General Cromwell has declared that he seeks only a solution to our troubles in whatever form it is presented.'

'I agree with him,' shouted one of the men in the side seats. 'It is treason to even consider removing the King.'

Shouting broke out again. I sneaked a glance over my

shoulder to see who was saying what – especially when the shouting was reinforced by a fist. I wasn't the only one to turn round then.

'SILENCE! Let our speaker finish.'

The muttering persisted, people shuffling about reluctant to sit down with an argument still to be won, but finally there was silence and the speaker began again.

'We have dark days ahead, good people. General Cromwell, who refuses to be swayed by the lies told about him, continues his efforts in parliament. He demands that the matter is settled, warning that unless a decision is arrived upon very shortly war will undoubtedly follow.'

This last bit completely blew it for me, because I thought they'd just had a war.

***

A torrent of noise erupted as we trooped outside, the entire congregation bursting into speech the moment fresh air hit them. The men gathered in one place, women in another. Teenagers wandered about in twos and threes, nudging one another and giggling behind their hands; while the little kids ran about playing on the bridge, incorporating its low balustrade into their game, and ignoring the anxious cries of, '*be careful or you'll fall in.*'

I took in a dozen deep breaths to wash away the smells, stretching my cramped limbs. I glared at the birds singing cheerfully overhead. Well, if God wasn't prepared to do anything about a country going to war, what chance had I got of persuading him to send me home, however hard I prayed?

SIX

There was a scream from the bake house. I dropped the handle of the butter churn, running through the kitchen to where Margaret stood, her right arm held rigidly in front of her, uttering high-pitched wails, while Beth, the cook, flapped her apron trying to stop her crying.

I reacted instinctively to the picture; a tin of newly cooked bread lying on the ground half-covered by a cloth.

'Water,' I shouted and, grabbing Margaret's shoulders, pushed her towards the nearest pail, plunging her arm in and holding it there.

'*Shush, shush*, Margaret, it's only a small burn. Let me see, dear.' The mother, who had been outside, appeared and calmly lifted the child's arm from the water. 'Why it's better already thanks to Molly's quick action. Now, hush, Beth will put some salve on for you.'

The wails continued increasing in volume as the little girl caught sight of the angry red weal on the inside of her arm, where she'd caught it on the bars of the fire. No oven-cloths, I thought resignedly, watching Beth skilfully remove the other bread tin from the ashes. She upended it, knocking out the newly baked loaf with asbestos knuckles.

'I don't want to make bread,' Margaret wailed, big crocodile tears dripping down onto her cheeks.

'Of course you do.' The mother hugged the young child to her. 'All well-brought-up girls learn how to make bread.

Now, stop crying; Molly has not uttered a single complaint about her hands and they must be so painful.'

Her grey eyes broke into ready laughter as she noticed the dagger-like glares Margaret was throwing at me from the safety of her skirt. I caught her glance and smiled back.

The service, yesterday, had lasted more than three hours – *I mean three hours!* In our day the congregation would have rioted after one. No wonder I felt knackered. It had taken the sight of the dinner table – groaning with enough food to feed a whole nation in Africa – to cheer me up. I swear there was a whole side of beef, two chickens, plus some sort of stew, and vegetables – swede and cabbage. And after, there were cakes and jellies.

If only HE hadn't been there I would have been in seventh heaven, but I know he doesn't like me – that's crystal. I could feel his eyes giving me *the look*. It's something I know well because Mum does it all the time. And I swear my hands hurt more when he's about – like Grandma and her rheumatism when rain's coming.

It took an absolute age for everyone to wade through all the food and, by the end, my back killed from trying to sit upright. I daren't relax; the wooden seat on my chair so slippery, the slightest slouch and I'd have shot straight off onto the floor. With that to worry about, I couldn't really do justice to the food. I noticed the mother watching me, a worried expression on her face. I wanted to tell her I was okay but, of course, I couldn't speak, could I?

While I waited I chanted my mantra. *It'll all be over soon and I'll be back home.* But even then I wasn't free. The table had to be cleared – the whole Sabbath thing meant that servants didn't do any work either, except I wondered who had cooked our dinner? Again, my hands saved me because I hadn't a clue where the kitchen was. Dragging my heels, I followed Agnes down a short corridor and into a large dungeon-like room at the side of the house, its ceiling a mass of hooks, on which rabbits and pheasants were hanging. I gazed at the bedraggled and bloody creatures; their necks lolling limply to one side, their eyes cloudy – and wished I was a vegetarian.

I got back to the parlour to find Margaret laying out embroidery silks. I gazed through the window longingly – it was a lovely afternoon. With a feeling of shock, I realized that even if I could get out of the house it wouldn't help. If it was Sunday in this house, it would be Sunday at the manor and the family would be inside, doubtless performing similar tasks. I would never get into the house without being seen. I nearly broke down then, and would have too if screaming could have helped in the slightest. How the hell was I ever going to get out of this half-world if I was stuck inside all the time? Devastated I turned away, hiding my face, knowing I had to stay here at least one more day.

Margaret had placed a handful of partially completed bags on the table. They were quite small, like the ones Gran uses for lavender. Carefully watching where she and Agnes sat, I picked up the bag Molly had been in the middle of embroidering. It was exquisite; tiny stitches of coloured silk formed the delicate structure of a butterfly, its wings already fluttering as it tried to escape the material holding it down. I didn't know much about her, but the butterfly was so real it confirmed what I'd already guessed – that she too wanted to escape and that was why she was always in trouble.

Panic took over as the parents re-entered the room; I could feel my hands trembling with fear. I could sew, I'd had to do it at school, but nothing like this; with stitches so intricate you could hardly see them. I felt cornered, like a rat in a trap. Even if I could hold a needle, my obvious lack of skill would bring down the wrath of God on me. The mother joined us at the table, while HE read aloud from the Bible. My heart was beating so fast and loudly in my chest, I thought it would burst through my rib cage. Any second now and he would notice I wasn't doing anything

It was the mother that came to my rescue.

'Husband?' she called across the room. He looked up frowning, marking his place in the book with his finger. 'Would it not be a good idea to send Molly out to look after Edward and the baby?'

She made it sound like a punishment.

'Yes, indeed.' He didn't speak, simply indicating with his other hand for me to leave the room.

I left before he had a change of mind.

Edward was sitting on a seat in the garden kicking his heels, while the nursemaid walked the baby up and down.

'I've been told to look after you,' I said. 'What are you doing?'

He looked up and smiled. 'I'm playing armies, do you want to play?' He moved aside so I could sit down, his small legs lost in his black tunic.

'When do you get to wear proper boys' clothes?' I asked on impulse.

The boy gazed at me curiously. 'Oh, you are funny, Molly, you asked the self-same question only last week. You know perfectly well I will not be breeched until I am six, when I become a man,' he added proudly.

He had four little soldiers made of wood and painted different colours; black, a sort of buff colour that I imagine the Puritans always wore, dark green and a scarlet one.

'I like these, who carved them?' I asked without thinking.

'What a silly question, Molly, are you quite well?'

'Of course I am,' I thought quickly, 'I'm playing a game of pretend.'

'What is that?' the boy gazed at me expectantly.

Great – works every time. 'I'm a stranger,' I explained. 'I ask questions and you tell me the answers.'

Edward's eyes lit up. 'Like you asking me about breeching?'

I nodded. 'Now you have to tell me who did the carving, stranger.'

He shouted with laughter. 'As you ask, stranger, so I will tell,' he replied formally. 'The man is Mister Higgins and he lives at the end of the street.'

'And would permission be granted to visit this man?' I asked, responding in the same vein.

Edward nodded furiously. 'Yes, we could go tomorrow after our chores are done.'

'And who are these?' I asked, picking up the soldiers.

'I think they are royalists,' explained the little boy, 'and these are parliamentarians.'

'Who's winning?' I said, making a mental note to use the word *parliament* in future.

Edward glanced furtively behind him. 'I let the royalists win mostly, I like their bright colours.'

Good for you, boy, never knuckle down to authority.

'And on my sixth birthday, Mother will give me another soldier.'

'Sounds like you're going to have a long wait before you can have a proper battle. Come on, let's kick a ball.'

The nursemaid looked up at this and smiled, but said nothing. I picked up the stubby leather ball lying on the ground and walked off down the path, Edward trotting eagerly by my side.

'I like the stranger game because my sister, Molly, never wanted to kick a ball,' he said. I looked down startled. Had he guessed?

The garden resembled a patterned jumper – like the ones Gran used to knit when I was little. Neatly clipped hedges had been planted in circles and squares and filled with plants and small bushes, the entire plot surrounded by a brick wall. We went through a gate at the far end onto open meadowland, where we could run and kick the ball. It did me good, getting rid of the aches and pains I had acquired sitting cramped up for three long hours. Finally exhausted, Edward picked up the ball and we walked back towards the garden.

He looked shyly at my gloved hands. 'Do they hurt, Molly?'

'Yeah, they do.'

'Molly, why does Father hit you?'

I looked down at his little face, his eyebrows drawn together in a frown. Again, I was reminded of Hannah, standing up to protect the rights of the girl who was being bullied, and I knew this kid would be the same. I shrugged.

'I don't really know. I think it's because I hate being told what to do.'

Edward seemed puzzled. I guess he's far too young to understand what independence means, so are Agnes and Margaret; although, from what I've seen so far, I'm positive Molly has grasped the ball and is running with it.

'When I become a man, I won't hit my children,' he added stoutly.

I hope you stick to that, old buddy, I thought, running round one of the circular beds in a fit of energy. Edward followed me enthusiastically.

'Molly, can we play the stranger game again?'

I looked down at the little kid. With a shock, I realised for the past couple of hours I'd actually forgotten where I was – *thanks Edward.* 'But it's got to be our special secret. Don't tell anyone.' The little boy nodded. 'And every time I ask you a strange question, you'll know we're playing our game …'

The problem with living in a century where language is so old-fashioned, I'd opened my mouth to add *okay* to the end of the sentence and had to hastily shut it again.

SEVEN

I should have known from the prayers, HE said before every meal, that Monday was a workday even for little Edward.

Once again Agnes woke me. For a brief second my mind was a blank; the girl in her petticoats, a shawl clutched round her thin chest, dark hair streaming down her back, a stranger – someone I'd never met before. Then I recognised the canopy of flowers above my head. Instantly, my icebound straitjacket closed in on me again. I felt entombed in a nightmare – only you wake up from nightmares. You may feel sick, battered and bruised – but you wake up. Here, no matter how often I chanted the words *this can't be happening,* it had happened and I had to deal with it.

I stumbled down the backstairs, silently cursing Dad for landing us in that hotel from hell in the first place, and Mum for never taking time off for a family holiday. I watched the frail silhouette of the young girl in front of me; not for one second did she flinch or hesitate when she opened the back door to be accosted by bitter cold and a penetrating odour from the privy. Shamefaced, I remembered the red, pulpy skin on her hands that first day. If she could survive this, then so could I.

We followed the same routine; my hands a tiny bit less painful. Scabs were beginning to form although, when Agnes replaced the bandages, the cloth was still heavily stained with yellow goo. But at least I managed to carry the pails without flinching, although I nearly died when the cold water touched my bare back. I can't believe someone hasn't invented hot water. If it isn't invented by tomorrow, I'm going to do it.

Today, the husband ate his breakfast alone – with Agnes and me waiting on him. As soon as he had finished, he left the table and the house; the mother waiting in the hallway with his cloak and hat. We joined the little line; Agnes and Margaret presenting their cheek to be kissed – me to curtsy. Outside his horse, already saddled and bridled, also waited; the entire gathering programmed into performing this daily mark of respect that god-fearing men like him demand.

Once his horse's hooves had faded into the distance, the mother smiled and, taking Edward's small hand, led him to his seat at the breakfast tale. I'm positive I'm the only person that saw that smile of relief, because I smiled too. I glanced up at the big clock on the mantelshelf. It said half-past-six. I guessed he was going to work, but I didn't dare play the *stranger* game with Edward while people were about. He's a great kid, keeps throwing me glances under his lashes. Still, I can't get rid of this strange feeling that, on some level, he knows I'm not his sister.

It was a morning of discoveries. I'd only seen the houses from the road when Dad and I had explored the village, catching sight of their small, neat gardens through sparkling windows. I wasn't particularly bothered about the inside of the house – feeling towards it as you do towards a hotel or holiday apartment; somewhere to dump your suitcase, sleep and eat, for a fixed period of time. Bigger than our house though, its interior was simply a collection of rooms – some little wider than a corridor, one opening into another like a house made from playing cards.

Clinging to Agnes like a leech, we trailed across the yard to a gate in the wall which opened up into a muddy farmyard. An open-fronted barn backed onto the garden wall where cows, pigs, chickens and ducks were milling aimlessly about – the ducks surprisingly living quite happily on dry land. Immediately they heard the latch click, they surged towards us expecting to be fed.

Agnes and I had butter and cheese to make, and the first shock of the day arrived when I learned that making butter and cheese involved milking cows. I stared in terror at the horned beast clopping towards me, its blue-veined udder swinging from side to side like a shopping basket strung from the handlebars of a bike, a string of white drool dangling from its mouth.

'I can't,' I stuttered and held up my hands.

Agnes glanced over her shoulder to see the mother following us.

'Ma'am, Molly ...' she began.

'Oh dear, Molly, I quite forgot your hands. The animals would kick up a storm if you touched them with those rough bandages. Can you imagine?' The mother laughed and picked up a brown-sacking apron from a hook on the back of the door. 'You may churn the butter instead.'

I joined in the laughter, not quite sure if the mother was seriously directing her sympathy at the cow or was teasing me. It was nice though. Despite the early hour, she wasn't grumpy and taking it out on the kids. I waited while Beth, grumbling all the while, hefted the milk from the previous day into a large wooden churn, before returning to the kitchen to supervise Margaret who was kneading the dough.

Edward was already trotting about the yard, his job to feed the animals and collect the eggs. Watching his painfully slow progress, I wanted to say, *you're too little, let me do it – go and play*; except he wasn't. And, if only he could've worn casual trousers and wellies, he'd have been super quick; the mud of winter clinging tightly to his wooden clogs. Still, he never quit. Determined to be useful, like his big sisters, he trotted backwards and forwards with his miniature pail of food, making sure he didn't miss any of the livestock.

Agnes and her mother spent the time chatting, their heads casually resting against the cow's flank, the jets of milk making little shushing sounds as they struck the sides of the wooden bucket, its wide base sinking into the soft mud with the weight of the milk.

I found myself continually coughing; the air, saturated with a smell of dung, stinging the back of my throat. *How could anyone live like this?* The monotony of the previous evening, hearing the clock tick out each minute as if it were an hour. I was used to every hour streaking past like a minute, with never enough time to finish my homework before going training. And the rush home for food and yet more homework, unless the evening ended in sparks flying and me stomping off to bed.

Here, the mother and Agnes had spent the evening sewing until it was too dark, even with candles. I pretended to read while Margaret played quietly on the floor with the baby. It was a nice baby, all chubby and cuddly. The husband smoked his pipe, occasionally looking up from his Bible to talk to his wife. Except, he didn't talk to her, he lectured. He wasn't even interested in the baby, even though it was another boy. And you could see from the shy looks Edward shot him, from underneath his lashes, he was simply dying for his dad to play a game of footy in the garden.

Living in primitive times is no excuse; they were a smashing family, even if you left Molly out. HE was so lucky and he didn't know it.

A glass of milk and a slice of cake, handed round by Beth and eaten in the kitchen, provided the background to yet another painful surprise. Fortunately Margaret's moaning, 'Do we have to do our letters?' forewarned me what to expect. Molly was the studious one – the teacher. Instantly, the feeling of being back in shark-infested waters swept over me again, knowing I would be forced to blag it. It was difficult enough trying to remember to speak properly.

'Agnes, will you remind me where we finished on …' I paused, trying to guess. 'Saturday?'

Agnes nodded and I breathed a sigh of relief.

'We are learning how to add up pennies and half-pennies but …' she sighed painfully. 'It is very difficult, Molly, I'm not as clever as you.'

You're finding it difficult! I hadn't the faintest idea what she was on about. 'Well, let's give that a miss for a few days and do some reading,' I said.

'I'm not very good at reading, sister,' Margaret admitted bravely.

Out came another Granism. 'Well, practice makes perfect.'

'Oh, Molly, you say that all the time,' groaned Margaret. 'But I am never going to be able to read.'

'Yes, you will. Now fetch your book and we'll read it together.'

Obligingly, Margaret ran off reappearing, moments later, with a large leather-bound volume. 'Mother says we can use her book,' she said, handing it to me.

It contained poetry by Edmund Spenser and was full of that weird spelling Dad loves. I wanted to cry, suddenly missing him. I swallowed and started to read, relieved to find I could actually understand the old-fashioned writing. I must have absorbed more than I thought from Dad's constant lectures on the history of the written language, although my pronunciation caused so much laughter, the mother stopped what she was doing and came in to listen.

'Mother,' exclaimed Margaret, 'Molly uses such funny words.'

She smiled. 'I have long since come to the conclusion,

Margaret, that Molly uses strange words only to discover if you are attending.'

I wondered then what had happened to the real Molly. Was she locked into my life? If so, I pitied her my mum after hers.

The great silver clock in the winter parlour had already chimed one when we eventually stopped. I felt shattered; we'd been working non-stop since before eight. The mother sent us upstairs to tidy ourselves for dinner and I flung myself down on my bed, wanting to sleep.

'Molly, *please* don't be late for dinner, Father will be so angry,' said Agnes, carefully brushing her hair and re-tying her cap.

I couldn't believe what I was hearing. HE was coming home; I really thought he'd gone for the day. If only someone would publish a timetable – heaven knows, I desperately needed one.

'I'm sorry, Agnes, I didn't mean to worry you. I didn't sleep well,' I lied, 'and my hands are aching.'

'Poor, Molly, I had quite forgotten. I will help you with your hair.'

She's a good kid, far better than me.

I had learned. I swept my curtsy my head gazing at the floor, not expecting to speak or be spoken to. I followed the stern back into the parlour and sat in my place, looking so angelic it would put anyone off the scent. I handed round the food, ate quietly, and waited politely until the parents had finished eating and left the table. Then I quickly carried the platters to the kitchen, beating Agnes to it, before joining the rest of the family in the parlour upstairs; its straight-backed chairs the unrelenting enemy of my spine.

It was a beautiful day and, after the husband had finished smoking his pipe, he informed his wife that he would like her to go with him to pay a visit to the pastor. She immediately got up to fetch her cloak and I grabbed the opportunity.

'May I go for a walk, sir?' I asked bravely, the first time I'd said more than, *yes, sir*, in two days.

He looked up, frowning, as if I had a colossal cheek even to speak to him. The mother had reappeared in the doorway and I glanced across at her, noticing she was holding herself absolutely rigid. If I had to guess, I'd say she was praying.

'A walk, young lady? I'll not countenance a walk which can only serve to put temptation in your way.'

'I promised Edward,' I replied with as much dignity as I could manage, 'we would go and visit the carpenter who made his soldiers.'

The mother moved then. I had guessed right, she had been praying. 'I see no harm in that, husband,' she said quietly. 'I believe Molly to have learned a valuable lesson.'

He nodded his head in that stiff way of his. 'We shall see; this is but the second day. You may go. I can trust my son even if I cannot trust you, whatever Mistress Hampton wishes me to believe.'

I got my walk but not as originally planned. Edward skipped happily by my side, every so often gazing up at me with a smile to ask the name of a bird or a plant. I puzzled him, I could see that quite clearly, and guessed that Molly had known about flowers. Had she embroidered the hangings on the bed? If so, someone so gifted was a sad loss and I, a poor substitute.

'Can we play the stranger game, Edward?' I asked, desperate to think of something that didn't make me want to howl.

He nodded cheerfully, his little legs running to keep up with my long stride. 'What is it you wish to ask?'

'Who embroidered my bed hangings?'

'You know quite well, sister,' he burst out. He stopped abruptly, took a breath, then started off again; the effort of making his voice sound grown-up very marked. 'It was the mistress of the house and her daughter, Molly. They were finished last winter,' he added eagerly.

'And have you ever been to your father's place of work?'

He nodded furiously. 'Last year. I went with Mama and my sister, Molly.' The words flew out in a rush as he ditched his spunky attempt to speak formally. 'And there are many houses and shops ...'

He prattled on and on. I felt content to listen, enjoying the innocent excitement in his small voice as he described the store, the clerks that worked upstairs writing figures in a big book all day long.

'And Father has a big desk.' Edward stopped to take in a breath, his eyebrows pursed in a frown. 'I don't think he uses it very much. Mama says he walks about the store talking to customers. I would like to do that when I have grown bigger, but Mama says I have to learn to read and write first.' Edward looked up at me, his face set stubbornly. 'I think that would be very dull work, writing all day.' He sighed. 'But I still wish I could go to the store. Father says I am too little – although I am now much bigger than I was last year, so I will ask him again.'

'What does he sell?'

Off he went again, enthusiastically listing the numerous items for sale as if they were something quite extraordinary, which I suppose for Edward they were.

'And I saw plates in a big chest. Mama said they had come across the sea from Holland. Where is Holland, Molly?'

'Across the sea – the Channel,' I replied somewhat unhelpfully. 'Is that where the blue pottery comes from?'

Edward nodded, continuing eagerly, 'And soon we will have drinking vessels made of glass – like the windows.' He chatted on, his whole-hearted enthusiasm infectious.

We had now walked the whole length of the village

street. Beyond us were trees and moorland without a house in sight, as if a guillotine had sliced away all forms of civilisation from this moment on. We had passed no one on our way, the street deserted. But dotted about on the open ground behind the houses, I saw people working, their small figures, clad in beige and black, doll-like.

The carpenter's cottage sat in the middle of a copse of elm. Set on the far bank of the steam, it was thatched like the rest of the houses in the village, the Elizabethan house the only one that was tiled. The low-beamed room was littered with lengths of wood; and wood shavings, blown about by the wind, covered the floor like a carpet of rushes. Mr Higgins sat at a bench next to the open door, the tools of his trade hanging against its whitewashed walls. I saw axes and saws, a row of chisels and a mallet.

'Master Edward and Miss Molly. This is a pleasure.'

He seemed elderly, his thin back bent from constantly stooping over his work. I heard a baby cry out from a room behind the shop.

That was one of the surprising things I'd noticed about the people, how quickly everyone grew old. So far I'd seen four ages: kids, teenagers, young marrieds, and then, like they'd slipped down a chute, ancients with black or missing teeth. No way could I imagine them playing golf like my grandmother or jetting off on holiday to the sun.

'We've come to see if you have any more soldiers?'

He shook his head. 'No, Miss Molly, I only carve them if asked. There is no call for such toys in a small village.'

'No, I suppose not,' I replied disappointed. I wandered about picking up things and looking at them. 'What do you make mostly?'

'As you see.' He pointed towards a chest on the floor, one side as yet unfinished. 'It is to be given as a wedding gift.'

I bent down, noticing how the flowers came to life under

his chisel. He had drawn the pattern in ink on to the planed surface and was now cutting into it, section by section. 'Have you ever made a fire screen?' I said.

He smiled as if we shared a secret, raising his eyebrows, and I guessed I'd asked another dumb-fool question. 'The screen, I have been making for Sir Richard, is now complete.'

'May I see it?' I asked eagerly.

He looked at me curiously and pointed to a brightly-coloured, rectangular piece of wood on a square base. It was the same one.

'Is this the family?' I asked naively.

'But you know this, Miss Molly,' rebuked the man.

'No, she doesn't, Mister Higgins,' piped up Edward. 'We are playing a game called strangers. Molly pretends not to know things and that way she finds out if I know the answer, because I want to be very clever and go to school.'

Wow – what a reply – I wanted to hug him, I was so impressed.

The carpenter fell for it hook, line and sinker. He smiled broadly. 'You have always been inventive, Miss Molly. This is an excellent way to teach and keep a child's interest.'

To my delight, he told Edward all about the screen, pointing to the people and giving their names.

'And, what is that?' I asked, once again trying to identify the small object peeping round the skirts of the lady.

'A monkey, Miss Molly. You have good eyes.'

'Does Sir Richard own one?'

'No, indeed not. No one does, except for fine ladies in towns like London. I spent five years there, working on one of the churches. Its owner took it everywhere, even to church. A strange animal, with nimble fingers exactly like our own. Now, where it is possible, I add it to my work – as a mark that I carved the piece,' he replied proudly.

'See!' He pointed to the half-finished chest, a monkey's head peering round the trunk of a tree.

It was a fascinating little shop. I wanted to stay longer but Edward was getting bored; not at all interested in the wooden box Mr Higgins was showing me, in which he'd used delicate slivers of wood to create a pattern of linked diamonds.

'This is a jewellery box, Miss Molly. I first cut the pattern by removing fine layers of wood, replacing them with the inlay which I glue into place.'

'Is the wood English?' I peered closely. The box was fab and I wished it belonged to me.

The old man shook his head. 'Not these. They come from the new countries. They are very costly and, as you can see, I use them sparingly.'

'What do you mean by new countries?'

'India is one of them and Barbados, which is an island very far away across a great ocean.'

'Mm, I know, I've seen pictures,' I said without thinking. *Oops!*

Strangely, my blunder didn't even merit a second glance.

I listened intently while he told me about English woods, elm and ash which were used for carriage wheels, while oak was carved into furniture because it was so hard. He wasn't in the least bit boring either, not like Dad who drones on for hours, until you want to stick your fingers down your throat in a desperate bit to escape.

I turned to go, Edward eagerly pulling at my hand.

'Is that an Adze?' I asked pointing to a short hoe-like object hanging from the wall.

'Indeed, Miss Molly. How did you know that?'

Edward gave a whoop of proud laughter. 'There, I told you Molly knows everything.'

We said goodbye and were walking up the street again, when I suddenly had an idea. 'You wait there, Edward, I'll only be a minute,' and ran back to the shop.

The carpenter had already started work on the chest

again. He glanced up as I panted in.

'How much would it cost to make another soldier for Edward?'

'For you, Miss Molly, a sixpence.'

I didn't know what that was, but I knew someone who did.

'Could you paint it in bright colours, please? How long will it take?'

'A few days, I will work on it in the evenings.'

'And can you put him on a horse?'

The old man shot me a bright, sparkling glance before looking pointedly at my gloved hands, the bandages still showing. 'For you, Miss Molly, he will be on a horse.'

Wow! I actually had a friend – that's a first.

I smiled my thanks and rushed back up the street to catch Edward. He was watching the ducks chase each other round the pond.

'Edward, what's a sixpence?'

'That's easy,' he replied. 'Half-a-shilling. Why do they do that, Molly?' he asked innocently, gazing at the drake dive-bombing his girl friends.

'Because they're happy,' I replied, narked that now I had to find out what a shilling was. Molly might be the fount of all wisdom, but the birds and bees are not on my agenda of suitable subjects for discussion with a five-year-old.

SEVEN

I woke in the dark and, for a moment, thought I was home. Then I remembered. Instantly, that feeling of being bound into a whalebone corset crashed down on me again. I grabbed my bed-curtains and yanked them back, determined not to give in to an overwhelming desire to burst into tears, and ran over to the window peering out. It was beginning to get light. I woke Agnes, who followed me down the stairs to the garden.

'Agnes, why can't we fill our cans at night before we go to bed, and leave them by the fire?' I said over my shoulder. 'It would save a job in the morning and the water will be warm to wash in. I really *hate* cold water. And,' I continued thinking time and motion, 'if we put water in the copper pan to heat *before* we go to the privy, we could use that as well. No one will know but us,' I added, just in case washing in cold water was decreed by HIM.

Her plain little face lit up. I was so glad, aware her life wasn't going to be anything much except for work. For her, hot water was a great step forward. Well, I'd promised myself if no one had invented hot water by this morning, I'd do it.

Today, everything was different again. It appears that on Tuesdays HE goes to Sherborne. I heard the magic words while I was waiting on him at breakfast, the mother asking, 'And what time should we expect you back, husband?'

I kept my face down, expressionless, my ears flapping in a desperate bid for clues as to why he went there – but he was to be away all day and that suited me fine.

I sang through the jobs, sensing this was the day of liberation. My hands still hurt but now I could ignore them. Dinner was eaten quite quickly and afterwards I asked the mother if I could go for a walk. I stood there awkwardly, my fingers crossed behind my back – like any ten year old – silently muttering, *'please, please'*.

'You will not go near the manor house, Molly.' She looked at me gravely, her grey eyes reflecting my own. I wanted to shriek out loud, to tell her, to trust her with my secret because I knew I couldn't lie to her. Why did she have to be so goddamned nice? I could lie to Mum and Dad and never think twice about it.

My heart thudded into my boots with a resounding thwack. *Oh no, not again!* 'I promise I won't go to the manor,' I forced the words out between clenched teeth.

She smiled then, knowing I wasn't going to get into more trouble. 'You may go, Molly, and enjoy your freedom.'

I walked up the village street towards the manor. Hopelessly, I gazed down the drive my footsteps slowing to a stop. I battled with my longing to push open the iron gates against my promise to the mother. What the hell did it matter, I would never see her again. Stubbornly, I grasped the gate and swung it half-open. I was going and nothing would stop me. But I couldn't. I stood there frozen like a bloody statue – unable to stir.

Before I could stop myself, I was flying across the fields towards the river; the wind drying the tears as they spilled over onto my cheeks, only slowing up as I spotted some boys playing near the stone bridge.

What the hell was wrong with me? Did a promise to someone I'd only just met mean so much that I'd give up the chance to get out of this hell-hole?

The two boys saw me and dived for cover behind the wall of the chapel. I shrugged and wiped my eyes. Stupid little kids playing pretend Red Indians. I took no notice as they crawled on their hands and knees through the grass, hiding behind dense tussocks, perfect cover for spy-kids. Angrily, I broke into a run again heading for the woods.

My wooden shoes were heavy, and I was gasping and out of breath by the time I reached the top of the hill where the trees began. I can't say I was looking where I was going, too busy cursing myself for being such a wimp. Next second I went flying, cannoning into someone who had stepped out from behind a tree straight into my path.

The words, 'Bloody hell,' cut angrily across the air.

'Holy shit,' I exclaimed at the same time. I stared down at my left hand, which I'd caught against a sharp stone when I fell, blood already seeping through the bandage.

It was the servant girl, the one who had bound up my hands. She picked herself up off the ground, her hands flying to cover her mouth. My glance met hers. She flinched away and an expression of absolute terror swept across her face.

We stared at one another, like two dogs circling – wary – wondering who would attack first.

I did.

'Have you seen a fire screen in the manor?'

'Yes!' gasped the girl. 'Did you …'

'YES, YES, ME TOO!'

I didn't know the girl but still I hugged her, tears pouring down my face. After a while, I sniffed and wiped my eyes.

'You first,' I said, still clinging to her hand like a lifeline.

'I come from London. We were on our way to Devon for the Easter hols. Mum and Dad like to sightsee on the way down, to break the journey,' the girl explained.

She looked a couple of years older than me, but I wasn't sure. People look different with their hair scraped back and wearing a cap – like me at swimming. In the house she always kept her face firmly fixed on the ground – again, like me. Together we resembled a couple of monks in a monastery.

Now she met my glance eagerly, the dull amber of her eyes sparking into life, wisps of blond hair escaping from her cap.

'How long?'

'Two years.'

'Holy shit! *Two years!*' I gasped. 'But I can't, I've got a swimming gala in June.' I thought longingly of the finals that were held yesterday, wondering who'd won. I hadn't, that's for sure. But if I got back I could still do the nationals. 'I can't stay here for two years. Have you tried to get back?'

She nodded.

'What's your name by the way?'

'Janet.'

'Okay, so what happened?'

'It was the day after I got here. At first I thought it a really great adventure – you know like you see on TV – but it wasn't. It was horrid and cold and scary. I spent the night in a barn which really spooked me.' She gulped remembering. 'That cured me; I just wanted to get home then. When no one was looking, I climbed through a window into the manor. There's a sort of circular stone in front of the fireplace; took me ages to find it, before the sun settled on it. I stepped on and I was nearly there,' Janet said. 'I could see the tunnel and the stone room with the religious pamphlets everywhere ...' I nodded my head furiously. 'I could feel myself ... getting thinner ... my hands fading ... then someone caught my arm and dragged me back.'

'*Dragged you back!* I don't believe it! So what happened then?'

'I was taken in front of Sir Richard. The man, that

grabbed me, is his steward. He accused me of being a witch.'

'Get real,' I gasped.

'No! Honest! I was that scared my knees were knocking. The steward said he'd opened the door and seen me muttering spells. He said he watched me change into a harridan – *as if!* I don't even know what that is. And he caught hold of my arm to stop me flying away.'

'You have to be joking!'

'One thing you'd better learn quick,' Janet said seriously, 'no one jokes in this village. Sir Richard asked if there were any witnesses who could confirm the story.'

'And?'

'He questioned me then. I told him I knew no one in the area and had got into the house in search of something to eat because I was starving. I'd felt faint … and that's when the steward found me. The man didn't like that one bit. When Sir Richard said I should be let go, you should have seen his face; especially when he was told to take me to the kitchen and get me some food. After that, I left and went back to the village. I was desperate. I didn't know what to do and then I saw Molly.'

'My Molly,' I interrupted.

Janet nodded. 'She looked okay so I asked her for money – I begged her for some money,' she hastily corrected. 'Molly must have felt sorry for me. She was like that; she took me home to see her mother. She gave me a job and a roof over my head. You're lucky – she's nice.'

I nodded. 'But she's not really my mother. I can't believe you've been stuck here for two years. How do you bear it?'

Janet looked down at the ground. 'I don't!'

'Can't you get back in?'

She shook her head. 'I've been trying. I get an afternoon a week on Tuesdays when your father …'

'He's not my father,' I almost shouted the words.

'Okay! For what it's worth, I wouldn't like him for a dad either, the way he treats Molly. Anyway, he's out every Tuesday so I come up here and watch.' She pointed out over the hillside. 'You can see all the way up the drive, almost into the parlour. But since the war, Sir Richard has pretty-much stayed at home and so have his family, *and* his steward. He's called Perkins,' she ended bitterly. 'He lives next door.'

'What do you mean, next door?' I said, thanking my lucky stars. If I *had* gone on down the drive ... I shuddered, recalling the feel of the leather strap against my knuckles.

'His wife and family live in the thatched cottage next door to you. You must have seen the kids – two boys and a girl?'

I nodded, more concerned with escape than the steward and his family. 'So how can I get into the manor, if you can't?'

'Richard – that's who.'

'Richard? But I don't know a Richard.'

'Richard Blaisdale,' Janet said. 'He's Molly's best friend. They went to school together. He's Sir Richard's eldest son.'

Oh that Richard. 'But, I'm not allowed near the house.'

'Then leave him a message under the bridge, that's what Molly did.' She pointed downstream where I could see the broken stones of an old bridge.

'How do you know all this?' I asked curiously.

'I bathed her hands often enough,' she said. 'She was always in trouble, couldn't keep out of it. Not like me. Ever since the steward accused me of being a witch, I've been ever so careful; but people still avoid me like the plague. They cross the road when I come past, muttering and crossing themselves, and the kids throw stones and yell that they hung the last witch and they'll hang me.'

I gasped at that. '*We've got to get out of here.* I'll get a message to Richard straight away.'

Janet smiled. The feeling of relief was so stupendous,

knowing we were no longer alone, we hugged one another again. Then, subsiding into childish humour, flung our arms into a noisy high-five. It hurt like hell but that didn't stop me collapsing into fits of giggles. It was so good to laugh, Janet's face going pink with the effort.

Nearby, a pheasant flew up, its feathers rustling noisily. I jumped up, hastily looking about me, aware that we'd been making a hell of a racket and could have been overheard.

'It's nothing,' said Janet, peering through the undergrowth as if she had ex-ray eyes. 'No one ever comes here; it's supposed to be haunted by the last witch.'

I crossed to the edge of the trees gazing down towards the chapel. The boys had finished playing their game leaving the field deserted.

'Was there really a witch?' I said, sitting down again.

She nodded. 'But years ago, I asked your mother. She said it was before she was born. She told me that people were very ignorant then – *as if they aren't now* – and thought anything different had to be evil.'

'You keep referring to her as my mother. I don't even know her name.'

'Ann, *Ann Hampton*. He's John. I don't like him much because of beating Molly. But, to be fair, he's never lifted a finger against the younger children. Molly is wild and clumsy and mutinous. She wants her own life and he's determined to break her spirit. He speaks in that stupid religious language too, always bringing God into things and quoting the Bible, but he doesn't behave much like a Christian. Oh, and by the way, don't forget to call your mother, ma'am. *It's all right*,' she added quickly, noticing my face had gone red, 'Molly always forgot.'

'But Margaret calls her mother,' I protested. 'So why can't I?'

'*Because*, stupid. Mr Hampton decreed it last time she got into trouble. Told her she had forfeited the right to be part of a Christian family with decent hard-working parents, *as if*!'

'Well, if I replaced Molly who did you swap with?'

Janet shook her head. 'No one – that's why people were suspicious. Your mother, Mistress Hampton, told me that beggars are often whipped out of town or even stoned until they move on – talk about uncivilised!' she ended angrily.

'So what year are we in?'

'Sixteen forty-eight.'

'*Sixteen forty-eight*! That's hundreds of years ago. *Bloody-hell*! No wonder nothing's been invented.' I scratched my head, wishing I'd paid more attention in history. 'They spoke about the King and Cromwell at the service in the chapel. And you said Sir Richard had stayed at home since the war. It has to be the Civil War, but which King – one or two?'

Janet looked at me, a puzzled frown on her face. 'One or two, what?'

'Charles – one of them was executed,' I said impatiently. 'He was – he is?'

I nodded furiously. 'I think it must be Charles the First. But, it can't have happened yet. They must still be fighting.'

'Who?'

'The Roundheads and the Cavaliers – that's who.'

I stared round at the peaceful countryside. From where we were sitting at the edge of the wood the ground fell-away towards the river, its sparkling water slithering along the valley floor like a glittering reptile. The distant hills were blue-rimmed and, from our vantage point, the open 'E' shape of the manor house resembled a scorch mark etched into the ground with a burning stick. Nothing stirred, only the tiny figure of a gardener pushing his barrow.

'I can't see any sign of war. Are you sure you've got the date right?'

Janet nodded. 'It's sixteen forty-eight all right, and April.'

'That figures, it was Easter at home. Have you ever seen them, you know – Cavaliers and Roundheads?'

Janet nodded. 'I saw a troop of Cavaliers last year. They were riding towards Blandford, but they didn't stop.'

'What were they like?'

Janet shrugged. 'Covered in dust. They were riding fast but they wore great boots. I watched from the upstairs window. I told your mother. She said the King had escaped from Hampton Court and taken refuge in the Isle of Wight, and the men were most probably going to his aid but, to be honest, I didn't take much notice.'

'No battles?' I felt disappointed.

She shook her head.

I glanced back over the fields towards the manor house, knowing somehow I had to break in – Janet too. To one side were the stables, where in another century my mum was working or the police were searching. I shivered. 'What do you think has happened to Molly? Do you think she and I swapped places? In which case, poor Molly, but at least she won't get beaten.'

Janet grimaced. She still carried about her traces of that rigid expression she maintained in the house, as if her smile muscles had atrophied. I could sympathise with her. I'd only been there a couple of days and already my face felt like it had been dipped in concrete. 'She went out on Saturday morning leaving her chores undone. All I know is Mistress Hampton was worried and went to find her, and you came back.'

'Are we alike?'

She nodded. 'Can't tell you apart. Okay, looking back there are differences but you aren't exactly expecting a double to appear, are you?'

I carried on asking questions, everything I could possibly need to avoid giving the wrong answers. What the family did in the mornings, the afternoons, the evenings. What

Molly was like? Our ages: Molly fifteen – like me, Agnes – twelve, Margaret – eight, Edward – five, the baby – not yet two, another on the way. John Hampton, Molly's father, a merchant with a warehouse in Blandford Forum, a prosperous market town, riding there every morning except when he went to Sherborne. Then he stayed away all day, not re-appearing until after five o'clock and, twice a year, he was absent for a week or so.

'Why?'

'He owns a ship which sails out to the West Indies every year.' Janet said. 'I don't know why he doesn't take the family – I mean holidays in Barbados in sixteen forty-eight would be dead cool.'

I giggled. 'Get real!'

'*Honest!* He does own a ship. And when it's sighted, he goes down to Weymouth and stays there till he's sold the cargo.'

'Cargo?'

'Spices and wood. Oh, and sugar. You know the brown stuff we get in the house.'

'I know what sugar is, lame brain,' I laughed again, feeling great.

We talked and talked, even about our real lives in the twenty-first century, our homes and friends, boyfriends, birthdays. That was when we discovered we shared a secret – not from friends, but definitely from our parents – an unobtrusive tattoo.

'They'd have chained me to the bed if they'd guessed,' said Janet, pulling down the shoulder of her frock to show me the horns of a very angry ram. 'I had to blag about being eighteen.'

'Aries?'

She nodded. 'And you?'

'Taurus – May 19 – top of my leg' I said hitching up my skirt. 'I wanted to pierce my nose to shock Mum, but my mates at swimming said it'ud look like a water fountain in Rome. I didn't have any probs though; no one argues age with someone like me.'

Janet giggled. 'My mum had a fit when she found out but she quite likes it now, although she's threatened me with death if I dare have any more.' She sniffed, trying to stop herself crying; her eyes awash with tears. 'Oh, Molly, do you think we'll ever get home?'

I nodded. 'We have to. No one can possibly live in this barbaric age. I don't know how you've survived this long without going mad. But I promise we'll get home.'

Janet jumped to her feet. 'If you're to write a note for Richard, you'd better run, it must be ever so late.'

I got up, turning to give my new friend yet another hug. 'See-ye,' I said and hurried down the hill.

'Not if I see-ye first,' came the unexpected reply.

I laughed, feeling ever so much better.

***

I ran home, straight to the winter parlour where we ate breakfast. It was deserted. I saw a quill pen and ink on the dresser but no paper. Why on earth couldn't I have landed in a century where notebooks and paper lay about everywhere, like in my house? I could hear the family outside in the garden and ran upstairs into the bedroom, pulling open the cupboard where I hung my clothes. That was the one question I'd forgotten to ask Janet. Where did Molly keep paper to write notes; there had to be some. Finally, I found it, tucked away in the corner of the cupboard – a small pile of neatly folded squares.

I had to hurry if I was to get out of the house again that night and contact Richard. I wasted sheet after sheet, trying to make the damn quill write. Someone was having a laugh, I mean no one can write with a nib that either scratches the

88

surface or splutters blobs of ink everywhere. At its best, my writing looks like a spider's just walked over the page – this was worse. The clock struck the quarter, making me jump and daubing the paper with yet another blob, but it had to do. It was well after five and already the sun was beginning to fade. I flapped the paper in the air to dry it.

Quickly putting my cloak on again, I walked back up the street and along the main track towards Blandford. Two hundred yards past the cross roads, I spotted the stile Janet had told me about. I leapt over into a ploughed field, its ruler-straight ridges taking me down the slope towards the river, my eyes searching out the broken stones of the bridge.

The sun had dropped behind the hills and now shadows, like long pointy fingers, crept across the grass. I clambered down the bank, wishing I was wearing jeans and trainers; the full skirts of my dress hampering my stride. Only a single arch had broken away, the stones tumbling down into the riverbed; the water running fast below my feet. My foot slipped on the wet rocks and, for one heart-stopping moment, I teetered over the swirling torrent, my arms whirling like a windmill. I peered timidly down at the stones checking all around to find my next step and reached out for the comforting roughness of the broken arch.

Where could I leave a note? There had to be something. I ducked under the bridge. In the gloom the water took on a mysterious identity, full of dark, moving shadows which shifted about as if they were alive. It felt spooky. I could sense eyes watching me but was too scared to turn round and check, gripped by that horrid sick-feeling you get when you think someone is following you. Shivering violently, I examined the stone face of the wall searching for a hiding place. I wanted to run, to escape into the sunshine with its warming rays. I was about to give up when I spotted a narrow shelf of rock, near the top of the broken arch. Balancing carefully I reached up, instinct telling me there was something there. I was right. My fingers touched a box and, pulling it towards me, I slipped the note inside.

Hastily, I turned back towards the sunshine, hunching my shoulders to try and make myself invisible. I wanted to run and had to force myself to move slowly as I painstakingly retraced my path, cautiously inching my way from one boulder to another, clumsy and awkward in the increasingly dim light – only expanding my lungs to take in a deep breath once I'd reached the safety of the riverbank.

EIGHT

It was another lovely day. The first omen that my luck was about to change was the water. I had woken early and, waking Agnes, we had run to the kitchen eager to see if my experiment had worked. It had; the water was nowhere near hot but, once mixed with the water from the copper pan, it was definitely tepid. Almost gaily, she and I had washed, the water feeling good on my skin.

The second omen was Mr Hampton saying *good morning* to me. I nearly cheered. 'Good morning, sir,' I replied respectfully.

I had paid my penance and was now to be readmitted to the human race, and I wasn't about to blow it. Not a flicker of emotion passed across my face as to what I was really thinking, a mask of politeness. Instead, I redoubled my efforts, becoming even more cautious in his presence so as not to give offence, my eyes and head firmly pointing downwards towards the carpet.

The third omen was my hands. Although I had knocked my hand on the stone yesterday, they were at last beginning to heal and I had removed the bandages. Now I could flex my fingers, it made eating so much easier.

It was no hardship to wait for breakfast until Mr Hampton had left for work. With him gone, suddenly it became a fun meal. Of course none of us spoke but Agnes handed the bread to Margaret with a little smile,

Margaret gave me a smile when she handed me the honey, and I winked at Edward as I passed the meat, the mother nodding and smiling too. I knew that in another life she would be talking, telling us about the jobs to be done that day, the health of the animals and our neighbours; kindly and cheerful in the gentle way she had. And, to be strictly honest, I actually enjoyed no one talking – a welcome change from my own mum setting about me the moment I got downstairs.

I hadn't given it a moment's thought but now my hands had improved, I was expected to take over the milking. Watching the mother and Agnes, it had appeared easy. Now, I found myself face to face with the huge beast, ignorant as hell, and no instruction book. I stared in horror – although, to be honest, I expect the cow felt worse than me. Copying Agnes, I sat down on the small stool and buried my head in its flank. Closing my eyes, I reached down and began to pull on the teats. Up-close it smelled like a sewer. The only way I could deal with it, and not throw up, was to pretend I was ringing church bells. Then the cow – stupid damn beast – only had to go and prove it wasn't housetrained, by producing a gigantic waterfall of wee. Horrified, I made a grab for bucket, the thought of wee-filled milk absolutely vomit-making. My face must have been a picture.

Still, it had to be done. I tried again and, to my surprise, the milk started to flow. Before I knew what had happened, the pail was nearly full. I'd done it – I'd actually managed to milk a cow. I felt so proud of myself I nearly shouted my delight aloud: *hey not bad for a beginner*. But I couldn't, could I? I started to josh about, making Margaret and Edward laugh. I'm not sure if Agnes knows how to laugh, she always seems so serious.

And the best bit of news of all; provided my chores were completed before our dinner at half-past one, I was now free to do what I wanted in the afternoon, unless it was the nursemaid's afternoon off and I was roped in to help look after Edward. Of course, it goes without saying, I wasn't to go near the manor, but today – having done my chores – I was free.

I walked nonchalantly through the village and along the lane, even stopping to pick a posy of flowers to put into water. Leaving the road at the stile, I climbed over making my way through the burgeoning grass towards the tumbled-down bridge. All around, the air rang with bird calls – melodious trills interrupted by loud, indignant squawking. I lifted my head and stared up at the trees. Overhead a fight had broken out between a couple of crows and a magpie. I expect the magpie was trying to break into the family home. There was a lot of noisy swearing and posturing before it flew off chased by the irate crows, their black plumage bright against the blue of the sky.

Inside, I bubbled with excitement as if something great was about to happen; which was stupid, because the only thing that would really be great is getting out of this twilight zone. Still, for some reason, I had butterflies in my stomach.

A young man sat on the broken stones fishing. He was tall, about as tall as me, and fair. He didn't hear me approach, intently gazing at the fast-moving water.

Was this *Richard? I wasn't sure!* Then I noticed his clothes; a jacket of dark maroon velvet with puffed sleeves – the velvet reminding me of the smoky surface on a freshly picked plum. Short, it was fastened with laces down the front, a white shirt with a wide lace collar peeping out below it. His trousers, also padded, stuck out all round and were tied at the knees with ribbons. Below them, he wore red and green embroidered stockings and shoes with heels *and* bows.

'Richard,' I called, scared silly now.

For a split second I might have thought his clothes laughable – as if he was appearing in a Shakespearian play and had wandered off set – but the thought vanished the moment he turned round. He had one of those faces that occasionally burst onto the big screen, with high cheekbones and a looming brow over deeply set eyes that somehow manage to look gloriously handsome even when frowning. Across the space of the bridge, the blue of his eyes was startling. It felt like a lifetime of winters had been replaced by spring. His face lit up and he leapt to his feet. Kicking aside the cloak lying on the ground, he rushed over and grabbed my hands – I flinched.

'*It's about time.*' His voice burst out of him light and infectiously eager. Was he really so over-the-moon at seeing Molly. 'I've walked down here every afternoon since I got your note on Saturday. And why send another? You know I would come everyday, and your writing... I could hardly read it – *what*?'

He stared down at my gloved hands, only the tip of my fingers visible. 'Has he been hitting you again?' I nodded. He raised my left hand gently in his, brushing it against his cheek. 'So that explains the writing; I did wonder. Come on.'

I still hadn't said a word but this didn't seem to matter. Seizing his fishing rod, cloak and basket in one hand, and still holding mine – very gently – in the other, Richard picked his way over the broken stones striding out across the meadow. I followed like a prisoner in handcuffs, fluffy golden pollen from the celandines gluing itself to the hem of my gown.

A rocky outcrop had become visible on the top of the hill, the ground rising sharply. Richard didn't stop or pause, or even speak, until we reached the summit and were out of sight of the manor and the village, and among the rocks. 'Sit,' he said, panting slightly. 'Tell me.'

The tall rocks formed a natural amphitheatre, a barricade, protecting it from the north winds. It was open towards the south and, in the bright air, the distant blue of the sky shimmered like the sea. At my feet a trickle of water erupted from the stones to form a fragile stream. Sparkling in the sunlight, it dashed joyously downhill to join the river somewhere below.

Although we weren't that high, it was a great vantage point. I gazed down into the sweep of the valley, feeling empowered like an invading army; the bright air dancing off the sparkling green of the fields. Off to my left the road ran parallel with the river stretched away into the distance. My eyes followed it, imagining regiments of soldiers heading into battle, the river racing along in time to their marching feet until it vanished from view beneath the overhanging trees.

To the north-east, a knot of dark fir trees enclosed the tall spire of a church, a cluster of thatched roofs revealing the presence of a small village – close by only if you are travelling by car.

The countryside looked empty, much emptier than I was used to. With a jolt of astonishment, I remembered that the distractions of our century hadn't been invented yet. There weren't any pylons ploughing their way across miles of country or wind farms sited on hills, or tall conical towers containing evil-smelling silage. Nowhere, could I hear the drone of a helicopter or find trails of silvery exhaust streaking across the sky, from a plane on its journey to some exotic destination. Here, only the wind ploughed its way across the country and the distant hills were covered in gorse; narrow cart tracks like pencil marks winding their way between outlying farms.

To the north, a ribbon of road cut its path towards me; the same road that Dad had dawdled along – with me, half-asleep but safe, in the back. I could even make out a herd of cows; blotches of brown and white munching on stray tufts of grass that had sprung up between banks of spiky gorse.

Another conundrum – the cows I had seen from the car had been black and white. Then I remembered – these weren't the same cows.

Arriving at the village of Lingthorpe, the road disappeared between two rows of houses, the tiled roof of Molly's house staring imperiously down on its thatched neighbours. Emerging from behind the walls of the manor house gardens it split in two, a narrow lane curving round past the gates. My first impression of the manor house, when Dad landed us there, had been of a building that had definitely seen better days; its drainpipes broken away from the walls, and chipped and flaking stonework that needed restoring. In the sunlight, it looked fresh, solid and determined as if making a statement that it was here for the duration. It faced south over the valley, its formal gardens, like mathematical equations, no longer in existence in modern times; the gardens at the Retreat casually laid to grass and shrubs. Behind the stone paths and neatly hedged borders was a small park of newly planted trees which, sheltered by the high boundary walls, already boasted a covering of spring leaves. My eyes homed in on the powerful gates. They were closed, a bulwark against interlopers. Beyond them, a short drive flowed up to the front door of the building; my pathway to freedom if I was to get home.

Once past the gates, the lane got lost beneath the meadow of flowers, re-emerging at the bridge over the river. Even at this distance, I could see how fast the river was flowing and, if we had any more rain – like the torrents that fell in the night – I had no doubt it would flood and break its banks.

Once again, I pictured the gossiping villagers from Sunday and the two boys borrowing the chapel walls as a prop for their game. Behind the whitewashed building, the hill swept upwards towards the now distant woods.

I sat down on the rocks, the sun hot on my shoulders where the rocks sheltered us from the wind.

'Give me the flowers, Molly, they will wilt in the sun.' Richard filled a mug with water from the bubbling stream, placing the flowers in it. I felt so awkward. It would have been nice to break the ice by asking if they came here often. I mean it was quite obvious they did.

'Fritillaries – your favourite. What about the ones you took for your garden, are they flowering yet?'

I gazed at the soft mauve and white checked flowers, six petals forming a bell-shaped cap which drooped down from the delicate arch of the stalk. I hadn't known their name, simply recognising them from the canopy above my bed, where they formed an oasis of calm. I had found myself studying them closely every night before I closed the curtains, their delicate shape proving an effective antidote against the nightmare world in which I had found myself. Hastily, I tried to recall what I'd seen in the garden.

I shook my head. 'Not so far, but if they don't grow I'll take some more from the meadow and try again,' I replied, hoping that's what Molly would say.

'Why didn't you come before, Molly?'

Handing me the pot of flowers, Richard stretched himself out on the hard ground, one leg crossed nonchalantly over the other. He looked so completely at ease as if, at any moment, he might doze off. I found myself staring. I didn't much care that Molly knew him so well, she probably wouldn't have bothered to even glance in his direction; I had never seen him before. He was slight with those long muscles that swimmers get, although I guess his were from riding horses. I wondered then what other sports existed in the seventeenth century apart from fencing, because he looked fit. I could imagine him running the London Marathon – although not in those clothes. Except the fancy clothes rather suited him, and even though I wouldn't have been seen dead in purplish-maroon, red and green, on him they sort of gelled together. I stared round the little rocky cove, the angular grey shape of the rocks standing clear of their green surround. *Yes*, he looked perfect. Okay, I fancy lots of boys, particularly the ones I swim with, and can fool around with the best of them, but none had ever considered me to be anything special. But this glorious person did … and he was my best friend. How lucky was that?

'Father was angry because I was at the manor,' I said, trying to shift my eyes away.

'Father!' he propped himself up on his elbow, his eyebrows slightly raised and a mocking twist to his lips, his blue eyes laughing as if I'd made a joke. I so hoped I wasn't blushing. 'But why take the risk? Cook told me you had been there, but she wouldn't tell Mister Hampton; I expect it was Perkins.'

'I needed to talk to you.'

'I'm here now, so talk away.' Picking up my right hand he studied the knuckles. Not used to wearing gloves, without thinking I had removed them. 'You'll be scarred this time, Molly, and will always have to wear gloves.' He kissed my fingers gently. 'I'm sorry.'

For a moment, my breath deserted me. I stared down at the little row of pink scabs beginning to dry and flake off, trying to ignore the sensation of his lips on my hand. Underneath, I saw a jagged white line where the leather had bitten into the skin.

'I'm waiting.'

'I …' I floundered in the sparkling depths of his eyes. How on earth was I going to tell this beautiful stranger I wasn't Molly; and worse, would he kindly get Janet and me into his house so we could go back to our own century?

We sat in silence. Richard seemed quite happy, not a bit disturbed by my not talking, as if it was a normal part of their friendship. Panic-stricken, I searched my brain for something to say but found nothing there. The ice chamber, I'd lived in for days now, had so many cracks it was beginning to melt in the warm sun. Confused wasn't in it. It was as if someone had taken a sword and sliced me down the middle. Part of me desperately wanted to tell Richard who I was and why I was here; the other part wanted to stay exactly as I was for evermore, the sun warming my shoulders, completely content and not wanting to change a single thing. I stared at his hands – the angle from wrist to knuckle long and shapely; his nails smoothly rounded, a stranger to manual labour.

'Will you tell me about the war?' I managed, finally breaking the silence.

I didn't think the question funny, but Richard did. To my astonishment, he fell about laughing.

'What's the matter?' I said my voice stiff with embarrassment.

'Oh Molly, it's no wonder I love you.' I flushed scarlet, fixing my eyes on the distant river. 'One minute you think it's a stuffy old war and the next you are asking me to tell you about it.'

'Will you?'

He nodded. The blue of his eyes made me think of the Mediterranean Sea. I have never seen it except as a computer image, but I have often imagined how it would feel to swim in ... a feeling of warm silk clothing your body.

'Why the change of heart?'

'The men were debating it in chapel on Sunday and I didn't understand what they were talking about. They sounded very serious. Some were saying that war was inevitable, but I thought the war had ended.' I guessed the last bit, hoping I wasn't about to make a fool of myself – yet again.

'It did, nearly two years ago now when the King was captured. Last autumn he escaped to the Isle of Wight, believing he would be safe. He should have gone to France,' Richard said, his tone bitter. 'Now, it is too late – and he has been held prisoner ever since.'

He looked serious as if it *really* mattered.

'So why a war?'

He paused and frowned at the ground. I knew he was arranging his words in a way that I would understand. 'After the first war, many of the regiments were left unpaid by Parliament. It caused a great deal of anger and some have changed sides and now give open support to the King. There are also rumours that the Scots are raising an army.' Richard started up, glowering fiercely. 'If that happens, even I would fight, for no Englishman can accept the thought of the Scots invading our country.'

Wow! *I'd never dare take him to see an England v Scotland Rugby match. I could see him creating a riot if the Scots were winning.* 'You wouldn't!' I gasped.

Richard grinned and lay back down. '*You know I wouldn't, Molly.* When has a sword ever settled anything? They fight … men die … and the side that has the greatest strength of arms in the field claims their cause was just. But why is the village becoming involved?'

'I don't know if they are,' I replied defensively. 'They were just talking.'

At least a million times a day since I arrived here, I wished I wasn't so ignorant. I wished it again now. 'But why is religion so important?'

'That's a strange question from someone who lives in a house dominated by religion.' Richard sat up and looked at me closely.

I wondered then if there was anything he'd spotted about me that was different. I hoped not – not yet anyway. At least, let me have a few more hours of this glorious charade. 'You forget making butter and preserves isn't exactly the ideal schoolroom for learning about anything.'

Richard shouted with laughter. 'I forgot your life was so dull. Even so, you have to know most of this. Surely Mister Hampton speaks ... Oh, I forgot.' He gazed at me, his expression concerned.

Wow, even a non-speaking father has its uses.

'Religion has divided this country for hundreds of years, Molly. My father remembers hearing of men – and women too – burned at the stake for non-compliance.

I shuddered, hardly able to believe what I was hearing. 'What does compliance mean?'

'Oh, Molly,' Richard groaned. 'What am I going to do with you? Your wretched sense of humour ...'

Humour! He has to be joking! I'd never even heard the word before.

'You would have made an excellent candidate for burning, with your refusal to obey Mister Hampton.'

Oh! So that's what it means!

'That is why my father advised the villagers to stay away from the conflict. He remembers when the King invaded Scotland, trying to force them to accept his religious views. Men were killed but nothing changed. He believes no one holding a religious view will ever change it, least of all as a result of persecution or war. And, until God descends to earth in a cloud of fire to show who has the right, it is folly to fight.'

'Does no one do anything except go to war?' I exclaimed, forgetting who I was supposed to be.

Richard flashed me a grin, ignoring my outburst.

Okay, so Molly made stupid dumb-assed comments. I smiled to myself, happy that he wouldn't think badly of me whatever I came out with.

'Besides, it is foolish for people living so far from London to become involved. It can only cause trouble. How can anyone outside London possibly know what is true and what is simply rumour?'

I let him talk, watching the shadows flit across his face as he mentioned a name or spoke about the power battle raging between the king and church, the army and parliament. He could have been a lawyer, arguing skilfully one case against another. Even so, it seemed awfully confusing with people changing sides as easily as I changed my hairstyle. Tossed aside were the moderates, who had tried and failed to create a more open society, with freedom of worship and a more equal political system. Now, the people left facing one another were like heavy-weight boxers with fists trained to kill. King Charles, who believed in his divine right to rule; the Presbyterians, the most powerful party in parliament, who were opposed to everything he said and believed. Dragging their supporters with them, it was their way and none other that must triumph, no matter who died to achieve it.

He lapsed into a silence, a silence which I was happy not to break, although a part of me wished I had found the courage to tell him who I really was. It would have been really great to chat about how things went on in my time – where fights in parliament had dwindled to polite slanging matches and no one got killed.

I watched the sun drift slowly across the sky, knowing I had to leave and not wanting to. 'Shall I see you tomorrow?' Perhaps by tomorrow I would have dredged up the courage to tell him I was an alien.

'Molly, look at your hands. If Mister Hampton sees us together – can you not wait until he goes away?'

'As if that's likely to happen,' I muttered, despair creeping into my voice. If I couldn't see him, what was I going to do?

'But you told me, only the other day, that he would shortly be going to Weymouth to see his ship dock.'

'I did?' I caught the excitement in my voice and hastily damped it down. 'Oh yes, I did, that's right.' Why hadn't

Janet told me about the ship's arrival? I'd kill her next time I saw her, landing me right in it. 'But there's been no news yet,' I improvised hastily, 'storms or something.'

'Can you not wait until he has left the village, Molly?'

Richard was right and, if what he said was true, it might only be a couple of days before I saw him again. Surely I could wait that long. I nodded. 'But how ...'

'I will be at the bridge on the day he leaves. If you cannot get away I will be there the next day and the day after that.'

Don't you have school to go to? The question stuck on the end of my tongue. I guess Molly knew the answer to that; I certainly didn't.

NINE

Yesterday, I didn't get to the bridge. Rain had appeared from nowhere falling in great torrents, and any thought of going out for a walk was instantly dismissed; but somehow the delay doesn't matter, my mood changing from deep despair to over-the-top-optimism, all because someone knocked on the front door.

We were in the middle of dinner when it started to rain, the parlour dark and gloomy under the heavy pall. At home I would have flipped a light switch but not here, even though it was difficult to make out the expressions of the parents sitting opposite me. Not that I wanted to look at HIM, with his sour face and cold sandy eyes, but I enjoyed looking at the mother, with her clear grey eyes that spoke volumes even during the silence of the meal.

There came this knock on the door. I stopped eating in surprise and, forgetting where I was, turned my head to look. Luckily for me so did my sisters and Edward; obviously visitors were an unusual event. Instantly, sharp knuckles rapped the table and, stricken with guilt, I quickly turned back. I stared down at the polished surface, my heart hammering. I don't know why, because I felt sure he wouldn't hit me for something all the children had done. I heard Janet go to the door and a man's voice asking for Mr Hampton. The husband rose and left the table, wiping his mouth on a napkin.

'Continue your meal, children,' said the mother.

But it was far too interesting an event to eat. I could see Margaret felt the same as me; both of us half-heartedly munching at our food, our ears pinned back, hoping to catch a word or two of the muffled conversation taking place in the hallway. Only Agnes showed no curiosity.

After ten minutes, with me watching the clock, the husband returned to the parlour and sat down, continuing his meal as if nothing had happened. By this time I was beside myself with curiosity. The rain tumbled down harder and, in the kitchen, someone laughed. My eyes on the table or not, I knew HIS face had just got grimmer. Obviously, the messenger was being fed and had been stupid enough to forget where he was. I felt sorry for him.

'Will you prepare a bed for Snape, my dear.'

The mother looked up. You could have heard a pin drop. 'Most certainly, husband, how long will he be staying?'

'One night only. Tomorrow, he and I will leave early for Weymouth. He brought me news that the ship has been sighted.'

'How long will you be away, Father?'

It was Edward! He might be little but he could see we were busting a gut trying to keep silent and – sensible lad – knew his father wouldn't thrash *him* for breaking the silence. I could have hugged him.

The husband frowned. '*Edward*, you know the rules of this house.'

'Yes, Father, and I beg your pardon,' replied the child innocently. 'But I was so excited at the thought of your ship safe and almost arrived in port.'

The husband smiled. Well, he didn't actually smile but he sort of stopped looking grim. I nearly fainted on the spot. The lightness in his face was so dramatic, making him altogether more youthful, and I could see that Edward would grow-up to look like him.

'Very well, Edward, but do not make a habit of it. Most likely I shall be away a week. I have to arrange for the cargo to be sold.'

'May I go with you, Father; I *really* want to see the ship.'

He smiled again.

Heavens above! Was there no end to the blessings being bestowed on us that day.

'It is good to see you are so eager but as I have already told you, Edward, you are not yet old enough to travel the distance. I will take you when you are eight.'

Edward sighed and I thought of the soldier which, perhaps even now, was being carved out from a piece of wood. He's such a great kid I wish I had ordered two – one for being a great kid and the other for finding out that the husband would be away a week. Then I remembered, I still didn't know what a sixpence was.

The sky rained cats and dogs. Because neither of the parents was with us in the winter parlour, I was given the task of reading from the Bible, while Agnes and Margaret sewed. Afterwards, I dared to introduce them to that expression. Edward laughed himself silly and I hastily shushed him.

I felt gutted at not seeing Richard. I stared out of the window telling myself that I was behaving like a ten-year-old. But I couldn't help wishing I was at home and could phone him; my insides aching with hunger even though I'd just eaten a huge meal. And it was so stupid. So ... he had blue eyes ... lots of people have blue eyes. A little voice whispered ... but not with a smudge of darkness behind the blue.

I turned away from the window. No one but a fool would put a step outside; Richard wouldn't be at the bridge even if Mr Hampton had been away. But with him in the house? Sadly, even I had to agree Molly took far too many risks. Dear Agnes, my source of information, told me that her father frequently took long walks along the river, and she worried he might see me heading through the field towards the bridge, and put two and two together.

We talked quite a lot that day, curled up on my bed with the curtains drawn, to shut out the rain rattling noisily down the windowpanes. By mid-afternoon it was so dark I could no longer see the strangely shaped words, packed tightly together on the flimsy paper, and since HE wouldn't let us light candles – I guess he doesn't care if I ruin my eyes – we crept upstairs and talked.

Agnes loves to talk, but never about herself. I'm so used to Blue and her dreams of going to Oxford or Jan wanting to become a model, it felt weird having to dig for information.

It was a strange conversation too, as it centred entirely round Molly; Agnes starting every question with, 'And what will you do then, Molly?' and 'What do you think about that, Molly?' It taught me a lot about the girl whose place I had taken. Perhaps it was the way Agnes talked about her, with such interest. They were best friends, okay, but Molly came across as someone so obsessed with what was happening to her, she never noticed her sister's devotion. I'd have given anything for a sister like that.

Were Molly and I alike? I didn't know, but somewhere in the back of my mind I hoped not, because I've got this nasty feeling I wouldn't like her. She seems hell-bent on doing what she wants and doesn't give a damn who gets hurt in the process. I know that sounds exactly like me. *But it isn't.* Okay, so I don't know all the facts about her yet. Why, for instance, she refuses to obey her parents when it causes so much pain, not only to her but also her mother. If Ann Hampton were my mother, I wouldn't do one single thing to upset her. Even worse, Agnes and Margaret are scared silly when HE's about in case he starts on them; and she doesn't bother about that, either.

I woke up this morning feeling quite calm and, for the first time, that awful feeling of blind panic has left me. I looked up at the nodding bells on the mauve fritillaries, peeping shyly from their carpet of purple, white and yellow, conscious that the vast iceberg in which I'd been trapped had gone – dissolved.

I kicked up my heels, trying to stand on my head, and bounced out of bed. I didn't bother to wake Agnes; she looked so peaceful. Outside, dawn was beginning to break. I sniffed the air, my eyes drinking in the streaks of peach and gold floating across the sky. Even the privy didn't smell after the heavy rain of yesterday.

Our visitor, Mr Snape, had a room on the ground floor, and Janet would wait on him. That started me off wondering what made him tick – HIM, I mean, not Mr Snape. I mean it was obvious he had money. The house was huge, but we only had two dresses – one for everyday and one for Sunday – and only *two* pairs of shoes! I don't know if the mother had any more, but I doubted it. Yet there was always plenty of food, way more than we could eat, and Beth heated water in the kitchen all the time, so why the cold water? I'm sure dukes and princes, even in 1648, didn't wash in cold water. And why did his daughters have to lug heavy cans up the stairs – after all Agnes isn't very big. Was it something to do with the puritan religion, that you can amass wealth but not spend it?

In a way, what was happening to me was similar to an exchange visit in a foreign country. You understand the every day things okay but if you don't speak the lingo, you really haven't a clue what's going on below the surface. Although, if I'd really been on holiday in France I could have phoned Dad and asked him – he'd know.

I giggled. That's a first, me actually asking Dad a question.

I carried up my two cans, returning for a second trip to

collect the two Agnes always carried. It wouldn't hurt her to get a few minutes extra sleep – after all she isn't as old or as strong as me, and yet she was expected to work as hard. And I owed her; all through the first nightmare days she'd been silently helping me keep out of trouble.

'Come on, lazy bones,' I shook her lightly on the shoulder.

'Have you been out already, Molly?' she asked, automatically sliding out of bed the instant her eyes opened.

I nodded, 'I've got the water.'

As we washed we chattered; at least it was Agnes mainly and not about much. After all Agnes doesn't know much imprisoned in this village, but I really blessed her gossipy nature, helping to fill in yet more gaps.

'I wish,' she began and stopped.

'What do you wish?' I said, not paying any attention.

Then the words hit me full on. This was the first time, since I found myself in that house five long days ago now, that Agnes had uttered the words, *I wish*. My mates and me, we say it all the time. It made me feel ashamed.

'That I could go to Blandford with you. I wish I could see what it was like for myself.'

'When am I going to Blandford?' I said, knowing Agnes doesn't care what stupid questions I ask.

'Stop teasing me, Molly, you know very well you will go there tomorrow with Mother – you always do when the ship comes in to port.'

I laughed with relief, saying flippantly. 'I will ask her; perhaps you can come next time.'

'*Will you really? Oh, Molly* – it would be so exciting to see real shops and houses, and the fine clothes that townspeople wear.' Agnes clapped her hands, a rare smile lighting up her thin face.

It struck me then how deadly dull her life was compared to a twelve-year-old in my century – yet she never complains.

She seems quite content to go on, day after day, milking cows and making butter. She isn't brilliant at reading either, and it doesn't seem likely she will ever go to school. Even if she does there are no good books and no telly or computers, only that awful embroidery. Besides, she'll never be allowed a career, except to make better jams and preserves than her neighbours, and worry about salting the meat. Then, at eighteen, she will be married off to some yokel, to milk yet more cows and salt yet more beef. It doesn't seem quite fair.

'Agnes, do we have any money?' I asked, turning round so she could fasten the buttons on my gown while I brushed my hair – its chestnut lights intensified by the chlorine they put in the swimming pool, which rots our cozies and bleaches our hair.

'I expect Mother will give you some for your journey, why?'

'Nothing – I just wondered.'

'You *do* look pretty, Molly,' she burst out, trawling up the endless row of miniscule buttons. 'I would so like to be tall like you.'

My brush froze in mid-stroke and I gazed at her gobsmacked. Me – pretty! A great lump stuck in my throat. I stared down at my long beige skirt which I'd classified as a passion killer. But it wasn't; the dress with its flounced overskirt actually looked okay, a hell-of-a-lot nicer than my long skinny legs – all blue with cold and covered in goose bumps – under my short school skirt. I couldn't see my face because there wasn't a mirror, but I know I felt happy, happy that I was going to see Richard; but never *pretty*, that had to be Agnes talking.

Agnes whisked her fine dark hair into a bun, pinning it severely, before tying her cap under her chin. Suddenly, it registered how different she and Molly were from the other two – the other three, if I included the baby. Margaret and Edward were as alike as two peas in a pod, their hair a sandy brown and their eyes hazel, identical in colour to the husband's. Agnes was small and thin, her eyes almost black under frowning black brows, while Molly was tall and big boned – like me – with eyes that were widely set under a chestnut mane of hair. I found myself hoping I looked like Ann Hampton. I wasn't sure about her hair because only wisps ever escaped from her cap, but she had beautiful eyes, like deep pools of clear grey water. What a strange mixture.

Of course, my own family weren't much better; Mum – blond with help, Dad – mousy; my sister – like me – dark brownish-chestnut, except she has light blue eyes whereas mine are grey with a dab of green.

The husband breakfasted with Mr Snape. Afterwards we waited patiently, lined up in the hall to say goodbye. He actually bent down and patted Agnes, Margaret and Edward on the shoulder but not me, for which I was grateful. I would have been sick if he'd touched me. I glued my eyes on the bag he was carrying, in which his clothes for the trip were packed, praying seven days would turn into forever.

He'd gone and, even without asking, you could tell it by sniffing the air. I wouldn't have been surprised to find the house smoking a joint, after standing to attention for months. No one said anything – I mean, there wasn't the sound of singing coming from the kitchen or anything – but you could tell.

'You will need to be ready quite early in the morning, Molly.'

I gazed at the mother stunned. She had spoken, she had broken the eleventh commandment – *Thou shalt not speak at meals.*

Edward looked up, his sandy eyebrows pursed in a frown, which meant he was dying to ask a question.

'Wait, Edward,' she shushed gently. 'You may speak when we have finished eating. I was quite wrong to break the silence; my only excuse is that I feel quite excited about our trip. So you see Edward, even grown-up people occasionally do silly things.' She smiled at me and I smiled back.

Edward did as he was told, but I could sense he was bursting with excitement, frowning fiercely at Margaret to hurry up when she began dawdling, kicking her heels and gazing out of the window.

'Margaret,' admonished her mother, trying to instil speed into her.

Margaret was always slow, always finishing last while we sat silently, our hands folded in our laps, waiting for her. I knew she was lost in her own little world and wondered what she was thinking about. Did she know about fairies and dragons? What about Barbie Dolls? I almost laughed out loud at that. I could tell her loads of fairy-tales and give her something magical to dream about, and I promised myself to do just that before I left.

The morning flew by. And, with him away, we ate our dinner much more quickly and, to be honest, the food tasted fantastic, even though we weren't allowed to speak. Nevertheless, it was almost three by the time I had finished clearing the table. I had to be back in the house by six, which left a little over three precious hours to spend with Richard.

He was waiting, as he told me he would. News travels fast in a country village. His plum-coloured jacket had been changed for a bottle-green one, with stripes of gold running down the sleeves. Today, he looked taller – edging me out by a centimetre or two. I glanced down noticing the heels on his shoes. Again, we headed uphill towards the escarpment, Richard talking madly. I felt as if I'd known him all my life and so envied Molly.

It was a lovely day – the sky was bathed in a soft blue haze, with shimmering fronds of lime green from the newly hatched leaves.

Then my conscience had to go and spoil it. *'Why don't you tell him now?'*

'*Because,*' I frowned horribly at the stony ground.

'*Have you forgotten your promise to Janet to get her out of here?*' The voice in my head continued relentlessly.

I had. I felt myself flush guiltily. I hadn't spoken to Janet since Wednesday and she'd completely slipped my mind. '*He wouldn't believe me,*' I retorted angrily to my conscience; bloody awful thing, always poking its nose in where it's not wanted.

'*So, is he going to believe you in a few days when he's used to the new Molly?*'

I couldn't answer that.

We didn't stop when we reached the rocks. Richard dumped his cloak on the ground and, grabbing my hand again, set off along a stony track. I was happy to go with him, although it was frustrating not knowing where, and not daring to ask. The track opened out onto a long grassy slope sprinkled with daisies, which flowed smoothly down into a valley. It would have been perfect for snow-boarding or tobogganing, with only a couple of steep bits easily avoided. I gazed down at the gentle slope wondering what we were doing there. Next second, I knew.

'Ready, Molly. *Go!*'

There wasn't even time to say, 'Go where?' All at once we were flying. And had I misjudged the incline – *no way was it shallow*. Within a few steps, I was clutched in the jaws of momentum, unable to stop, my arms and legs moving so fast they were out of control, my feet barely skimming the ground. I felt as light as the wind whisking off my bonnet. I let go Richard's hand, grabbing at the ribbons to stop it flying away, but kept running, trying to keep up with his pounding steps.

The ground levelled and he slowed, gradually pulling to a stop. He bent over, panting heavily, and turned his head sideways to grin at me. I stood there stretched up to my full height, breathing in the glorious sunlit air.

'Have you been practising?' he said. 'You nearly beat me.'

I shook my head and my hair, released from its tight cap, escaped and flew in all directions, a halo of chestnut lights. Hastily, I pulled it back from my face and twisted it into a knot.

'Don't put your cap on again, Molly, you know I hate it.' His voice rang with misery.

'And I get into trouble if I'm caught without it,' I retorted half-heartedly, wanting to be persuaded.

'But no one ever comes this way.'

Before I knew it, he'd snatched the cap from my hand hiding it behind his back.

I lurched forward to grab it and stopped. Embarrassed and confused, I stared at him unable to remove my gaze. He stared back, his eyes bewildered mirroring mine. He couldn't be looking at me like that, could he? I wanted to weep at my answer. *No – this was Molly he was staring at.* They were boyfriend and girlfriend and I had plonked myself down right in the middle. I hid my face under my hair, knowing I couldn't bear it if Richard only liked me because he thought I was someone else. But the only way I could find out was to tell him.

'Let's walk,' I said, my voice tight, and started back up the track hoping he'd put my red face down to running.

We strolled back up the hill. Richard picked flowers, giving them to me to carry until I held a great bunch.

'Stop,' I laughed in protest. 'There's too many.'

'Then we'll float them down the stream,' he said, bending down to grab some more.

I knocked his hand away and he set off up the hill, pretending to stoop down and pick more flowers, with me at full pelt after him.

We crested the hill, falling down exhausted from the steep climb. I filled the pot from our little stream arranging the flowers, and then splashed water on my face, drinking thirstily. I watched Richard float flower petals in a trickle of water until they disappeared behind the rocks.

'You're very quiet.' Richard glanced at me from his usual lounging position on the ground.

'Am I?' I hesitated and took a deep breath. The moment stared me in the face. The perfect opportunity to confess to being a stranger from another century – someone he'd never met before, and didn't know or care about. 'I …' It was impossible, a thousand times more difficult than it had been the other day. And I hadn't managed it then. 'I was thinking about Blandford – going there, I mean,' I quickly substituted.

He nodded. 'That explains it. But you always enjoy your day away from the village – I know I do.'

What did he mean? *He was going away too!* Or perhaps he felt relieved to be spending the day without me. Not having to worry in case we were seen. The frustration of not knowing, not being able to ask what he meant by that remark.

'Richard, when are you going back to school?' I said, searching for something ordinary to say.

'University, Molly, university. But I'm not sure if that will ever happen now.' He sounded upset and I knew it really mattered to him.

'I spoke to Father last evening. He doesn't feel it a good idea while he is so frowned upon. He feels we are safer to stay quiet, until either King Charles gets back his throne or the royalists are forgiven for supporting him.'

'Is he in danger?'

'Father? Not of being arrested; no, that hasn't changed. He fears if he brings himself, or any of us, to the notice of the authorities in London, he may lose his lands.'

'Has that happened a lot?' I said, beginning to relax again and feel more comfortable. He was so easy to talk to.

He nodded. 'Many of my father's friends have been

forced to leave England and have had their land sequestrated ... *confiscated*,' he substituted, spotting the question in my face. 'Their families are now destitute and survive only with the help of friends. George Goring, who commanded the Royalist troops at the battle of Langport ...'

'Langport!' I exclaimed, because we'd driven through there on our way to Millfield in Street. I added without thinking. 'There wasn't really a battle, was there?'

Richard nodded, giving me a very funny look. Suddenly, I felt convinced he knew the truth. I opened my mouth dreading his reaction when I confessed. The words shuddered to a halt on my lips. *Not today! I couldn't do it today.* This was torture – like being disembowelled alive then torn apart. I wanted to be with Richard, spend time with him. Being liked by proxy may not be much but it was something. Except, it was more than that. I also wanted my day of freedom with Ann Hampton. I wanted to bask in the warmth that she generated towards all her children; desperate to experience the tight bond that everyone says exists between a mother and daughter. After that I'd tell him – *promise.*

'Yes, he had to flee the country and now lives in Spain. He serves their king now. This is not a good time to be a royalist, Molly. You are much safer to be like your family.'

The moment had passed; my sigh of relief transforming itself into a guilty smile. 'But won't things get better now the war is over?'

'It would seem not. Father is the most loyal of persons but even he has become exasperated. King Charles refuses to treat with either parliament or the army, playing one off against the other. It is a dangerous game he is playing.'

TEN

It felt weird not seeing any cars – as if the world had ended and I was the last to know about it. I might have begun to accept my journey back through time, still I nearly freaked when we emerged from the narrow lane and trotted out onto a wide, well-used road, without looking. I glanced left, frantically expecting a juggernaut to come hurtling round the bend. Instead, birds sang loudly in the hedgerows, competing with one another for choir of the year, while the river tumbled along the side of the road keeping the horse and cart company.

Outside, I was dressed in the sober hues of my Sunday best, but inside bubbles of excitement welled up, and my feet felt so itchy it was all I could do to stop myself breaking into a dance. I waited impatiently while the mother dawdled outside the front door, kissing the family and leaving instructions with Beth and Janet and the nurse; everyone lined up to see the mistress of the house leave, exactly as they did for her husband.

At last we were moving and I felt like flying – as light as a bird. An intense feeling of pure happiness swept over me. Even my dreams of Richard, which had dominated my sleep, faded into the background at the thought of having her all to myself for a whole day. Braving my ignorance, I asked about the villages as we trotted through them, for the sheer pleasure of watching the grey eyes gaze back at me with a smile.

We passed the carter, with his usual assortment of strange and bulky objects overflowing his cart. Some days he even carried people – a sort of postman and bus driver combined. Today, it was a goat and some chickens which were clucking indignantly. I caught a glimpse of beady eyes and a series of dishevelled heads mixed up with fluttering wings, like a three-headed monster. They looked ever so comical, although I don't expect the chickens thought so tied up in a bunch by their feet. The carter, ignoring the noise, puffed away at his pipe, his horse plodding its slow way along the lane.

By contrast our horse was positively world-class. It trotted smartly along and, what with the newness of my surroundings and our non-stop talking, the journey seemed to take minutes, although I guess it was well over an hour. As the town came into sight other carts joined ours; the mud road dwindling away replaced by cobbles. I burst into laughter as a parade of vegetables, cabbages, swede and turnips, performed acrobatics in the air caused by the jolting of the cart over the lumpy cobbles.

That was the big thing missing from this century – vegetables. Our dinners were mostly meat with not much of anything else. I had discovered a root cellar tucked behind the barn, where potatoes and carrots were stored for the winter. It was almost empty and I had assumed there wouldn't be any more until the new crop in the summer – but perhaps I was wrong and you could still buy them in the towns. Swede I didn't mind but I found turnips coarse and peppery, even when served with a honey glaze. Sometimes, Beth served a fruit sauce with the meat, instead of vegetables. That was one of Edward's jobs, to turn the apples in the larder; Beth making apple sauce from ones already going-off. Stacked behind the fruit, I had seen rows and rows of pottery jars – all neatly labelled – apple, damson, plum and blackcurrant – and I guessed that was another job waiting for Agnes and Molly when the fruit ripened in the summer.

Although the countryside had appeared empty, I realised now it couldn't have been, judging by the number of carts descending on Blandford. Saturday had to be market day and families were off on an outing, like our occasional trips to the shopping centre when I positively had to have new clothes. The day was cold, a change from the sunny warmth of the previous one. I smiled as the idea crossed my mind that Richard had ordered that day of sunshine especially for us. Today you needed a thick jacket, a keen wind blowing; the sun soaring in and out of white-edged clouds racing to reach the horizon. The women were warmly wrapped in long cloaks or coloured shawls, under which their spotlessly white aprons peeped out like a badge of office. And they wore bonnets or caps, like the mother's and mine, for no one – not even children – went bareheaded. Clutching a wicker basket to their chest, they sat upfront with their husbands continuously shouting across the carts to their friends, in what appeared to be an on-going conversation.

By contrast, the men were almost completely silent and appeared to spend more time talking to their horse – heavy-legged, clomping beasts more used to pulling a plough than a cart – than their wives. Some of the men were really old too, with young and pretty wives. Sometimes it was easy to see why; two generations of kids – one lot almost grown up, the other still babies – sitting quietly in the back of the cart.

I felt so relaxed and comfortable with Ann Hampton that once or twice, I almost blew it. She must have thought I'd contracted lockjaw, opening and shutting my mouth like some species of codfish. I gazed at the people converging on the town, dying to discuss the difference between them and modern folk. It wasn't only their clothes that made them different. It wasn't even their faces, deeply lined with rough skin, as if they constantly battled with bitterly cold winters and scorching summers, it was more their whole outlook on life. They plodded like the horses, as if life was something you had to get through – not have fun in. I don't expect there was any spare cash for fun anyway, their clothes worn; the elbows and sleeves of the men's jackets shiny with use and the leather traces, running through their hands, stitched and wearing thin.

A cart carrying baskets of bread joined the procession. This surprised me a little. In my ignorance, I had thought every household baked fresh every day, like us.

I loved making bread; it was the one job I really looked forward to. The warm smell from the loaves hits you full in face, as you take them from the fire – the scent, out of this world. And Beth, if she was in a good mood, would let me bake a small piece of dough into a bun, handing me a dab of butter so I could eat it the moment it was cooked.

Perhaps town's people bought bread? I guessed Margaret would if she lived here, because she's now got this phobia about burning herself again, which is why I swapped my chores for hers.

The bread cart moved on, replaced by something distinctly foul smelling. I grimaced at the mother, screwing up my nose, and turned round to look. Two carts away a pile of cowhides were contaminating the good smells of the morning.

I looked about me eagerly as the cart rattled and bumped over the river bridge, the pony automatically slowing its pace on the uneven stones. There were houses on both sides now. Tall and short, tiled and thatched, some built with their upper floors jutting out into the street, their wooden beams created a patchwork of shapes and colours – like a packet of Liquorice All-sorts. Huddled together for support, the long street descended, step by step, down a steep hill. And, not only did they lean sideways, they slumped forward on the verge of toppling into the road, their rooftops close enough to shake hands.

A window opened above us. Automatically, I ducked as a stream of liquid from a chamber pot narrowly missed two pedestrians, who leapt for safety under the leaning houses.

The mother smiled. 'Living in towns can be quite dangerous, Molly.'

'Why is it permitted?'

'It isn't. The town's ordinance states that slops should be emptied at the back but servants are often lazy.'

She certainly knew how to drive a horse – none of that silly *walk-on* stuff that TV-actors use. This pony responded to a flick of the whip touching her flank, the cart weaving in and out of traffic – and there was lots of it, no one much bothered which side of the street they drove. It was chaotic, creaking cartwheels competing with the yells and curses of their drivers, horses whinnying, and people shouting at the top of their voices. There had to be accidents, even though the traffic moved at a snail's pace.

I was silent, eagerly watching, my eyes flittering from side to side, greedily taking in every inch of this new world.

She pointed to an inn halfway down the street where we were to leave the pony. We passed under an archway into their yard and stopped. I got down, glad to stretch my legs. It was a sprawling barrack of a place, drifting backwards on both sides of the archway into a malodorous stable; the rumps of half-a-dozen horses sticking out into the yard. Angled black beams showed where the building had been extended, with no two windows in the whitewashed wall on a level – reminding me of the little doors in an advent calendar.

A man appeared, dressed in that universal covering of brown which made me think of pig sties. His face was stolid, without shape or form, a face that definitely belonged to this century. Not like Richard's. Despite dressing like a play-actor, he could have easily fitted into the twenty-first century; his whole demeanour modern and full of life. There was nothing about him that would invite curious stares or comments in my world. But the groom carried an air of in-built subservience about him. Even with modern clothes, and a modern haircut, he wouldn't have fitted. Keeping his gaze tightly on the ground, he quickly removed the animal's harness leading it off to the stable. Then, doffing his hat politely, held open the door for us to enter the building.

It had been sunny outside and my eyes took a moment or two to adjust to the gloom. We were in a large room, dimly lit, the light trapped between dark beams, so low I had to duck. Rays of sun streaming through the leaded windows created parallel shafts of brightness, highlighting pockets of dust suspended in the air. Despite a blazing fire, the room still gave you that cold feeling as if you needed an extra sweater, its floor of dark grey slate swallowing any brightness thrown out by the flames.

Rows of high-backed benches, their seats narrow like church pews, stood against the wall, a plain wooden table placed between them. Their high backs created an illusion of privacy, shielding guests from public gaze. But the dark wood greedily absorbed any spare light and made the room darker still.

'Would you like to try chocolate, Molly, or your favourite apple and honey drink?'

I blinked – this was really living it up. And she was so different, chatting to the innkeeper, completely at home in these strange surroundings. 'I'd like to try the chocolate, please.'

'And I will have coffee,' she said. She leaned forward, her hand on the table touching mine. 'I confess I look forward to this the whole year.'

'You should keep a store at Lingthorpe, ma'am.'

She didn't answer that; she didn't need to. I guess HE wouldn't allow it. Instead, she told me how coffee had come in from Holland some years previously but was generally only to be had in London. However, since Blandford was on the coaching route, the Landlord at the inn now kept it for a few special customers.

'Of which you are one,' I said.

She smiled, her face rosy and happy looking.

I didn't much like the chocolate – bad choice. It was rather strong and sickly, but I got it down and then needed to visit the closet – which, wonders of wonders, was actually an inside job; a seat with a hole in it stuck out in a room at the back of the inn, but still dreadfully smelly. I haven't a clue where my sudden fixation for loos and water has come from. Jan and Blue would laugh themselves silly if I told them that the greatest of all modern inventions was the flushing toilet, but it really is if you don't have one.

Market Street, where the inn was located, was one of three main thoroughfares. HIS store was in East Street and, at the bottom of the hill we swung left, the road beginning to wend its way back up the steep slope again. I was astonished at how big the town was. I mean, what with plagues and fires and wars, it was pretty amazing there were any people left in England at all. Of course, it had to be the biggest building in the street. Raised above the roadway, it loomed over the houses on either side and looked exactly like him – everything from the solid beams, holding the construction together, to the dusty boards on the floor, beige in colour.

The ground floor was open to the street, a long wooden counter stretched across the gap. Behind it, wooden shutters lay against the wall, next to a cupboard with rows of tiny drawers in it, which I took to be the equivalent of modern-day shop-fittings. Two ladies were waiting to be served. They greeted Ann Hampton politely, before turning back to complete their purchases; their clothes so dull it was anybody's guess whether they were servants or titled ladies. I was dying to see a real-live Cavalier wearing thigh-length boots and a fancy waistcoat, or a lady in a velvet gown, with feathers in her hat – but so far, nothing remotely like that had come into view.

As I watched, the shop assistant plunged a metal scoop into a large barrel, bringing out what looked like brown dirt – but which, I had an awful suspicion, was actually brown sugar. He took it over to the counter where a sort of iron contraption stood, rather like a scarecrow with metal plates for hands. By the time he had attached the scoop to one side, I'd worked out that the heap of round, revolting-looking things on the counter were actually a pile of very dirty iron weights; the smallest about the size of the plug in a washbasin, the largest – bigger than a triple-burger, only heavy and solid. Each weight rested neatly on top of the next one, like those bright-painted Russian dolls that fit inside each other. He sat the scoop on one side, adding weights to the other. When it balanced, he poured the dirt into a small cloth sack which the customer handed to him.

I so hoped I was wrong about it being sugar, because the store looked a breeding ground for serious germs, and catching the Black Death was not on my itinerary of, *must things to do when visiting the 17th century.*

I followed the mother up some open wooden stairs into a barn that was even dustier than the ground floor, with dribbles of brown powder decorating every available surface. Wooden barrels had been stacked in one corner and lengths of wood, reminding me of Mr Higgins, the carpenter. He had used wood from the West Indies to create the delicate pattern on the jewellery box, and I wondered if this is where he had bought it.

A trap door opened, crashing down on the dusty boards, and a workman appeared. I jumped and coughed as the powdery flour lifted, filling the air with a thick dust. He hefted one of the barrels onto his back, tossing it down a chute.

I wanted to have a closer look and find out whether the man, stationed with his cart below the chute, had been engulfed in flour. Edward nearly had hysterics describing the farmer's face when the barrel had burst open drenching him in flour – he's such a sweet kid – but the mother had disappeared up yet more stairs and I hastily followed.

I emerged at the top of the building, the roof tiles so low they snagged the cotton on my cap. Up here, it would be boiling in summer and absolutely freezing in winter, far too cold to work despite the carpet on the floor. I had noticed a closed stove on the ground floor, where customers waited to be served. However efficient, it still wasn't powerful enough to warm the entire store. Then I remembered the lengths of wood stored on the first floor, and realised that having a fire on the upper floor wasn't exactly a practical idea, but I still felt sorry for the people that worked here.

A boy, not much older than me, with his back to the window for light, was busily writing in a huge ledger using an immensely long quill pen. He looked up curiously and stood up. He didn't speak, simply nodding his head in greeting, immediately sitting down and starting work again. Edward had said *two clerks* and I gazed round the room catching sight of an old man, only his legs visible behind the high-fronted desk. As soon as he saw the mother, he got to his feet and came over, clasping her hands affectionately in his.

'Miss Ann – it is always such a pleasure.'

She laughed. 'Jonathan – it is the greater pleasure for me to see you are still alive and well. Every year I expect to see you retired.'

The old man was dressed in rusty brown – which had probably started life as black, his clothes old and worn like him. Below his trousers white stockings gathered in folds along his spindly legs, and he wore black pumps. He shook his head, to which wisps of white hair were still sticking, his once-blue eyes peering short-sightedly. 'It is best to keep working in such troubled times and I will do so for as long as the master finds me useful.'

'And your wife, Jonathan?'

'Fair to middling, Miss Ann – neither of us is getting any younger. However, we have made one advantageous change this year. Our eldest grandson has taken over the house with his new wife, and we have retained two rooms for our use. Now, while we are working, the ladies are company for one another. My grandson is a good lad. You will find him on the lower floor – covered in flour,' he added, a twinkle in his eye.

'Miss Molly,' he exclaimed and gave a little bow. 'How you have grown this year and begin to look so much like your dear father. Now, I expect you want your money; I have it ready for you.' The old man turned back to his desk, mumbling forgetfully into a row of pigeonholes set in the top.

In six days so many peculiar things had happened, I'd learned not to allow my mouth to gape open like a fish, but *money* – this was something else.

The mother caught my expression and smiled mischievously.

'What a sensible man, your dear father; a crown every year until you are fifteen and, from your sixteenth year until you are twenty-one, a whole half-sovereign. What wealth for such a young lady. What good things you will be able to buy,' the old man mumbled aloud. 'Now where have I put it? Ah yes! Here you are, Miss Molly, please be so kind as to sign my book to say you have received it.'

Beaming, he placed a large gold coin in my hand. I looked down, aware it was money but feeling exactly as I did when I went to Spain – helpless – without a clue how to work out what it represented in English pounds and pence.

'Thank you, where do I sign?' A finger, all knotted with rheumatism, like my Grandma's, pointed to the place on the ledger.

There were eight signatures already on the page. I stared at these records of Molly. First, the badly formed, printed letters of a small child, improving year by year; the last few written in a neat copperplate which mirrored the delicacy of her embroidery. I tried very hard to copy her writing, but the end result wasn't as good. I wanted to cry, feeling somehow that I'd let her down.

'May I look round, ma'am?'

'Yes, dear. I shall be busy here for several hours.' I heard the chink of coins and guessed she also had a present – no wonder she'd been excited.

I still felt weird, those signatures of Molly dancing in front of my eyes, and my chest heavy as if the real Molly was trying to get back and couldn't – like me. I shivered, wondering how anyone could describe HIM as *your dear father*. Okay, so it was kind to give me money, but I'd have preferred no money and no beatings, and I knew Molly would, too.

ELEVEN

I stared down at my hand and it smiled back at me, my nails making pretty little half-moons under the coin in the centre of my palm. I glanced back to where the mother was chatting and laughing at the old man's jokes.

'Excuse me, but could you change this into smaller money for me – shillings and sixpences, if possible?'

The old man beamed. 'And I thought you had forgotten, Miss Molly. I have them ready for you.' He counted six shillings and eight sixpences into my palm, the feel of them, dropping one after the other, like an electric current surging through me. At last I knew what a shilling was. The little coins were small and made of silver, each one bearing the head of Charles the First, his hair long and wavy – except I guess it was a wig. I turned them over seeing letters round the edge enclosing a coat of arms.

'What are you going to buy, Molly?'

'A game for Agnes and Margaret – they hate reading so much.'

The mother looked at me then. I mean *she really looked at me* – her grey eyes studying me as if she could see right through my chest wall into my heart. I held my breath, hoping she hadn't guessed. I couldn't bear it if she started to treat me differently – like a stranger. After a moment she smiled and sighed. 'You are growing up, Molly.'

I ran down the wooden stairs, my feet clattering and

banging on the heavy boards, free to look about the town by myself. I needed some retail therapy. I giggled, hastily changing it into a cough, spotting the shocked faces of the two ladies at the ground floor counter. So! Who cares if I laugh, they'll never see me again. Smiling broadly, I went down the steps into the street, straight into a film set.

In the middle of the cobbled street two men were having a great chat, leaning back on their horses as if they were sitting in an armchair. As if on cue, other people entered the scene; a man pushing a handcart, another driving a broken-down old nag, women heading purposefully along the raised pavement towards the market.

Here, crowds of people milled round the little stalls in the hope of catching a stall-keeper's eye. I saw bread, meat and eggs, cloth, ribbons, needles, thread, pots and pans – allsorts. There were bottles of a strange-looking medicine, which the man swore would cure anything, and I was almost tempted. A stall-keeper began to shout his wares, while a group of children jostled to get the best view of a street entertainer, already surrounded by a crowd of on-lookers. At that point, I wouldn't have been surprised if a chorus of dancers had leapt out of the crowd, followed by a loud voice shouting, 'CUT-PRINT IT'.

As I passed, the door to one of the houses on East Street opened and a lady emerged. At home I would have said *some woman* – but this was a true lady. In a glamorous, dark-green cloak and dress, she wore a hat like a big baby's bonnet with feathers and carried a long stick decorated with ribbons, which she obviously didn't need like sunglasses on a winter's day. When the two men spotted her, they swept off their hats, the feathers in them lightly dancing in the air on their way towards the ground, bowing with the greatest elegance. I hid an envious smile. It was impossible to imagine men in our century, never mind young guys, behaving with such style. I suppose women had to lose something when they demanded equality.

Eagerly drinking in all the sights, I carried on down the street heading for the market hall; a circular building standing up on stilts, benches and stalls sheltering beneath it. Inside, I bubbled with excitement. What I was seeing was a world-exclusive. No one else living had ever seen this – only long-forgotten writings and waxen-faced images summoning up pictures of the past.

Surprisingly, I felt totally at home wandering about, even though I felt somehow different from everyone else. So strong was this feeling, I almost expected people to stop and stare as I walked past; exactly as me and my friends would have done if we had spotted a celebrity walking down the street. Yet, none of these people even bothered to give me a second look. To them I was nothing noteworthy. It felt wrong in some strange way.

A clatter of horses' hooves drowned out the sounds of the market and a troop of horsemen rounded the corner of the street, their coal-black mounts slowing to a careful walk as their hooves met the cobbles. I stared, unable to believe my eyes: Roundheads! And exactly like the illustrations in our school history books; with round helmets, a piece jutting-out at the back to protect their necks, and carrying lances. Over their dark jackets, they wore a metal breastplate and they had on leg shields, which Dad had said were called grieves.

My Grandma says kids, meaning me of course, are so pre-occupied with themselves they only see things that concern them. Now, I understand what she means. The first few days here, I was so spaced out I never saw anything. All of a sudden, I can pick out a million details about this one troop of cavalry. How, for instance, the lance carried by the rider in the eighth row has lost its pointy bit.

The men looked shabby and unkempt – not smart like our modern soldiers. Even their breastplates had lost their bright-silvery sparkle, dulled into a bluey-brown like petrol leaking into a dirty pool of water. Some were dented and split as if they'd recently been in a fight. Despite everything, though, they still looked magnificent; their horses' coats running with sweat and white foam lathering their chests – as if the troop had come a long way and fast.

'Molly, where have you been? Hurry up.'

Richard's voice, exactly as I heard it in my dream last night. Unbelieving, I swept my glance round the crowded area searching, convinced my ears were playing tricks. Then I saw him. My heart leapt into overdrive, beating furiously like a call to arms. He was lounging against one of the uprights supporting the conical-shaped roof of the market hall, partially obscured by a gaggle of men. Arguing loudly, they were tossing their arms about in wildly extravagant gestures, forcing passers-by to keep well out of range for fear of being knocked down. I caught some of the words flung into the air – King was one, Cromwell another.

He strode across the market place, a joyful smile on his face. My head swirled and I felt light-headed as if I had stood up too quickly.

'It's a common enough sight, Molly, these days.' Richard nodded at the riders. I could tell from his expression that he felt dismay at their presence. I tried to say something comforting, but my tongue had wrapped itself in knots – and I stayed silent. I wanted to ask, what are you doing here? I didn't know and, surprisingly, I didn't care. I'd just been given a most precious and unexpected gift – a few extra minutes to spend with him. It felt like I'd just won first prize in a competition that I didn't even know I'd entered.

The riders swung into East Street, their mounts clattering up the steep gradient towards the Salisbury road, leaving behind steaming piles of dung. Pedestrians glanced up, drawing back to avoid being run over, but otherwise no one paid them any attention. Richard was right. I guess after six years of war it was a common-enough sight.

He didn't take my hand, his manner more reserved than it had been the previous day and, for a moment, I thought I'd upset him. It was only when I noticed men and women walking separately, not touching, that I remembered this was a different age where different rules apply.

Richard led the way through the town, retracing the route the cavalry had used, clearly marked by the mess the horses had left behind. Market Street and East Street had been paved which made for easy walking; but once away from the centre of the town, the pathways dwindled and the streets narrowed, becoming densely packed with unassuming little houses, stacked one on top of the other higgledy-piggledy. Neither of us spoke; a frown furrowing across his brow. I wanted to ask why but I still seemed incapable of forming words.

No one bothered with us, not the slightest bit interested in two young people walking sedately towards the bridge in the distance. I was still thanking all the gods, I hadn't gone up the street instead of down, when I caught sight of a reflection in a pane of glass – the young woman elegant in black. With a sense of shock, I realised it was me.

Richard was dressed differently too. His jacket and trousers were of a rich brown cloth that looked smooth to the touch and, although his jacket was fastened with large buttons, a broad white-cotton collar folded over the top, there wasn't a trace of embroidery or embellishment anywhere. Even so, he retained that modern look. The way he stood casually leaning on one hip, his lively expression, even with his hair tied into the nape of his neck, the only attention he would have attracted in my century was screams of admiration from girls.

I lingered in the open doorway of a workshop, astonished to find it full of strange little men with beards, wearing chimney pots on their heads; a shire horse harnessed to a cart waiting patiently outside. I couldn't believe what I was seeing. People making things! I heard a loud whirring sound. Startled, I noticed the man nearest the door using a machine with a foot pedal. I desperately wanted to ask about it but didn't dare in case Richard flew back at me with the ominous words; *Who are you? You don't belong here. And what have you done with Molly?*

It was so unfair that on the day I discovered history, I was stopped from asking in case I was exposed as a fraud. It's like I've just woken up from a long sleep that has lasted all my life because all of a sudden I'm looking at things and actually registering them – and I can't do a damn thing about it, except stay ignorant.

'Hurry-up, Molly, we haven't got long.' I felt a touch on my arm, like a thousand volts of electricity. 'Good morning, Mister Jenkins,' Richard called, politely nodding to the figure working the machine. Above him, I saw a series of ropes and a pulley and, on the workbench, a vice with claws holding a half-made chair leg firmly in its grip.

The man stood up and doffed his hat. 'Good morning, Master Richard, Miss Molly.' He gave a little bow. 'You are both so tall these days it's difficult to remember you used to be little enough to put up on the back of my horse.'

Richard laughed. I smiled awkwardly, feeling a bit like a freak in a circus, and hoped Mr Jenkins wouldn't ask me a question because I definitely wouldn't know the answer. Turning hastily away, I patted the shire horse and it stamped its foot in pleasure, its legs encased in their traditional white ruffles. Raising his hand in a salute, Richard crossed the road, swapping sides with me, making sure he stayed on the outside. To be honest, I found this rather bewildering because there wasn't exactly any traffic; then a cart trundled past and a shower of water flew up from a hole in the road. I guess it's considered good manners for men to get wet rather than ladies in their floor-length gowns.

Gradually, the hurly-burly of the town retreated into the

background. There were still a few houses but no shops. We cut across the meadow which ran behind them; our steps evenly matched. Molly would have been familiar with the path we were taking. After all, she had lived here as a child; I hadn't.

It hadn't warmed up much. The wind constantly dragged the sun behind vicious-looking clouds that ate away the blue, until even a sailor would have had trouble finding enough material for a pair of trousers. It certainly wasn't a day for sitting about. I didn't care though. I was gloriously and unexpectedly with Richard; nothing could possibly top that, but I was still grateful when he found us a dry spot, under the stone arch of the bridge, out of the wind.

Today, though, it wasn't only his outfit that had changed. He was different; withdrawn, as if wearing a plain style had prompted him to adopt a new, more formal manner. I felt he had stepped away from me and we were sitting separately with a wide space between us – not shoulder to shoulder, our bent knees touching. The two previous occasions, I had felt so relaxed in his company it was like being curled up in the most comfortable chair in the house watching telly.

Now, although we chatted and laughed, words remaining unsaid floated in the air and, several times, I caught him glancing surreptitiously at me. Once again, I felt convinced he had guessed my secret – that despite all evidence to the contrary, I wasn't the genuine article, the real Molly whom he so obviously loved. The thought was so devastating, I wanted to cry. I stared fixedly at the far bank gripping onto my tears, waiting nervously for the inevitable bombshell to drop.

It didn't come; Richard seemingly content to skim stones across the water, the smooth surface of the missile repeatedly bouncing before inevitably losing momentum and sinking.

Was he waiting for me to confess? I began searching for the courage to admit the truth. It should have been easy. My best friend – someone to whom I could say anything, no matter how outrageous. After all, that's what best friends are for. And what would be the worst that could happen? That he believed me or that he didn't? If he did, I would lose him but get home. *If he didn't* ... my heart sank, like the pebble he was tossing into the river. In my mind's eye, I watched it spiral down through layers of silt to be lost on the bottom. *If he didn't believe me, I would still lose him.* He would think me ridiculous and childish making up crazy stories, a poor thing worthy only of contempt.

I remembered Janet telling me how, at first, she had considered her trip back through time a real good laugh. My first feelings had been those of disgust and loathing. Now, I could appreciate the magic of my situation. This world, even dominated by discontent and war, was like one of those happy dreams that you want to continue for ever. When your alarm goes off, bringing you back to earth with a bump, you whisper – a few more minutes please I was having such a lovely dream. Except this dream was becoming increasingly dominated by the thought of losing someone very precious.

Desperate to delay the inevitable I burst into speech, gabbling on about stopping in the market on our way back to buy presents for the children.

'And I mustn't be late. Mother and I are going to dinner.'

He'd been silent for so long, it was a surprise when he did speak.

'You remember the other day, talking about the war?'

My spirits soared joyfully, like a lark bursting into song; I had been granted a reprieve.

'Mm. What about it?'

'Do you think there ever could come a time when we were on different sides and hated one another?'

'*No!* Do you?'

He shied another stone into the water, not replying.

'*No, Richard!*' I cried out, forgetting for a moment who

I was supposed to be.

He swung round at that and grabbed my hand, holding it tightly. 'Not willingly – I agree. But Father was talking last night about relatives who live in London, friends from boyhood who have turned their backs on him. He was saying to Mother, if things get worse he may need to send us to France.'

'But not for long?'

He reached out for my hand again, absentmindedly running his fingers lightly across the back of my scarred knuckles as if checking that the bones were still in place. 'We were nine, Molly, when war broke out. Two years ago, no one came out the victor. But the squabbles have not gone away. Quite the reverse. They have intensified, with both sides becoming entrenched, more and more bitter as they remember the slaughter that took place throughout the six years of conflict. So many dead, so many families destroyed. Men don't forgive – not easily. It will take a generation – perhaps even longer. Father believes this can end only one of two ways – the abdication or death of the King. And, if he goes, so do the rest of his followers – ground into the mud under Presbyterian rule.'

I knew it ended in death – but I couldn't say. 'But you keep telling me you aren't involved.'

'We're not. Father has never taken sides. But such is the pressure from the church and parliament, they are forcing everyone to take a stand and speak out. I can see no end to this – except you on one side and me on the other. *Oh Molly!*' He groaned as if physically in pain. '*Everything's changing.* It might not look it, living in that pigsty of a village where nothing ever happens; but friends are becoming enemies. I don't want that to happen to us.'

It won't, ever! I wanted to say it aloud, because I knew for certain it wouldn't be politics that separated us; it was time that was our bitter enemy. I sensed it now, lurking behind the pillars holding up the bridge, waiting to pounce.

'But I'm not on that side, whatever it is,' I burst out wildly.

'Puritan.'

'*Puritan – yes – yes – puritan – that's right*. No! I'm following my mother's example. She's a proper Christian.'

'Married to fanatical puritan.'

There it was said – my father, John Hampton – the bogey man.

I had to get back. I saw the pain in his eyes, but what was the point of staying? He felt unhappy because of the war. I just felt unhappy.

Richard left me at the bottom of East Street and I wandered back through the market. I had promised a gift for Agnes and Margaret and, however miserable I felt, I couldn't let them down – not when they'd been forced to stay at home milking the cows. I passed a stall selling painted wooden dolls and stopped, attracted by the bright colours. How Margaret would love one of these.

'How much are they?' I asked nervously.

The man behind the stall looked up. 'You have money?' he said, his tone rude and off-hand. I nodded. 'Well then, one shilling.'

'Don't you listen to him, Miss Molly.'

I turned round startled on hearing my name. A woman stood there smiling at me. She had a round cheerful face under her bonnet, but without make-up her eyelashes were sparse and her features blurred into one another. She was dressed in a plain green gown and, over it, she wore a sort of half-length skirt, drawn-back at the front and gathered at the waist. Round her shoulders she wore a shawl, which she had pinned together to keep it from falling off.

'Is it a year already,' she gossiped. 'How time flies. And you so tall and so like your father. You will be going to the church, Miss Molly?'

I nodded dumbly.

'And your mother?'

'She's at the store,' I burst out, thankfully knowing the answer to that question.

The woman beamed, her cheeks glowing as warmly as the friendly smile in her eyes. 'Then, I shall go straight to the store to pay my respects. Now, don't you take any cheek from these ruffians. Bill – this is Molly Blaisdale as was.'

The man behind the stall bent his head, tugging at his hair. 'Sorry, Miss Molly, I didn't know ye, I won't charge ye more than nine-pence.'

My iceberg was back – except now it felt like a suit of armour, my arms and legs surrounded by a coat of rigid chain mail. Like a robot, I pointed to the doll and handed over a one-shilling piece – taking back three copper coins. My mouth opened and shut, 'thank you,' I said. The man tugged at his hair again.

Mechanically, I moved to the next stall, watching in silence the words, *this is Molly Blaisdale as was,* drift slowly across the air from one stall to another, the stallholder's mouth slowly smiling as I pointed to some gingerbread and peppermint drops, my hand offering two pennies.

The words spun round and round in my head: *Molly – Molly Blaisdale that was.* Only the real Molly knew the answer to this one – and she wasn't here to ask.

TWELVE

I wandered about picking up stuff from the stalls, gazing at it intently although I never saw it. I wanted to cry, to hide away, my lovely dream-world in tatters. No longer interested in the gaily-decorated stalls, I walked back up the street to find Ann Hampton waiting.

'Did you enjoy the market, Molly?'

I looked up at her as she tucked my arm in hers, exactly as she'd done the day we first met, and I wondered if she knew her daughter sloped off to meet Richard. I had a sneaky feeling she did – and didn't mind. The words Molly Blaisdale burned a hole in my chest. But how could I ask?

'I bought Agnes this game because she couldn't share our treat.' I pulled out the box of draughts which I'd found in the market. 'It's called Jeu de Force – do you know it?'

She nodded.

'And I got a doll for Margaret.'

We walked back down towards the market, where she bought flowers – a great handful of violets and primroses – before veering off into a narrow lane that meandered along the side of a hill, a church clearly visible at the end of it. I hoped there wasn't yet another service to sit through. After Sunday, I was all-churched out. And, after today's revelations, I couldn't have stuck it. I just wanted to go home and hide away under the bedcovers.

The church was a typical old building and, reluctantly,

I'd seen millions of them. Set high on a hillside, a tower and battlements to protect it from attack, its walls had already cracked under a wind that tore relentlessly down the valley. Perhaps, because of my dad, I could value something from our modern life, where money is made available to restore old buildings. We passed beneath a wooden porch, scored with millions of holes made by ravenous woodworms – one of its uprights little more than a honeycomb. I opened the gate and stepped onto a narrow flagstone path that wandered between gravestones, where wild daffodils and dandelions had seeded in the mossy grass. Some were already broken and leaning, the exposed hillside providing no protection from winter gales.

The mother sat down on the stone seat against the wall of the church. I dropped down beside her, not quite sure if my legs would support me after reading the inscription on the headstone nearest to us.

In loving memory of James Henry Blaisdale.
1606 – 1638
Beloved husband to Ann and father to Molly
He gave his life to save another.
Perished at sea April 1638
Sorely Missed

There was a verse as well but I couldn't see it, my eyes blurred with tears; which was stupid because this was Molly's father, not mine. I brushed them angrily away. At least the mystery of the market place was sorted and HE wasn't anything to do with me, which made me well-glad.

Helplessly, I watched the tears drip down the mother's cheeks and silently slipped my hand into hers, wanting to comfort her.

'I have never spoken to you about your father, but I made up my mind to do so this year because you have suffered so much, I cannot bear it to go on. And, it seems to me that in the last few days you have become so different ...'

You can say that again.

'What do you remember of him?'

'Not much,' I replied truthfully.

'I knew your father from childhood although he was older than me. We grew up here in Blandford Forum and were married when I was little more than seventeen. My father had wished me to wait, but I threatened to elope,' she smiled sadly. 'By this time the route to the East and West Indies had been opened and ships were bringing in spices and sugar. Soon after you were born, your father bought his ship – it is called the Molly, you know – after you.'

I didn't, but I wished the real Molly was sitting here – not me. She should be the one the mother was talking to. I felt so envious of her surrounded by all these amazing people. But what had happened – had we exchanged places? Was she locked into my life? When she returned would she appreciate, as I now did, that life isn't made up of stupid everyday conveniences. If you are loved, you can be happy living in the North Pole. Even as the thought grabbed me, I got this horrid feeling that Molly isn't coming back; we didn't change places. I felt sad because now she would never get to know this wonderful lady.

'It was such a happy time, Molly; we had ten marvellous years and I even travelled with your father on one of his voyages.' She laughed. 'I was miserably seasick, but it was worth it to see these strange lands. We travelled first to some Spanish islands off the coast of Africa and then across an ocean, so vast that I feared we would never see land again. I admit I was terrified, but after four weeks at sea we came upon this magical island – Barbados – it is called, basking in a blue sea and covered with strange trees and flowers. And there were fish that flew and whales, and the

sun shone every day. At the next possible opportunity, I will
show you my book – I pressed flowers and leaves to remind
me. Since we have lived in Lingthorpe, I have been so busy I
had forgotten all about it.'

Yes, milking cows and making cheese, I thought angrily.

'We anchored in Carlisle Bay, living on the ship because
your father insisted the climate was dangerous. It did not
look dangerous but he said people succumbed to strange
fevers, especially in the summer months. Nevertheless, it
was a voyage I cannot forget. We had left you with your
grandparents and were away three months. You cannot begin
to imagine how much a small child grows in that time.
After that, I did not worry about his voyaging across oceans,
because I knew the ship was strong. They only undertook
two voyages a year, in the months between December and
June. Your father explained that in the autumn time great
winds rise up in that part of the world. Their only warning
is a period of calm when ships cannot make way and lie
there for days on end with their sails flapping. The winds
rise so fiercely that a ship has no time to reach port, and its
only chance for survival is to head into the storm. Sailors
know only too well if they try to run, the seas will swamp
them.'

She paused, her gaze fixed on a clump of daffodils, their
delicate yellow petals translucent in the fleeting sunlight.

'Then one day, the ship arrived in port with the news
that your father had drowned. I thought my heart would
break.'

'Then why did you marry again?' I said, my tone as
bitter as the oranges they were selling in the market. 'Surely
you don't love …'

The mother put out her hand to stop me talking. 'There
was the business and the ship to be dealt with. I don't
understand commerce and you needed a father.'

'Not like him, he hates me.'

'Only because you go against his wishes. He is a good man at heart.'

'How can you say that, ma'am,' I shouted angrily. 'He beats me.'

'Oh, Molly, please call me mother, today; I hate ma'am.'

I flushed. 'I'm to blame for that as well, aren't I?'

She didn't reply, even though what I said was the truth. Instead she said, 'It wasn't always like this – don't you remember?'

I shook my head. I don't care if Molly did remember, *I* didn't and *I wanted to know*.

'He was a friend of your father's. I knew him well. He was a kind man although, even then, he said very little. His wife had died giving birth to their second child, leaving poor Agnes alone. It seemed sensible; I needed a husband and he needed a wife. We married.'

She stopped – her head dropping down as if the memories were making it too heavy to hold upright. 'Margaret was born and then I lost a child – a son. You were only eight, Molly, too young to remember these happenings. But this is when everything changed. Overnight, your stepfather became a man obsessed by religion. It was as if he was trying to placate God, to prevent his smiting the family again. We left Blandford Forum and moved to the house in Lingthorpe.

'It has not been easy for any of us, Molly, for I too was used to a freer life. I wasn't brought up as a puritan. My father was, what we would call now, an Independent. His views on life those of tolerance and kindness.'

'Why don't you leave him then?' I burst out. 'There's money – the store belongs to you now.'

She gazed at me astonished.

'Child, sometimes you ask the strangest questions – almost as if you never listen when I talk to you. Have you not understood that on marriage all property passes to the husband; that is why the ship belongs to you.'

She could tell by my face that I hadn't a clue. Actually, I was trying to work out why the hell she had married again, only to lose everything.

She explained that my father, wanting to make sure we were okay whatever happened, had left the ship to me. As a single woman, I could hold property. The profits from each cargo were held in trust until I was twenty-one, with the proviso that once a year, after the ship had come safely into harbour, I gave my mother ten guineas and me, until I was sixteen, a crown.

'I don't want the ship, you can have it – and then you can divorce him.'

The mother's grey eyes looked shocked, all the colour vanishing from her face. 'Molly – people believe you can burn in hell for even thinking such a thing.'

'I don't believe that. If God exists at all, he makes you go through hell on *this earth* – while you're alive,' I shouted, remembering the bullies who had made my life so miserable in junior school. 'Not when you're dead.' But it was no good trying to initiate her into twenty-first century morals – I knew that.

She clutched my hand and we sat lost in angry and helpless thoughts. I knew, too, that she didn't keep the money she got at the store; he took it – his right as a husband. I swore under my breath, the most foul words I could think of. There was no way out for her, I could see that – unless he died. For a second hope flared – he could, Molly's real father had.

'Where did he die?'

'He was drowned off the Scilly Isles. One of the young boys fell from the rigging and your father went in after him. He managed to get him to the rocks, but the sea took them.'

She turned to look at me. 'Molly, John Hampton is a good man; I would not have married him otherwise, you must believe that. Perhaps in time, when the bitterness created by these wars has passed, he will cease to be driven by his religion and return to the way he used to be. We can only pray for that, Molly. And you can help.'

I looked up then.

'Molly, dear, I am telling you all this for a reason. For the past year, you have set yourself against your stepfather and it has brought trouble to every member of the family. Not only you, Molly, we suffer too because we love you. And it has made your stepfather worse. Look at your hands, child.'

I glanced down at the scars across my knuckles.

'Now I have told you of your good fortune, surely you can be content with your circumstances, knowing there is a way out for you. Will you do that, Molly? I am certain once the war has ended, he will permit you to see Richard.'

I shook my head, stubbornly. 'He won't, Mother.'

Hindsight is a very useful thing; somewhere in the back of my mind, I vaguely remembered that the Puritans became top dog under Cromwell and I'd be an old woman before the king won his throne back.

'I never remember, is Richard my second cousin?' I said, changing the subject.

The mother smiled sadly, arranging the fingers of my left hand as if she were counting them. 'Second cousin once removed. Your great-grandfather and his grandfather were brothers.'

I let out the breath I'd been holding.

'I'm so sorry, Molly, I know how dearly you care for Richard and, if things had been different, you might have married but ...' She shook her head.

Then, patting my hand, she got to her feet. 'Enough of these daydreams. Life is not made of daydreams, child, and we must deal with it, as it comes. Please say you'll help me and cease to plague your stepfather.' She knelt down, placing the primroses and violets in a stone dish buried in the top of the grave.

'It would be easier for you all if I wasn't here.'

The mother gasped, her hand flying to her mouth. 'Don't ever say that, Molly, even in jest. I cannot imagine life without you; you give me strength to carry on – and the children adore you.'

A cold wind caught the edge of my cloak. I turned away, so she couldn't see I was crying too.

THIRTEEN

We talked all through dinner. I'd expected silence to reign as it did at the house, but not a bit of it.

Ann Hampton chose the food, ordering fish for me. It arrived on a large wooden platter, complete with head and fins, which was something of a shock because I've only ever eaten fish when it looks like something else – fish fingers covered in red stuff or in batter from the chippy, swamped with vinegar and salt.

I was given a knife and a fork with two prongs. I wish I dared ask how you pick up peas with it.

I tried one of the oysters she'd ordered, making her giggle like a schoolgirl at the expression on my face, my throat refusing to swallow the disgustingly slippery object.

'Try chewing it,' she suggested mischievously.

Heroically, more to make her laugh again than anything else, I bit into it. If I'm honest it wasn't that bad – rather like eating chewy sand and seawater – I made a few more faces before swallowing, content to see her smile, even though the landlord was darting some fairly shocked looks at our table.

She whispered across the table. 'Such levity is not expected in ladies of the puritan persuasion.'

I translated that to mean he'd probably decided we were related to lap dancers.

She talked about her childhood in Blandford Forum and

how, when fishing in the river Stour, she had fallen in. Henry, who was her best friend, despite always getting her into trouble, had shouted angrily at her before hauling her out. Hoping to escape punishment, he had spread her dress and petticoats on the bushes to dry while she sat in her shift.

I began to wonder why she was telling me stuff like this. I mean, Agnes had said this was an annual outing. Surely she had talked to Molly? Perhaps she hadn't. Perhaps she was talking because I was asking. 'And what was your punishment?' I said.

'Father was always so kind,' she replied gaily. 'I had to sit on a chair – very still – and think beautiful thoughts.'

'Is that all?' I exclaimed startled, scraping up the last of the fruit pie and cream

'Have you ever seen a child sitting still for five minutes – remember Edward. It is almost impossible, Molly.'

She was so different from how she was in the house. And, when I compared her to the women I'd seen in the village, from a different planet. She had a sort of air about her, *posh*, I'd call it. Except she wasn't posh, she was more … I remembered the word I'd been searching for – sophisticated.

I felt so relaxed in her company, I actually felt like a nice person – all those edges and prickles, and hurt places that I wore round my shoulders at my real home, disappeared. I felt could talk to her about anything, positive she'd never be shocked or critical, and wished she really was my mother.

As we headed for the stables to collect the pony, I gazed back over my shoulder, needing to plant my memories solidly, wanting never to forget: Richard, staring angrily after the troop of Roundheads, his expression desolate; Richard, skimming stones into the grey water of the river, bitter about being parted from Molly – not me. I closed that image off – unable to look at it. The thought of saying goodbye to him … *never to see him again* … was like a kick in the stomach. I felt my breath flutter painfully before stopping altogether. Quickly, I replaced the image with a happier one: the inn with its high counter where the owner stood, only the lower half of his head visible beneath the dark brown beams of the ceiling; the polished wooden tables, sitting unevenly on the grey slate of the floor; the roaring fire, with its pile of logs stacked under the chimneybreast, minute flames of brightness reflected a dozen times in the tiny leaded panes of the window; and two figures, a mother and her daughter, laughing at each other's jokes.

If I came back to the town and searched, would it all still be here? The inn, with its dark rooms, its little tables, polished so brightly you could see your reflection in them. Would the bridge spanning the river still be standing? Or would it all have vanished.

Visions of living in Blandford flashed through my mind. I'd have loads of money when I was twenty-one, the mother had said so. I pictured Agnes and Margaret, with Edward running behind, setting off for school. They turned back to wave; Ann Hampton standing in the doorway, a gentle smile on her face. I set my jaw stubbornly. It was only a matter of waiting. I could stay; no one would know I wasn't Molly, and then I could marry Richard and live happily ever after. It could happen. I could make it happen.

***

When I went to the privy Janet was waiting. 'I've been trying to catch you alone for two days,' she whispered.

'Sorry,' I mumbled, shifting uncomfortably from foot to foot. 'It's been difficult.'

'How did you get on with Richard – will he do it?'

I jerked awake – aware of my stupid, stupid promise to get us out of here. 'I haven't actually asked him yet,' I reluctantly admitted.

149

'You haven't …' Janet almost choked. 'But you said we'd get out of here,' she wailed. 'We've only got two more days till the master gets back. What *have* you been doing?'

'It's been difficult,' I repeated. I stared at her, guilt-ridden, desperate to escape her accusing look. 'Anyway he's not back till Wednesday, we got a message.'

'*Haven't you got it yet?*' she spat the words at me. 'Once he's back you're grounded – like me.' She stared at me suspiciously. 'You haven't changed your mind have you? You can't *want* to stay here – can you?'

I blushed, my face flaring beetroot red, and I prayed Janet couldn't see it in the dark.

She peered into my face. 'You *stupid cow* – it's Richard isn't it. You've fallen for him. *Oh my God, Molly, you're crazy!* What do you expect to happen – to be allowed to marry him and live happily ever after – I don't *think* so.'

'Don't be bloody stupid, Janet, of course I haven't fallen for him – I just need the right time, that's all; it isn't easy, you know.'

'And being accused of being a witch or being beaten is?'

'You're exaggerating,' I said, my voice now as angry as her own. 'No one believes in witches any more, you said so yourself.'

'*Molly?*' I heard my name being called.

'Molly, *I beg you*,' Janet whispered. She glanced furtively over her shoulder, as the footsteps drew nearer. '*Molly, for God's sake, get us out of here before it's too late* – it's not safe.'

I marched back into the house, my lovely exciting world smashed to smithereens with a sledgehammer. Janet was right – *of course she was bloody right, I knew that.* But why am I the only person in this crazy world not allowed daydreams? Mum spent all her time destroying them and now Janet was doing the same. I thought of Richard then – and the minutes we'd lost sitting in silence, pushed apart by the prejudices of war and religion, the bright pictures quickly fading away.

I knew, by the startled expression on the mother's face, I was looking defiant as I entered the parlour. I could feel one of my moods coming on, that deep black pit in which I deliberately foul things up, knowing I'll be punished and in a senseless way looking forward to it, so I could shout triumphantly – *I told you so*. I tried to stop it – like Blue had showed me – by taking deep breaths and thinking of cool water, but the uncontrollable anger continued to build, pushing its way out of my chest. I knew, too, that if I gave way to it, HE'd get to learn of it and punish me, however hard everyone tried to conceal it. I didn't care, because I was *never* going to see him again and Molly was *never* coming back.

But if Molly wasn't there and he needed someone to punish, would he start on Agnes? I couldn't bear that. I glanced across at Agnes, sitting quietly by Margaret's side. She'd been happy to see us return, her thin, sallow face lighting up. Molly, the only source of gaiety and fun she found in the world. I stopped dead in my tracks – my anger gone – evaporated.

'Ma'am, may we play *Hunt the Thimble?*'

The grey eyes searched mine. I wanted to tell her it was okay, my anger over. She smiled, handing over the thimble from her workbasket.

It was a lovely evening – like Christmas – the house full of laughter. We played *Blind Man's Bluff*. The baby, whose name was John – poor thing – tottered round after us, his little legs collapsing as he cannoned into charging, giggling children, hell bent on escaping about the room, sitting down plop on the ground. But even he had caught the party spirit and, instead of wailing like kids do when they fall down, he gurgled happily. Then, with Edward on my knee, I told them the story of the *Ugly Duckling*. Margaret clutched her doll, as if she would never let it go, and Edward, his eyes shining brightly, grasped his new wooden soldier. A general in the cavalry mounted on a horse, his flowing cloak painted black, with a red jacket and trousers and a black hat with a green feather in it.

When the children were in bed, I showed Agnes how to play draughts. The pieces were great, although the board was a bit tricky. It kept coming apart; still it wasn't bad for a seventeenth-century design.

'Now you can teach Margaret,' I said, closing the board. Then I remembered my promise.

'Ma'am?' I asked. 'Agnes would like to come with us to Blandford Forum next time we go; she'd love to see the shops.'

'Would you, Agnes?' The girl nodded eagerly. 'Then, of course you may come.'

Agnes' face lit up. She didn't smile not really – I think she's become too scared to smile, flinching every time her father appears, terrified he might pick on her – but you could tell she was happy, because the corners of her mouth softened.

I picked up the candle – *to light us to bed* – said the nursery rhyme. The mother was tidying away the bright silks. It was only just after eight-thirty; a ridiculous hour to go to bed even if I did have to be up at the crack of dawn.

'Goodnight, ma'am ... Mother.'

'Goodnight, Molly, dear.' She paused. 'I'm so sorry, child, you deserve better.'

I followed Agnes upstairs, once again blinded by tears, unable to bear the thought of being in that house a moment longer.

FOURTEEN

As I ran downstairs in the early morning light to get our washing water, I heard footsteps on the back stairs and, a second later, Janet appeared. She was dressed for the role of grandmother in a school play, a long nightdress covering her from neck to toe with a granny shawl pinned tightly round her shoulders. We looked at each other for a second then spoke simultaneously.

'*I'm sorry.*'

'I shouldn't have called you a cow,' she said, giving me a hug.

'I deserved it,' I replied gloomily. 'It's my fault not yours. I never gave a thought to how you felt, wondering if you were going to be stuck here for the rest of your life.'

'Peeling vegetables,' she added.

We made our way into the washhouse; I pumped while Janet held a jug under the stream of freezing cold water.

'Fill them at night and leave them by the fire,' I told her. 'They're not too bad then. I tell you what though, of all the things I miss, a hot shower's at the top of the list.'

Janet didn't reply, lost in thought, and I wondered what it was she missed the most. Then, words burst out of her like a dam breaking.

'I've even thought of killing myself,' she said, her face all screwed up. 'I get this nightmare. It's always the same one; a crowd of people surging round me, closing in. I wake up screaming. I'm so freaked I don't want to go out in case it comes true. And, I'm sure I'm being followed.'

'You can't be serious?' I was horrified, never imagining for one instant she felt like this.

'You try it, Molly,' she continued angrily. 'Okay, John Hampton may be a scumbag, but it still means you're safe. I'm a servant – no one gives a shit about me, except Ann Hampton. Haven't you noticed, she's always thinking about other people even servants. And every time I get real bad, she notices and says something kind or does something extra nice for me. I'd despaired of ever getting home and when you spoke to me ... it was like a miracle. I couldn't believe it, Molly, and part of me still doesn't.'

She put the jug down on the ground, water slopping over the edges. 'Every morning I think – today is the day and then, when nothing happens, I go to bed convinced it will happen the next day. But when I didn't see you, I thought you must be avoiding me because you'd changed your mind about going back.'

'I wasn't avoiding you,' I said uncomfortably, my head swirling with guilt and confusion. Was it so wrong to want a little happiness? 'I was trying to make Mr Hampton believe I'd learned my lesson. To be truthful, I haven't a clue what to say to Richard. *Beam me up, Scotty*, doesn't seem quite right somehow.'

I led the way back to the kitchen and sat down near the fire, my legs tucked under me. 'How do you tell anyone in this Godforsaken place that you belong to another century and you want to go back there – and please can I borrow your parlour for five minutes?' I prodded the kitchen fire miserably.

'But you've got to find the words, Molly. What's the alternative – a lifetime of drudgery for me and for you – with Molly's father ...'

'He's not her father,' I snapped.

154

'Not her father? What do you mean?'

'Molly's mother was married before – to Henry Blaisdale, Richard's second cousin or something like that. And he was married before, too.'

'So that's why.'

I nodded. 'Mother says it's because he lost his wife and child and got religion. It's all so confusing I don't know what to think any more. She told me I'd have a lot of money when I was twenty-one, because the ship belongs to me, not Mr Hampton. He makes his profit from buying the cargo and selling it on. Mother has a cousin in Blandford. He looks after the money for me.'

'Don't you mean Molly, you keep saying *me*.'

I shook my head. 'See how confusing it is.'

'Is that why you thought about staying?'

'I guess it is, except that I never thought of staying – honest.' The word echoed loudly inside my head and I hoped Janet wasn't paying too much attention, otherwise she'd guess I wasn't telling the truth no matter how much I swore to the contrary. 'I just wanted an extra day to be happy in. I'll try and see Richard today. With Mr Hampton out of the way, I should be able to get out.'

'Do you think Molly's coming back?'

I didn't want to answer that. I got to my feet. 'I must hurry and take our water up. See you later.'

Janet gave me a worried smile. I didn't blame her. If I'd been in her shoes, I'd have given me a worried smile too; my brain buzzing with so many conflicting ideas, I didn't know what the hell I was going to do.

155

FIFTEEN

I had been there seven days. This time last week I'd felt scared and bewildered, frantic to find a way out. Now, I walked leisurely down the road with my family, surrounded by neighbours, all of us on the way to church.

In that same week spring had burst upon the scene, transforming trees into sparkling green banners, a kaleidoscope of colours from light to dark. I laughed down at Edward, as we strolled down the path between banks of daisies and gold celandines; he was chattering away about silly things like any five-year-old, every so often throwing hero-worshipping glances in my direction.

I was wearing new shoes too. We'd seen them in the window of a shoe shop in Blandford Forum. They were dead cool, very soft leather with big buckles, so I confessed to Ann Hampton that my Sunday shoes were tight and perhaps these would fit me. The storekeeper explained that they'd been wrongly measured and the lady didn't want them. They fitted brilliantly so I bought them, the mother laughing at the expression on the shopkeeper's face when I paid for them with my own money. Since I'd already reached the conclusion that Molly's stepfather would doubtless expect me to hand over anything I had left, I figured the more I spent the better I'd feel.

This time I didn't need to tiptoe nervously into the hall clutching my Bible, as I'd done the previous Sunday. Now I felt confident enough to look about me, the mother nodding and smiling to neighbours. She handed me an orange stuck with cloves and I raised my eyebrows in thanks, thrilled we shared this silent communication. A great warm glow surged through my body at the thought that she and I were friends.

It was unbelievable and magical and fantastic that, after a lifetime of being picked on and told you weren't good enough, suddenly to have someone who likes you exactly as you are. It doesn't matter to her that I'm too tall and speak badly and sometimes I'm funny and sometimes I'm rude and grumpy – she likes me. *No, she loves me.*

The pastor droned on. But this time, I really didn't bother to listen – who cared. After all John Hampton wasn't there to frown at me. I held an orange to my nose, the sweet musk of the cloves masking the smell of unwashed bodies, my face a study in eager concentration.

It wasn't much of an orange, the skin withered like the apples I'd seen in the market yesterday, with their brown skins, but it was precious because Ann Hampton had taken the trouble to get it for me.

Behind my mask I was having my own battle. Not a battle between good and evil, which the pastor was talking about; this was a battle of two voices, both shouting at me. And I hadn't a clue which was the good voice and which the evil, or whether both were good or both evil. But I couldn't get rid of them no matter how hard I tried.

As soon as I made up my mind what I was going to do, the voices started up again – the words repeating themselves over and over again, like the line of a song you can't get rid of. I desperately wanted to stay, but at the same time I wanted to go home and swim. I also had Janet to think about, remembering how guilty I had felt the previous evening. But above everything, I wanted Richard and Ann Hampton and the children in my life, *and* I didn't want to go back to my parents.

My nails pierced the skin of the orange, releasing its pungent sweetness. I couldn't think like that. What had the mother said in the graveyard? *"Enough of these daydreams, Molly. Life is not made of daydreams, child, and we must deal with it, as it comes."*

She was right. It wasn't possible. The only thing that was possible was to find my way back to my own life and take Janet with me. I came to with a jolt, hearing the words of the Lord's Prayer: *Lead us not into temptation and deliver us from evil.* I felt they were praying for me.

The man who stood up to talk was a newcomer. Despite his attire, the wide dome of his black hat looming over a white collar and black jacket, he seemed more like a soldier; his face dark and swarthy with deeply etched lines on either side of his mouth, and his hair cut real short compared to Richard's shoulder-length locks.

'Today,' he paused. 'Today, war has once again broken out.' A deadly hush swept over the chapel, the silence so intense that everyone sat up. The villagers stared at one another their eyes fluttering nervously.

I could understand him all right, every word clear as a bell.

'Berwick and Carlisle have been seized by the traitor royalists, who have declared both towns for the King, and the perfidious Scots are preparing once again to invade England.'

There were groans at this and some of the women began to pray, their hands clasped in front of them. This seemed to me a bit over the top. Scotland is a long way from Lingthorpe and it was hardly likely we would find Scottish troops descending on this peaceful little village.

'There is worse, my good people. Colonel Poyer, Governor of Pembroke Castle, has declared for the King and troops from Colonel Langhorne's Horse and Foot, even as I speak, are joining the traitors.'

A man leapt to his feet at the back of the church, shouting his objection. He was quite young, his hair fair and cut to just below his ears. 'You lie! The Colonels are no traitors. I fought with Colonel Langhorne and a more honest man never lived. For five long years, he fought loyally for Parliament, as did I.'

You could feel his anger, darting swiftly like an arrow towards the soldier. The congregation swivelled round in their seats, eager to see who was going to back down first. Ann Hampton caught my eye. She stretched out her hand; I grasped it.

It was the soldier at the front who spoke. 'Here speaks a loyal Englishman and I salute you for it. Nevertheless, it is true. General Cromwell is even now riding to do battle with those who have broken the peace. May God speed his endeavours. And Lord Fairfax will shortly be marching north to disperse the Scottish threat.

'My mission today, good people of England, is to seek men who will join Lord Fairfax, for no self-respecting Englishman can stand idly aside while Scottish troops push southwards into our homeland.'

'Excuse me, sir.' A young man got up, shuffling his hat uncomfortably round and round in his hands. 'Excuse me, sir; may I ask a question of the military gentleman?'

The soldier nodded.

'I served voluntary-like for three years and came back unscathed. I was one of the men at Newmarket, when Colonel Cromwell petitioned Parliament for us to be paid our dues. You remember, good sir, the men of the horse were owed nearly half-a-year's pay and I had eighteen weeks pay owing to me. They paid us eight weeks and expected our gratitude. And they did not agree to that until the army marched on London, forcing them to pay us. Why should I serve again? I have a wife and three children to support. If I am not there, who is to feed them?'

'I also am owed money,' shouted the fair young man.

Another man leapt to his feet. 'I have heard that Colonel Foyer only allied himself to the King's cause because he has despaired of the promises of Parliament. He has placed his trust in the King knowing that if he is killed his family will not starve, for none of us here have seen Parliament's gold.'

'Ay, that's right.'

There were murmurings all round the chapel. You could feel the anger growing.

'You will be paid, soldier. Do you not trust Lord Fairfax?' The fair young man nodded. 'Then join with a clear conscience.'

Several men got up at that and two boys; the one that had had his ears boxed the previous Sunday, and another. Neither was any older than me. I could hear women crying quietly and understood now why they had prayed when they heard the news.

'Is that the same Lord Fairfax who failed miserably to get us our just dues?'

An older man stood up. He looked unsteady on his feet and I thought he'd been drinking until I saw the crutch under his arm. 'I lost a leg at Newbury. Does Lord Fairfax care about that?'

There were shouts of, 'No' and then another man called out, 'And, if we support Parliament what then? You have told us, time and time again, Pastor, that they seek to curb our freedoms and we will be forced to become idol-worshipping Presbyterians.'

I sat there blessing John Hampton for being away. If he'd been in the chapel glaring, I wouldn't have been able to turn round in my seat to see who was shouting – even ignoring the mother's warning hand on my knee.

Mostly, though, I watched the women. I would have had lots to say if it had been *my* husband that was thinking of going off to fight and, even more, if I'd been the mother of that kid. They sat there without saying a word, a few still silently sobbing, their aprons clutched to their eyes. You could see how unhappy they were by their white faces and their hands, clinging to the children. Being a woman in this century stinks.

'Ay, that's right. That's what Parliament wants, idol-worshipping Presbyterians.'

'That's a lie – it's the King that wants to make us into Presbyterians, not Parliament.'

A quarrel started between the two men, the entire congregation trying to hear the arguments for and against – including me. I was fascinated; war and religion really meant something to these people.

The pastor rose to his feet. He had a plump, pasty face which had never seen a battle. The others who had spoken were – like the soldier – quite lean, whereas the pastor had even lost his battle with his belly. He held up his hand, but no one took the slightest bit of notice, the noise growing into a tornado of sound.

'SILENCE,' he roared.

He got it too. I nearly jumped out of my skin.

'This is not a quarrel about religion. Time enough for that later. Now our country is at war and Colonel Jennings seeks men for his army. I see among you many volunteers but, before you decide, I have a message for you from Sir Richard Blaisdale.'

'Why didn't 'e come hisself?' shouted a voice from the back.

'He met with Colonel Jennings last evening. On hearing the news he wanted to come himself, but felt that his presence would not be welcome and would lead to a falling-out between you all.'

I thought they had managed the falling-out bit pretty well, even without Sir Richard.

''E's right there,' shouted the same voice from the back.

I tried to see who was shouting, but there was a crowd of men on their feet, talking and arguing.

'Let 'im keep his messages – royalist traitor. We know what to do with traitors – be'eadin's too good for 'em. If 'e wants us to listen, let 'im first send his own son or go hisself to defend our country.'

'JUDGE NOT LEST YE SHALL BE JUDGED,' roared the pastor. 'BEWARE YOUR WORDS FOR THE LORD IS A VENGEFUL GOD AND WILL SURELY SMITE THOSE WHO BLASPHEME WITHIN THE SANCTITY OF HIS HOUSE.'

In ones and twos the men sat down again, the pastor waiting until quiet had been restored.

'You are quick to condemn Sir Richard, but is this not the man who has refused to enclose common land so that you are able to graze your animals, as your families have always done? Is this not the man who has permitted us to worship in freedom? And is this not the man who has kept your village safe from war, warning that brother will rise up against brother, and sons will rise up against their fathers? DO I NOT SEE THIS HAPPENING HERE TODAY?' he roared.

Every word was directed right at someone and I could sense the uncomfortable shuffling as it struck home with deadly accuracy.

'And when,' he continued quite calmly, 'those of you that did go to war chose a side against his advising, is this not the same man who took no vengeance on your wife and children? We have heard tales a plenty of families forced from their homes, families whose children have been slaughtered, but not in our village. Has any family been evicted from their home – I ask them to stand up if they have? Stand up, so all can see what a villain this Sir Richard is. Who are you to call him traitor?'

He paused and looked round him, the level of embarrassment in the building so strong I wouldn't have been surprised if the walls had collapsed outwards like a pack of cards. Even I felt uncomfortable and I hadn't had anything to do with it.

'PRAY!' he thundered. 'PRAY YOU MISERABLE SINNERS FOR GOD'S FORBEARANCE TOWARDS YOUR TRANSGRESSIONS,' and then, in a voice of quiet calm, he said a prayer.

He was *so* great – I'd never in my life heard anything like it. Even when the head of our school lost his temper in assembly, it wasn't as good as this.

The pastor told us to go then, ordering the men to take their quarrel outside, for he would not have it in a house of God. I'm sure I wasn't the only one who was thankful it was over. I felt shattered, as if I'd been the ball in a game of ping-pong.

I followed Ann Hampton and Edward out of the chapel into a great gossiping horde of men, once again arguing loudly. Agnes, Margaret and I, holding hands, wormed our way through the tightly packed groups, back across the bridge to wait for them.

It had rained in the night and the river was swollen almost to bursting. Usually it wandered along forming bright rivulets and you could see the soft-brown shale banks on the bottom. Now it was cloudy and covered with froth and dirty-white scum, while miniature waterfalls poured through a damn of sticks and grass. It looked as angry as the men eyeballing one another outside the chapel.

There was a group of kids playing on the bridge. I glanced up and grinned, nudging Agnes. One of the boys had leapt up on the parapet, showing off to three girls. No one was taking any notice, the adults too busy chatting, but I watched – in case he stumbled and fell. He leapt down and I turned away.

On the opposite bank a game of tag had started. I gazed down at Margaret. She was scuffing the ground with the toe of her shoe, a wistful expression on her face as she watched the children darting about, shrieking with merriment. I knew she wanted to join in.

Suddenly, I caught the sound of a scream, its high-pitched tones over-riding the rough voices of the men bellowing at each other. I glanced up in time to see the flailing arms of a young girl toppling backwards into the torrent. Her head remained above the water for a second. I heard a second scream and then she was gone.

I never hesitated. Before she'd even hit the water, my shoes and bonnet were off. I dragged at my dress, hearing the buttons split away from the material and, in a bound, I was on the bridge, flinging myself into the river after her.

The water dragged furiously at my petticoats, gluing them to my legs. I tugged at them pulling one of them off then, taking a deep breath, duck-dived. The current grabbed me and I fought to stay still, my arms and legs madly back-peddling as I strove to get my bearings. It was like peering through a thick net curtain, the cloudy layers swirling about and refusing to stay still even for a second. It was pretty gross. The speed of the flow had dredged up millions of stones from the shale beds, their sharp edges bouncing off my body and I guessed I'd be black and blue by the time I got out.

I touched bottom and, grabbing the shale to hold me down, walked myself along the gravel bed. It was dark, the sun not powerful enough to penetrate the debris-strewn layers. Way above my head, I caught a glimpse of the surface, the sky a shadowy grey. I searched the murky water, feeling the current press heavily against my eyeballs. I knew the girl would have sunk like a stone, for even my legs found it difficult to kick, my single petticoat weighing a ton and hampering my movements – and I was used to swimming in clothes.

I was out of breath, the pressure on my lungs unbearable,

my brain instinctively yelling at my muscles to move, to breathe in. I glimpsed a shadow and something dark loomed up ahead of me. I made a grab for it but missed. I had to go up. I could feel myself choking. I needed air – like yesterday. Bubbles burst out of me as I headed upwards, my mouth gaping open like a fish sucking in the oxygen. I upturned my bare feet, scything them viciously through the air to kick me downwards at speed, slanting my dive to follow the current. I grabbed some fabric, a leg, and then an arm. Heading for the surface again, I burst into the air – like an underwater rocket – streams of water flying off me in all directions as I pulled the girl to the bank.

A hand reached down and, blindly, I pushed the girl up out of the water and, clawing at the bank, followed. She'd been laid on the ground and surrounding her – but not too close – was a vast crowd of black-clad mourners.

Why wasn't anyone helping, why were they standing there like statues – just looking?

I crawled to where the girl lay. Somewhere behind me, I heard a moan and a woman cried out, like an animal in pain.

'She's not dead,' I shouted. 'Someone help me.'

No one moved. The letters *A – B – C –* flashed across my eyes. I'd done it often enough with a doll; now it was for real. I checked her mouth and pushing her head back pinched her nose, at the same time covering her mouth with my own. I blew softly – one, two breaths. Locking my hands together, I pressed the heel of my hand into her chest bone, creating a rhythmic beat, and pushing down her chest wall. I reached five and blew in again.

I didn't notice the silence surrounding me, so engrossed in keeping up the rhythm. All at once the girl coughed and my hands jerked into the air, releasing her chest. I rolled her onto her side as she vomited up the river water and started to cry, pulling her knees up like a baby.

'There, there – you're okay,' I said, patting her on the back. She began to shiver with cold and, all of a sudden, I became aware I was half-naked – my hair strewn all over my face and back – surrounded by a crowd of strangers. I looked up, my expression of triumph wiped off as I sensed the ferocious hostility leaping through the air towards me. I felt like an animal surrounded by a pack of snarling dogs.

What had I done? I'd saved a child from drowning, that's what I'd done.

The pack stepped back, leaving two people in the circle with me – the father and the mother. She had her hand across her mouth, her eyes fumbling for mine.

'She's all right, honest,' I said.

For what seemed like an eternity no one moved or spoke – but it could only have been seconds – everyone staring at me. Then, from the back of the crowd, came a sort of growling noise.

'Mama, Mama, did you see, she flew like a witch,' I heard the shrill, excited tones of a child.

Then Ann Hampton was at my side, pushing her way through the crowd, laughing.

'Well-done, indeed, Molly. Thank heaven, your father taught you to swim when you were but a small child. And you see, good neighbours, what book learning has done for my Molly. She reads about things we could never understand.' Removing her cloak from around her shoulders, she wrapped it round me. 'She knew the child was not dead – and *see* – she was right.' She lifted the little girl, taking her to her mother. 'Here is your daughter. She needs to be kept warm, put your shawl round her to stop her catching a chill. You should take her home quickly, for she has had a bad shock.' She called into the crowd. 'Has someone a cart, the child cannot walk and must be kept warm. There, Mistress Perkins, away with you. Keep her in bed until she has recovered from her ordeal.'

166

The mother pushed the woman and the child, still crying noisily, into the crowd. It parted in front of her, the husband following.

'Come along, Molly, I had better get you home, you will catch your death of cold.'

Her hands were trembling and she put her arms tightly around me, as if to shield me from the crowd. Agnes ran up carrying my dress, her hand full of broken buttons. I quickly put the torn garment on over my wet petticoat, burying myself in the mother's cloak, her arm once again holding me tight. She led me through the crowd and, rather like Moses parting the Red Sea, the men and women stepped back to let us pass – with Agnes, holding Margaret and Edward by the hand, following.

SIXTEEN

We hurried home; Edward and Margaret almost running behind us. No one spoke, the silence deafening.

'Molly, go straight up to your room and get yourself dry. Agnes will stay with you. Margaret, go and play with Edward, there's a good girl.'

The mother pushed me through the door and followed me in, calling for Janet. Agnes and I went upstairs, water still dripping from my sodden clothes onto the wood of the stairs. I quickly took them off and started to rub myself dry. The river water had been cold, but not half as bad as walking home in the bitter wind. I shivered violently and rubbed harder. My new shoes had chafed my feet, my stockings lost somewhere in the river, and my heels were bright red. I flinched as I touched them.

'What's the matter,' I whispered to Agnes. 'What have I done now?'

She shook her head looking frightened. I began to feel even more worried until I remembered that Agnes nearly always looked scared, it was her normal expression.

Footsteps sounded on the back stairs and Janet appeared carrying a water jug, steam rising from it into the cold air of the bedroom.

'Molly, what the hell were you thinking ...' she burst out.

She saw my face grimacing ferociously and stopped dead.

Not now, I mouthed – pointing.

She glanced furtively to where Agnes stood half in and half out of the cupboard, searching for clothes for me to wear.

'Excuse me, Miss Molly,' she continued loudly. 'I spoke out of turn but I was worried when Mistress Hampton told me what had happened. She says to soak your feet in the hot water to stop you catching a chill.'

I wasn't about to argue, desperately needing a diversion to cover up Janet's stupid outburst. I could have killed her, positive she'd blown it. And, right at this minute, I couldn't cope with questions, sitting there in a petticoat – with only my old shawl, which I wore in the mornings to go to the privy, wrapped around me, and my teeth chattering.

Janet poured the water into the bowl – all the time glaring at me, while Agnes took out my old dress from its hook in the cupboard – all the time looking at me. We could have been acting in a play; one in which the actors cast elaborately furtive glances from side to side, asking the question: *which one of us is the murderer?* But it was so stupid, no one had been murdered; quite the opposite – I had saved someone. But I needed to break the silence before they exploded.

'So what have I done wrong now?'

There was a knock at the front door. We stared at each other, our faces white with fear.

'Janet ...?' But she was gone, running down the stairs to open the door.

I heard the pastor's voice followed by Ann Hampton's, then silence as they moved out of earshot into the salon. The water had lost its heat before the voices reappeared. I heard the front door open and close again, the mother's footsteps on the stairs.

'You are such a thoughtful child, Agnes,' she said, immediately noticing that Agnes was painstakingly repairing my dress where I'd torn the buttons. I hadn't seen it and I'd been in the same room as her for at least half an hour.

'Would you see to Margaret and Edward, I will help Molly dress. We will be down in a few moments, you can tell Beth.'

Agnes curtseyed obediently and, picking up her sewing, left the room.

I sat there waiting, completely out of my depth – exactly as I had been when I first arrived. All I knew was that I'd never seen the mother look so worried, not even when I was being beaten.

I couldn't bear the suspense a moment longer. 'I don't understand,' I burst out. 'What have I done? What's so terrible about saving a child's life?'

'*Nothing!* Absolutely nothing – you did exactly what your father would have done. When I saw you, I felt as if I were on the ship watching him, and I've never been so frightened in all my life.'

'So why were the people angry?'

She looked down studying her hands. 'They believed the child already dead. Now they are saying you invoked supernatural powers to bring it back to life. It would have been kinder if the child had died, Molly.'

'*Kinder for who?*' I snapped out the words, unable to stop myself. 'I cannot believe you would ever think a child should die because of a bunch of superstitious villagers.'

'No, Molly, I do not believe it, but I am not a villager. The pastor came to us the moment he left our neighbours' house. Mistress Perkins sent for him because her husband is determined to cast out the child, saying that it was not God who saved her but the devil. The pastor has tried to convince him that the child had simply swallowed too much water and that she would have revived without your help. But even if Mister Perkins becomes reconciled to the child's survival, stories will be told about her as long as she lives. If anything unusual happens, such as a house burning down or crops failing or a stillbirth, people will blame her. Janet has suffered badly from the superstition of the villagers, as she will tell you.'

'Is that why you pretended to laugh?'

She nodded glancing down at her hands again, and I guessed there was some more nasty news.

'The pastor asked me to send for my husband. He has also sent for Sir Richard.'

I remembered then that Richard had told me his father was going away.

'Because I saved a child,' I said indignantly.

'No,' she replied. 'After we had gone, the men fell to arguing about the rights of the King. A fight broke out and someone was badly hurt. Feelings are still running high. It will be worse still if the man dies, as the pastor feels is likely.'

She lifted her hands into the air in a gesture of helplessness. 'It is what Sir Richard has always feared; the village has forgotten what was asked of them – to stay out of the quarrel. Yet it is understandable for men to remain bitter about their loss of wages, when they have served their country loyally. The women, whose husbands and sons have already left to join up, feel bereft and look for someone to blame for their loss.'

'But none of that has anything to do with me,' I protested.

The mother shook her head. 'Of course, it has nothing to do with you. That is why the pastor is so concerned, because the people are linking the two events. You have to remember, Molly, the villagers are peasant farmers, who wish only for three meals a day and a warm hearth to sit by at night. They thrive on monotony, content with their daily lives – secure. Change is resisted and anything new or different is to be suspected, because it awakens feelings they cannot understand.'

'So I am to blame for these women losing their sons and husbands to war,' I said, my voice as bleak and bitter as the wind now hurling itself against the windows.

'Your stepfather will be here tonight or tomorrow morning at the latest. He is well thought of in the village and he, together with Sir Richard and the pastor, will calm the angry villagers and soon all will be back to normal, you will see. We simply have to stay at home today and be quiet.'

She helped me cover the blisters, but I couldn't put my shoes back on and was forced to wear my clogs, which didn't particularly matter since it would take Agnes at least a day to mend my Sunday dress.

Then it hit me. The dramatic events of that morning, and the anger of the villagers, had actually made it possible for me to stay. It was like someone had taken a pair of scissors to a black curtain and let the sun in. If the villagers were up in arms about the war, the obvious solution would be to send me away to the relatives in Blandford. I knew the mother wouldn't let Molly suffer as Janet had done, too terrified even to set foot out of doors. And, since none of this was my fault, I didn't have to wait in fear and trembling to be punished. With the village gone pear-shaped, John Hampton would be positively eager to get rid of me. And later, inheriting all that money, who knows what might happen?

My only problem now was Janet; she *had* to get back. She'd suffered enough and, anyway, *her family* were at the other end of the time-chute. Everything I cared about was here.

For a moment I allowed myself to gaze at the world through my own special pair of rose-tinted spectacles, a luxury I had banned from my life ever since I discovered exactly how uncaring my own parents were. I was eight and ill, very ill, and Mum and Dad had gone to work leaving

Meg to look after me – that was when I knew. Now I could see a happy Molly, surrounded by a loving family of brothers and sisters – and Richard.

I've never been much good at lying, that's one of my problems. If, like Meg, I could have told my parents what they wanted to hear, perhaps they might have given me an easier time – but I couldn't; I always came flying out with the defiant truth. Now, I needed a crash course in lying if Janet was going to believe me. I had to convince her I was hell-bent on getting back so she'd suspect nothing. And when we got to the manor she would leave and, once back, wild horses wouldn't get her to return.

Excusing myself, I headed towards the privy, signalling to Janet in the kitchen behind Beth's broad back.

I knew my face was still white from the cold of the water, which helped. The words spilled out of me, as fast as I could push them. 'I'll meet you at the back of the house.'

'How will you get out?' she said breathlessly, as if she'd been running.

'Pretend to be sleeping.'

***

Janet was waiting, impatiently walking up and down. I had used the pretence that I felt cold, shivering violently all through dinner to get me out of Sunday sewing. Quickly stuffing Edward's pillow lengthwise down my bed, I tiptoed down the backstairs and out through the garden into the fields behind.

We didn't talk, though Janet kept flashing worried little glances in my direction. I knew she was scared about being seen. I hoped that was all and she hadn't twigged I was staying behind.

We kept to the open meadowland behind the houses, deserted on a Sunday, but even so we moved cautiously, keeping low. We passed behind the cottages, so different from their neat and tidy fronts; a jumble of shacks and lean-to sheds housing animals and a privy.

The afternoon was overcast, the sun hiding behind sulky grey clouds and the meadowland, under its grey pall, had become a wild, unfriendly place. I found myself starting at every sound, my head jerking round to see if we were being followed; and a cow snorting was enough to send me scurrying behind the nearest bush. But fair's fair, I made them nervous too, watching them step hysterically backwards as I ran past them, although what they had to be nervous about – *they* hadn't got the whole village after them.

Away to my left I could see the main road keeping pace with us. We cautiously cut back towards it, crossing it and retracing our steps until we stood opposite the gates of the manor. They were closed.

'So, how do we get in?' whispered Janet. She knelt down on the wet grass only her head showing above the bank. It might have been stupid to whisper, there was no one about, but I felt exactly the same, a bag of nerves – gazing furtively over my shoulder, constantly checking.

'Richard mentioned a wicket gate.'

We gazed hopelessly at the long lines of the wall. Not for the first time, I found myself wishing that inhabiting Molly's life had also given me her knowledge.

'Well, which way – left or right?' I said.

'I don't know, do I; the gates were open.'

I sighed despairingly. It was like a multiple-choice question, with a fifty-fifty option. Whichever way we chose, danger loomed; both sides taking us straight back towards the High Street which we'd just spent the last fifteen minutes avoiding.

'We go right,' I tried to sound positive. 'The gate has to be in the wall nearest the river – that makes sense, nothing else does.'

Hesitantly, we followed the line of the wall and it was there, about half way along, camouflaged by a massive oak tree. Carefully, with my finger under the lip to stop its telltale click, I lifted the latch.

We found ourselves in a walled garden, neat rows of fruit bushes and newly growing vegetables filling the open space. I glanced up at the house where windows overlooked the garden. If anyone happened to look out they would see us, but it was a chance we had to take. We ran quickly down the path towards the stables.

'What now?' Janet gasped, as we reached shelter and darted under cover.

Outside the front door, a carriage drawn by two horses stood waiting. As we watched the entire family appeared; Lady Blaisdale, Richard, his brothers and his sister, even the nurse with the baby waiting on the doorstep. I nearly shouted with joy; they were going out. The problems of the village belonged to the village, not the gentry. The carriage set off down the path, the gardener opening the gates, while the nurse and baby vanished back indoors.

'She'll take the baby upstairs,' I whispered. 'Give her a minute.'

I guessed the time to be about four; a good time for visiting between dinner and supper. There were other large houses in the area. Richard had pointed them out to me, mentioning the names of families I was supposed to know. I wondered if there were any girls at these fine houses; girls who wore their hair neatly twisted into ringlets; girls in silk gowns with full skirts that whispered along the ground, and lace on the sleeves and collar. I glanced down at my dress, streaked with mud from crawling through the wet grass of the meadow, and scowled angrily.

'What's the matter?'

'Nothing, let's go.'

We entered the manor by the side door, exactly as Dad

and I had done that fateful Saturday, when we came in for breakfast from our rooms in the stable block. For a second or two, it felt like I'd never left, simply gone out for a stroll in the country. Then I remembered; that was over a week ago. My brain mashed into scrambled egg, leaving me sick and dizzy, as it tried to unravel the conundrum of the past which is now my present; and the future, some three hundred and fifty-seven years distant, which was my life until a week ago. Any minute now, if I wanted it, I could be back in that life. I may hate it but at least I could rely on the reaction of people around me, and all this would be a dream. I slowed my footsteps then sped up again. There wasn't a decision to make – *I was staying.*

I remembered where the parlour was and a second later we were there. We leant back against the closed door, scared out of our wits, our knees knocking. I listened anxiously for the sound of pursuing feet from the corridor but heard only silence – we'd actually made it.

I gave Janet a sort of half smile. 'You go first,' I whispered.

She didn't argue. In this matter of life or death, she presumed that neither of us had any intention of playing the hero. Besides, she was far too anxious to get home. Pointing downwards at the stone, she stepped onto it.

Nothing happened!

Her face changed – utter disbelief sweeping over it. I ran across the room peering down at the circular stone. We both stood on it, turning to face the fireplace, turning to face the door, face the window. We moved the fire screen – *nothing – nothing* – NOTHING!

Janet giggled hysterically, her hand flying to her mouth to stem the noise. Covering her face with her hands, she collapsed, her body rigid with shock. I simply felt cheated, the decision on my future once again whisked away. Pulling wildly at my hair, I tried to focus my thoughts and recall the exact sequence of events before I fell down the time-chute.

'For God's sake, Janet, pull yourself together; crying won't get us out of here.' I bent down and yanked her hands away from her face. 'There's something – something different. Try and remember.'

She gazed up at me, her face all screwed-up like a lost kid.

'Janet, it's the sun. Did you have sun?' I hissed urgently, suddenly remembering how warm the sun had been and my feeling cold.

She stared across at windows reflecting only the grey of the afternoon clouds. 'Then it's no good – all this for nothing,' she said, sounding as if the world had just ended. She stood up and began stamping her feet on the stone, trying to bulldoze a response out of it. She glared at the window; willing the clouds to move aside and let the sun through. I put my arm round her.

'No big deal,' I said lightly, as if it really didn't matter. 'We got in once; we can do it again, easy. But next time, it'll be sunny.'

Her feet were super-glued to the stone and I had to drag her away. I guess if I'd been stuck here for two years, working as a servant and terrified of my own shadow, I wouldn't have wanted to leave either. She'd got in and wild horses weren't going to drag her out again.

I felt curiously carefree, all those little voices, which had been nagging at me ever since I came back from the outing in Blandford, vanished. So I couldn't get home, it was nothing to do with me. I had tried; I had done my best.

With a sense of shock, as if the thought had been dredged from the deepest corners of my mind, I remembered Mum and Dad. I'd never given a moment's thought to the pain they might be experiencing. Pain, I shrugged, inconvenience more like. They'd get over it and, at long last, they would be able to work without interruption. There was nothing I could do about it anyway.

There was no sign of anyone in the house. I guess the maids – like the mice who play when the master's away – were taking it easy. Idly, I wondered what they did in their spare time without a telly. Definitely not country walks; not when they had to get up at the crack of dawn. If it was me that had to wash clothes by hand and brush carpets and use cold water to wash the dinner plates, I'd be sleeping every chance I got.

We reached the wicket gate safely and Janet cast yet another lingering glance at the sky. I knew she'd have waited forever if there'd been the slightest sign of sun but there wasn't, the sombre clouds thickening with spits of rain now beginning to fall.

I opened the gate to the lane, flinching back as I spotted the dour figure of the steward – Mr Perkins – his arms folded, waiting.

A shrill voice piped up. 'I told yer, I told yer I seed 'em.'

I know I went white. My hands fell to my sides and we stood there, for all-the-world like a couple of ten year-olds caught smoking in the school toilets.

'What are ye doin'?'

'I came to see Richard, Mr Perkins,' I said, my voice high-pitched and quivering with nerves.

'Callers don't use the wicket, they use the front gate. You an' that girl …' He pointed at Janet as if she was a bit of filth he'd just scraped off his shoe, the nails on his fingers black and pitted, 'were up to no good.'

I noticed his eyes, narrow and cunning like a weasel.

'You was in the parlour with 'er spells.'

'That's ridiculous, we were looking for Richard. You know perfectly well we're friends.' I caught Janet's sleeve, taking a step round him.

He ignored me and, swinging round, pushed his face at

Janet. Gross – his breath would have floored a skunk at twenty paces. 'I know what I saw. You may have fooled Sir Richard with ye innocent ways, but I know ye're a witch and her too,' he jerked his head at me.

Janet, terrified, took a step back while I took a step forward, drawing myself to my full height.

'That's nonsense,' I said, staring him straight in the eye, trying to tell myself this was simply another bully I had to face down.

Bully or not, he wasn't backing down. I watched nervously as he hitched up his trousers, hiking his belligerence up a notch at the same time.

'We'll see about this sneakin' about. My boys saw ye cavortin' together – let's see what the pastor has to say.'

He grabbed my arm and I pulled away.

'Don't be so stupid, Mr Perkins, I can't see why you're making such a fuss. You know I often meet with Richard; we've been friends since we were children.'

I might have been speaking to a brick wall for all the notice he took. He grabbed my arm again, his nails digging viciously into the flesh. I looked at his face, almost spitting into mine. Lines scalded their way downwards, like deep furrows in a newly ploughed field, ending at the corner of his mouth, others criss-crossing his forehead. This wasn't about me seeing Richard or saving his child; this was because Janet had made him appear a fool in front of his employer. He wanted revenge and he didn't care how he got it; the worst type of bully possible, and I knew he'd stop at nothing to regain his pride.

Janet knew it too; her face ashen, her eyes wide and staring. With a gasp of fear, she pulled free and ran.

'Janet stop, he can't hurt you.' I shouted and then, without thinking, I yanked my arm free and ran after her.

My wooden clogs were heavy and slowed me down and I scrunched my toes to stop them falling off. I would have been better bare-footed, except my feet were already cut and bruised. I heard thuds on the ground behind me and increased my pace, trying to catch Janet. I wanted to call out – *Janet, Janet, not that way, run towards home where it's safe.* The words hammered in my chest, but I hadn't enough breath to shout them.

She reminded me of a wounded animal running haphazardly in circles; aimlessly darting from cover to cover, anything to escape its pursuers. She reached the bridge flying across it, the door of the chapel banging open. I ran in after her and stopped. She was crouched near the front of the chapel, where the pastor had stood to address the congregation, her eyes staring.

'We're safe,' she panted. 'We're safe in the chapel.'

She hadn't been running heedlessly after all; she had purposely sought sanctuary.

My chest heaved too; not with the need for air but with fury that one person – one single bullying person – could create such mindless fear in someone else. I put my arm round her. 'He can't hurt us, Janet, we've done nothing.'

'Molly, you're so stupid. Of course he can,' she screamed at me. 'This isn't the twenty-first century. Men rule here; you're a woman, of less worth than an animal. This may be sixteen forty-eight but they're still barbarians and if they don't understand something they're scared shitless, and they lash out. Can't you see that?'

I didn't agree but there was no point saying so, she was way beyond thinking logically. Still, I tried.

'Come-on, Janet,' I said casually. 'After-all things aren't much better in our century. We've got people like that snivelling bully, Perkins. Only in some ways ours are worse, because they use knives and guns to get their own way. Most of the people here are decent and hard-working, kind and loving,' I added, thinking of Ann Hampton and Agnes.

'That's crap! Just because you're in love with Richard

and have a nice mother, you think living here's all lovey-
dovey. She tried to tell you about saving that kid, Molly;
she tried to warn you. She knows what they're like in the
village – you don't. You haven't lived here for the past two
years, being spat on and given funny looks whenever you
walk down the road.'

Everything in me screamed that she had to be wrong,
because if she was right we were in big trouble. We sat there
not saying anything, hardly daring to move, but there was
no sound from outside and no one came in.

'If we wait here, Janet, they'll find me missing at home;
someone will come looking.' I gave her hand a squeeze.

I don't know how long we sat in the chapel, watching
the light change becoming gloomy and then dim, while the
sky outside grew dark. The hours ticked by and I began to
feel hungry and stupid. Mr Perkins had wanted to frighten
us and he'd succeeded big time. Here we were cowering in
the chapel while he was at home, sitting in his armchair by
the fire, a contemptuous smile on his face. And no one had
come looking for me, so I hadn't been missed. Perhaps the
mother thought I was better off sleeping, but if we were to
escape a beating, we needed to get back as quickly as
possible.

I got up and stretched, tip-toeing to the door to listen.
All was quiet. Janet joined me.

'Come on,' I said. 'They must have gone by now. Let's
go home.'

Cautiously, I pushed open the door. It was dark and
silent – nothing moved. I stepped out, Janet following.

The door slammed shut behind us, the noise making me
jump. A torch burst into flame, illuminating the faces of the
men waiting patiently for the fox to crawl out of its den.

SEVENTEEN

I forced myself to glance casually round at the faces which, lit by torches, resembled a bunch of ravening wolves. By my side, Janet was trembling.

I grabbed her arm. 'Look,' I hissed fiercely into her ear. 'They daren't hurt us. Just don't show you're scared.'

I was a fine one to talk, a pain like stitch soaring through my middle.

My head high, I started forward dragging Janet with me. 'Head up,' I hissed again.

The crowd parted. I looked beyond them to the bridge. If we got to the bridge we'd be okay, for there was the pastor, calm and unruffled, certain in the knowledge that God was on his side. It was going to be all right.

The crowd behind us surged forward, surrounding us. I felt a fist digging into the small of my back. I shrugged my shoulders viciously trying to rid myself of the hand prodding me forward, forcing me into a half-run, the men behind us stepping on our heels as they jostled and shoved.

'Get off,' I snapped, turning round to glare.

'What's all this?' The authoritative tones of the pastor's voice boomed out over the heads of the crowd. 'The village is ringing with rumours that you have discovered a coven of witches and have them cornered in the chapel. I came to see for myself. I see no witches. What I do see are two frightened girls.'

'These be the witches.' It was the steward. He looked real pleased with himself. He'd waited a long time to get his revenge and restore his standing in the village, and he wasn't about to let this opportunity slip through this fingers. 'I warned ye about this girl.' He pointed at Janet, who was attempting to look brave and defiant, her hands clenched into fists at her side. 'Ye didn't believe me then, so I has 'er followed.'

A picture of two boys playing Red Indians, and the startled bird in the wood, flashed across my mind. *Holy Shit!* We were for it now, what had we been talking about?

'They was in the witches' wood, laughing an' talking in a strange tongue,' he continued. 'They was dancing, yelling an' singing out to the devil. All of us was witness to what they did to my girl,' he pointed at me. 'First, she drowns 'er in the river ...'

'That's a lie,' I shouted out. 'She fell in – you saw it, all of you.' I stared round into the faces of the crowd pressing against my shoulders. Their eyes were bright with anticipation of what was to come, almost drooling with eagerness to hear the next filthy lie. '*But I didn't,*' I protested.

'You all seed 'er,' roared the steward confidently. 'She was dead on that bank an' that witch breathed 'er own foul air into 'er – you seed 'er.' He pointed, his arm stretched out like a vengeful arrow, swinging round the circle of men and women encouraging their answering yells. 'You watched as she planted a witch's heart into the child's chest.'

I closed my eyes wanting not to be there, to pretend it wasn't happening.

'You can't believe that,' said the pastor. 'You can't believe your own child has become a witch, surely not?'

'She'll not live in my house again an' pollute my sons,' spat the man, 'whatever Mistress Perkins says.'

Again the crowd murmured its agreement, bolstering the man's ego to giant proportions.

'My mother explained that,' I shouted trying to make myself heard. 'I read it in a book.'

'Show us the book, then.' The voice came from the back of the crowd. Instantly the mob joined in, the chorus of voices louder and louder until no one could be heard.

The pastor raised his arms into the air appealing for quiet. 'If there is proof of witchcraft, it must be presented before Sir Richard. You cannot take the law into your own hands. The girl can produce the book then. But it is not witchcraft to go into the wood and dance – that is not proof of witchcraft.'

'She has the mark of the devil on her arm,' piped up a voice, its shrill tones soaring easily over the dark mutterings of the crowd.

I froze, the blood draining from my face; Janet white as a ghost beside me.

'That's silly,' I shouted angrily, forgetting to be frightened in the rotten unfairness of it all. 'You all saw my arms this morning when I rescued the girl. 'There's nothing on them. *Did anyone see anything on my arms?*' I swung round on the crowd copying Mr Perkins. 'And did you hear what I said, Mr Perkins. I said *rescued*. Your daughter wasn't dead, she was just full of water, and I pressed on her chest to make her cough it up. You saw her all of you. She vomited the water and then she breathed on her own. She couldn't have done that if she'd been dead.'

There was silence, the sound of talking died away. I could feel a hundred eyes glued to the back of my neck, their owners considering my words. I closed my eyes, rocking back on my heels, the air flooding out of me in relief that it was over.

'It weren't 'er, it were the other one,' the same voice shouted, its high-pitched tones reverberating round my head; *it were the other one, it were the other one,* and I knew instinctively that the gloating tones belonged to the steward's son.

A large hand reached across me tearing away the left sleeve of Janet's gown. There were gasps as the horns of the ram appeared and, once again, I heard the ugly growling sound I'd heard that morning.

'There's the proof, what more do you need, hang 'em.'

'She's got one too – it's on 'er leg, I seed it.'

Bloody little tow-rag, he should have been drowned at birth.

We were helpless; the crowd out of control and dominating even the pastor. I heard a voice calling for a trial, another for a hanging, another for burning. The pastor trying desperately to shout them down, only one man among so many.

But just beyond the crowd I had a friend, a friend nobody knew about, and I'd be safe if only I could reach it.

'Janet, I'm going to get help. Don't worry, I'll come and get you,' I shouted into her ear. Then, attacking everything standing in my way with my fists, my feet and my head, I forced a path through the bodies and, leaping onto the low wall which spanned the bridge, dived in.

The water closed over my head; strangely not as cold as this morning but warm and safe. I hated leaving Janet, but only a real good swimmer could survive in this water. I let the heavy weight of my skirts drag me down to the bottom, the light from the torches on the bridge penetrating the top layers and lifting the gloom. Calmly now, I pulled at the buttons on the back of my dress, tugging it down over my ankles. Poor Agnes, I expect she was still diligently sewing my Sunday dress back together again.

Taking to a river twice in one day is not to be recommended and, despite the initial sensation of safety and warmth, I shivered as I ditched my petticoat, pinning my cast off clothes to the bottom of the river with handfuls of shale. I turned and swam a couple of strokes underwater into the darkness of the bridge. Softly, I lifted my face into the air and, taking a deep, silent breath, sank down again. I had seen enough; the light from the torches circling the river bank below the bridge. I had faced that way when I dived in; it was logical to search there first, knowing everything floated downstream on the current. But I had no intention of being where they expected. The torches spread out along the bank, those in the distance only pinpricks of light through the water. I turned and headed upstream.

The flood of that morning had eased and the river idled more quietly, as if ashamed of its fury and wanting to make up for it by making sure I came to no harm. I held my breath pretending I was swimming the last leg of the relay and allowed my lungs to reach bursting point before heading for the bank. I lifted my nose clear, gathering some life-saving oxygen.

I had gained perhaps twenty metres and, if any of my pursuers glanced upstream beyond the bridge, they would have seen me. I submerged and swam on. Despite knowing the greater the distance between me and the mob the safer I would be, I desperately wanted to keep checking, to discover what point the search had reached. It was a strong, almost overwhelming compulsion; I simply had to see for myself whether anyone was interested in the black blob that had just risen above the surface. But what if the light from their torches picked up the white of my face? I disappeared below the surface again until, unable to control the urge, I raised my eyes above the level of the water and glanced downstream. The bridge loomed blackly against the bright fire progressing along each side of the bank as the hunters scrutinised every blade of grass, every ripple, every sound.

Beyond me, the river disappeared into the darkness of a bend, its outline blurred. If I could reach that, I'd be safe. I pulled myself strongly forward against the lingering current. Finally, exhausted, my lungs starved of oxygen, I headed for the bank. There was a clump of reeds growing close by, their roots in the soft mud, and I tucked myself into them, waiting.

I was cold but strangely enough I wasn't frightened, even when I saw more torches cutting across the field towards the lower river, intent on searching further downstream past the ruined bridge. A stray breeze caught my bare shoulders and I dropped down into the friendly water leaving just my face exposed, the least freezing of the two options.

I don't know how long I'd been in the water. Every moment or so I raised myself up, the air bitter against my increasingly cold body, to check on the progress of the pursuit – identifying two distinct groups of searchers. Those way downstream were too far away to worry me but the second group were once again standing by the bridge, not more than sixty, sixty-five metres away.

I couldn't believe they weren't giving up and heading home to their warm fires. In their shoes I would have done so long ago, convinced I was dead. Well, they might just get their wish for I soon would be if they didn't hurry up and quit. I could see the great black mass of bodies quite clearly, the light above their heads like a birthday cake with candles. They were talking; they hadn't given up. The black mass turned and the torches began to move upstream again. Some bright spark had finally realised I could swim.

I couldn't think about Janet; now I had to save myself. Somehow I had to get home because I knew, beyond any doubt – as much as I hated him for his bullying ways – Mr Hampton wouldn't let any harm come to his family. He belonged to that breed of grown-up who, to the public eye, appears a model of rectitude. He might be an ogre towards his family but God help anyone else that tried it on. Mr Hampton would go to the ends of the earth to protect what belonged to him, and that included his stepdaughter.

I submerged, watching the pinpricks of light grow larger. The huddle of men separated into individual silhouettes, each with a light. They were carrying long sticks which they were using to prod the river bed, like one of those machines that flattens out hot tarmac on the roads; up down – up down – up down, deep into the shale. There was no way now I could slip past them; I was cornered.

I heard voices shouting, the men nearest to me swivelling round to see what had happened. It was my chance. I slid out of the reeds, crawling up the bank on my stomach. Keeping low, I headed across the field away from the river and the searching men. There was a small hillock and I flung myself behind it. The men turned back and slowly, full of purpose, their torches pursued their relentless march towards the reed bed where I'd been hiding not a minute before.

My shift was filthy, covered in black mud, and I knew I wouldn't be seen against the ground. Copying the slime-balls who had stalked Janet, I slid silently out from behind the small hill and, using my elbows to pull myself along, crawled away. I was gaining height, beginning to look down onto figures that were becoming foreshortened by the angle of the slope. The sheer terror, which had swept over me when I left the safety of the water, started to subside and I moved swiftly, my knees and elbows stinging from contact with the wet grass, and my teeth chattering. I forced them together, aware that the slightest sound would carry in the quiet night air and give away my new hiding place.

I watched the two groups of men, those upstream now searching the reed bed where I'd hidden, poking into the vegetation on either side of the river. Thank God I'd moved when I did; I would have been caught like a rat in a trap.

The second group were way downstream, past the broken bridge. Now they also were coming back, scouring the riverbanks closely, and prodding at the middle of the stream with their long poles, their torches creating circles of brightness in the water. They stood on the broken bridge talking, their torches illuminating that small stretch of river like day.

There came a sudden cry, another and another, until the air was full of noise. One of the silhouettes gestured frantically beckoning to the men upstream. Abandoning the river, the searchers broke into a run, their torches zigzagging erratically over the uneven ground. Quickly, they converged on the broken stones of the small bridge.

What was it? Had my dress floated downstream? Puzzled, I watched the men forming a human chain, clinging tightly to the outstretched hand of the man behind. Two men, at the front of the chain, clambered laboriously over the broken arch and down onto the stones, lowering themselves into the water.

I shivered, running my hands vigorously up and down my arms, trying to get my blood circulating round my frozen body.

More shouting; the sound of splashing, then a swell of noise above which I could hear the shrill wailing of women. They lifted something from the water, slowly passing it along the chain until it was safely on the bank.

It was Molly; they had found Molly.

EIGHTEEN

They had gone because there was nothing more to search for; the chain of angry hunters, transformed by death into a group of mourners, their torches carried high above their heads. I could see them quite clearly, walking slowly two by two, taking Molly back home. They turned their backs on the now-silent river, which had held on to Molly only giving her up when she was needed to save my life.

It was dark again; stars, previously eclipsed by the torches, now the only light in an otherwise empty sky. I listened anxiously. An owl hooted making me jump and I heard a fox bark; but the humans had gone. I struggled to my feet, my legs numb from crouching on the wet ground, and hobbled painfully down the hillside towards the broken bridge. I was crying. Tears dripped down my cheeks onto my sodden shift, which had wrapped itself round my legs, making it difficult even to hobble – a huddled mass of snivelling, freezing humanity, crying for the loss of my fairytale ending.

What was I going to do? I felt like a puppy abandoned at the side of the road by its owners – totally lost, without a single idea in my head as to how I was going to survive. I sat down on the stones by the bridge, gazing aimlessly at the water, trying to tug my exhausted brain back into gear. What day was it? I vaguely remembered going to chapel, but was that today? It felt more like a week ago. But that couldn't be. A week ago I'd just arrived here but that felt like a year. *Poor Molly.* She'd been missing since the day I appeared and no one knew.

The events of the past week began to take shape. I thought back to the day I'd left a message for Richard under the bridge and found the wet stones slippery and dangerous. I could easily have fallen and hit my head. Is that what happened to Molly? I began to cry again; this time tears of sadness for Agnes and Edward, *and the mother* – I daren't think about her, it was too painful.

'Molly!'

I caught at the whisper like a lifeline. 'Richard?'

Unable to believe in miracles I half-turned, staring over my shoulder. Something moved in the darkness and a figure emerged from the field. I stretched out my hand as if I'd been thrown a lifejacket. 'What are you doing here?'

'Waiting for you.'

'But I'm dead,' I said stupidly.

'No, you're not, but you soon will be if you don't get warm.' Bending down, Richard draped his cloak gently round my shoulders, the heat from his body enclosing me like a pair of loving arms. He sat down and, tucking its edges under my legs, began to rub some life back into them.

'You know?' I said, beginning to feel as if I might live, after all.

'That you're not Molly? Yes, I know.'

I couldn't see his expression in the darkness but I wanted to cry again. I had lied and cheated; he might save me but he'd never forgive me, not now – not now Molly had been found.

'Look, Molly, or whatever your name is.'

My nose began to run as company for my eyes and I sniffed, wiping it with the back of my hand.

'I don't want you to say anything until you're warm and safe. Promise me.'

'But Janet?' I protested.

'She's home and in bed asleep, I trust. Now, promise me.'

I nodded.

He got to his feet and, wrapping his arm round my shoulders, helped me up. Slowly, we staggered across the cold hard stones of the bridge and into the flower meadow. Beneath my feet were the delicate stems of Molly's favourite flower, the mauve fritillaries; too small and fragile to be seen in the dark light of the starlit sky. I wondered aimlessly if, like Molly, they too were dead; their fragile stems crushed into the mud by the clod-hopping boots of the villagers.

My bare feet were now so cold I couldn't actually feel the ground at all, a blank space at the end of my legs, but I knew that the sharp pebbles on the riverbed had cut into them, although I had no idea how badly. Still, at this moment, my feet were the least of my worries. My legs and arms were refusing to work together, to synchronise; my legs jerking one way, my arms another. I never knew walking could be so exhausting, each step a penance for one of my many sins. I gritted my teeth, doggedly putting one foot in front of the other, Richard almost carrying me. A couple of times I nearly told him to leave me to sleep, the words on the tip of my tongue. Suddenly, I spotted the solid outline of the stable block and then, as if wafted on a magic carpet, I was in a lamp-lit room sitting on a bale of hay, with Richard holding a cup of something to my mouth.

Obediently, I took a large mouthful. *Wow, it was like nought to sixty in two seconds flat!* I choked, spluttering in my efforts not to cough out loud in case someone heard. The liquor was so strong it literally took my breath away, stinging the back of my throat, the fumes billowing down my nose and making my eyes water.

'What was that?' I croaked.

'Brandy.'

'Haven't you got any milk?' I fanned my mouth.

'You should have sipped it,' he rebuked, getting up. 'But it will make you feel better, less tired. Try and sip a little. Then you should get dry and get some clothes on.'

'Where are we?'

The room looked warm and inviting in the lamplight, bales of golden hay scattered over the floor.

'In the old gardener's cottage. Molly and I use – I mean used – it on wet days. But you're quite safe here and it's warm.'

It was. Built next to the stables, you could feel the heat from the horses radiating through its thin walls.

'I've brought you some clothes – they're mine. Molly sometimes wore them for a dare, and there's food. I'll go and get you some milk.'

I know I looked haunted. I felt it, scared to death about being found again.

Richard knelt down on the floor beside me.

'I promise you, no one ever comes here; it's quite safe.' His troubled blue eyes stared into mine. 'Believe me; I would never let anything hurt you.'

He got to his feet vanishing round the door. I could hear a horse moving, stamping its feet on the other side of the thin partition wall. It was a comforting sound. I stripped off my wet shift. Richard had left a cloth on top of the pile of clothes and, for the second time that day, I rubbed every inch of my skin until it glowed, putting on the frilled shirt and breeches of a Royalist. I was still cold and hastily put on the jacket, wrapping his cloak round me again. The warmth had brought my feet back to life with a vengeance and now my toes burned furiously. I dabbed the cloth carefully at the bits of skin that weren't covered with scratches. Cautiously, I began to inch the stockings over my toes, shuddering as the rough wool touched my heels. I rolled them up my legs, carefully lifting the wool over the worst scratches. There were garters to keep them up and a pair of shoes with bows. Surprisingly, they fitted.

I heard Richard come back, his low whistle announcing him before his head appeared round the door. In one hand he held a comb and, in the other, milk in a tall jug. I drank thirstily and started on my hair, thanking him for the comb.

'Warm?'

I nodded. 'Getting there.' I took a deep breath. 'How long have you known?' I said.

'Thinking back, it must have been that first day …'

I groaned, rocking myself backwards and forwards, my arms clasped round my middle.

'What's wrong? Are you ill?'

I shook my head. 'Oh, why didn't you say something?' I clasped my head in my hands. 'If only you'd said, all this could have been avoided.'

'But I didn't know,' Richard protested. He got to his feet. I watched him slowly pace across the floor, his head bent, his hands working round and round. In a way, I felt relieved he wasn't watching me, unable to cope with seeing the warmth in his smile fade, regarding me impartially as he would a stranger.

'I thought it was all imagination. That, at long last, Molly was letting go of her anger and prejudice against her family.'

'Even her mother?'

He nodded, turning his eyes on me. Troubled eyes, but still the eyes of a friend. They hadn't changed – not yet. 'Particularly her mother – she resented so much her marrying again. But wanting to know about the war … that was extraordinary. You see, Molly thought her own problems far more important. You are so very different.'

My head jerked and I yelped as the muscles in the top of my shoulder went into spasm. Richard was instantly by my side, his hand reaching out, concern and anxiety flooding into his face.

'I'm all right, it's only cramp,' I said, rolling my shoulders. I reached up to massage them.

He knocked my hand away and, grasping my shoulders began kneading them with his long fingers. I closed my eyes, feeling the knots begin to break up and subside.

'I thought we were identical.'

The hands stopped.

'You are...' Richard stepped away, his glance so penetrating it was as if he was memorising every cell in my body. I bent my head and stared at the ground, the pain in my chest much, much worse than the cramp had been.

'Although, now I can see many minute differences; the way your hair parts, the way you glance up under your lids as if you are accustomed to your hair falling over your face; and your nails are not broken the way Molly's were.'

I stared down at my hands. Of course, I'd been wearing gloves the day I first met Richard, he would only have seen the tips of my fingers.

'But even had I noticed them,' he continued talking, 'I wouldn't have given it a second thought. Someone you have grown up with, who you see most days ... like a brother or a sister ... do you actually ever look at them? No, this was Molly – as close to me as any sister. It was only when we were climbing back up the hill. You hung back – staring at me with eyes that didn't belong to my friend.' He began pacing again. 'It was like being struck by a bolt of lightning. I never thought of you in the same way again. You had become this amazing stranger – yet, you were still my Molly. I found it hopelessly confusing. *You must have noticed.* What is your name?' He said the words gently, as if it mattered.

'It's Molly – the same.'

I've never actually seen anyone do, what they call a

double take, but Richard did one now; his head jerking backwards, his eyes starting open with astonishment.

'But when did you know – for certain?'

'When I heard how you saved Perkins' little girl. Molly could swim but she had become terrified of water – her father drowned, you know.'

I nodded. 'I saw his grave …' I stopped and looked at him. I didn't want to talk about death. A feeling of guilt, that I had survived while Molly had died, pressed down on my head like a visible weight. Trying to ease my conscience I said, 'Will you tell me about her, what she was like?'

'As a child, she was exactly as you are now. She never once considered anything could harm her, and neither do you. Brave, fearless, infuriating, but unbelievably enchanting.'

I felt my breath falter and stop.

'I'm the older by nearly two years but there never was a difference. We used to go to school together, only that was stopped for Molly when she moved here. She hated being a girl because it meant she couldn't do things.'

'What sort of things?' I asked.

'She dreamed of becoming a botanist. When she was little, her father told her stories about the islands in the West Indies. Occasionally botanists travelled with the ship, bringing back plants and seeds, and her father promised she would go, too, when she was old enough. It was her dream to become educated. She would have asked to go to university, if women had been permitted. Of course, it couldn't have happened, her stepfather would never have allowed it. He considered women only good for keeping house, making butter, cooking, and caring for children.'

I heard the bitterness ring through his voice. Poor Molly, if only she'd been born in my time. At least, she could have gone to university.

'It was not ordained by God for women to be educated …' Richard stayed silent for a moment, a brooding frown breaking the symmetry of his expression. I bit my lip, wishing I'd been able to bring my mobile from the future to capture his expression; his eyes tormented under frowning brows, his jaw square and determined.

'It was his bigotry that eventually destroyed Molly. She became determined to defy him. I begged her to let it go, but she could not. Her stepfather was unjust and wrong in his treatment of her and, whatever the cost, she was determined to win the battle.'

'And now she can't,' I said sadly.

'I didn't know anything about it,' Richard continued, 'until one of the boys that works in the stables came to find me. He told me you were trapped in the chapel and the pastor had been sent for. By the time I got there, you had disappeared into the river. The pastor immediately ordered them to search, threatening eternal damnation if anything happened to you. It sobered them up I can tell you, but too late. It took something as terrible as your drowning – I mean Molly …' He gazed at me, his eyes full of misery. 'It's very confusing.'

I nodded.

'It took you plunging into the river, preferring to take your chances in that torrent, to make them see sense. Perkins disappeared in a hurry, but Father will deal with him tomorrow. He will lose his job and good riddance. Other people came from the village to help and Mister Hampton was with them. He had been sent for and had just arrived. He joined the search party while someone took Janet home.'

'But he doesn't even like me,' I protested.

'No, he may not like you, Molly, but you are a part of his household which is his responsibility. It would go against his conscience to let anything happen to you.'

So I was right, anything not to lose face. But it was a hollow victory; I might have been right, but it wasn't worth Molly dying to prove it.

'And Janet?'

'She was crying and very scared but the threat of damnation did its work; no one will harm her now. I didn't join the search. I went back to the house to fetch clothes, convinced you would make your way back to the bridge eventually.'

'You still didn't think I was dead, not even when they found Molly?'

Richard gazed at me very steadily, his deep blue eyes burning a hole in my heart; his voice serious and sad. 'After that day, Molly, I spent the entire night worrying about the conflict to come; determined whatever took place we would eventually be together and nothing, not even war, could separate us. Scarcely a day later all of this happens, and I learned you were dead – drowned. Yet, in the back of my mind, something was saying that this couldn't be.'

Richard collapsed onto a bale of hay, burying his head in his hands. 'The thoughts I had ... did not make sense.' He continued talking, his voice muffled, as if he wanted to speak yet despised himself for sounding weak. 'It was as if I had two voices in my head. The one telling me that I must feel grief because my childhood friend had died. The other insisting that however unworldly, unbelievable, there had to be two of you. One had died, yes, but not the stranger. Somehow she was still alive and if I hurried down to the river ... I could not believe my thoughts. I felt as if I was going mad and yet ...' Richard leapt to his feet and began pacing again, round and round like a caged lion. 'I know it was wrong, but the voice continued to insist ... if it had to happen at all ...' He subsided onto the straw bale, his gaze wild and tormented. 'I can't get out of my mind the picture of poor Molly being dragged out of the water.'

I could feel his pain. He'd lost something very precious, whatever he said to the contrary. One day he would come to terms with it, but not yet. I slipped my arm through his, my head against his shoulder. 'The rocks were really dangerous under the bridge. Hating water as much as she did, Molly was very brave to risk it. I guess she was desperate to get in touch, because she'd been banned from visiting the manor. She was probably hurrying when she slipped and hit her head. 'Did you keep her note?'

Richard nodded. 'Yes! Yours too! I was comparing the writing.'

'Sorry about that. Go on, you were saying.'

'I watched the villagers, the search was so thorough I thought there was no way anything could escape them. I told myself again and again that you had to be a good swimmer to try and save that girl.'

'You're right, I know water,' I shrugged. 'It never once occurred to me that I could drown.'

'I'd nearly given up when I saw you crawling down the hill towards the bridge – it was the best sight I've ever had in my life.'

My face suddenly felt very hot and I nearly burst out crying again. I swallowed hard and drank some milk – hurriedly.

'Now, I need to know about you. Who are you and how you came here?'

'But will you believe me, if I tell you? I promise you it's the truth, but it won't sound like the truth. It's more like something you'd tell to a child – to scare them into being good. And I wouldn't blame you if you did think I was a witch,' I said miserably.

He nodded, his face set. 'I'll believe you, Molly.'

So I told him. I could see my hands shaking up and down in my lap, as I struggled to find the right words, knowing whatever I said would end up sounding like a big fat lie.

'Something happened in that house that brought me here, from another time, to take Molly's place.' I bit my lip trying to find the right words. 'I've got this strange feeling it only happened because Molly had already had her accident. Perhaps I came here to finish something she was meant to do – but I'm not sure about that bit.'

I could see bewilderment in Richard's eyes as he struggled to cope with what I'd just thrown at him.

'It makes a sort of sense,' he said slowly. 'It also explains why you sent the second note, and why you were in the house when Mister Hampton had expressly told Molly to stay away. But … I can't understand how a person can travel from a different time; from a different town, possibly.'

'I don't understand either,' I said. 'That's the bit that gets me every time I think about it. In the age in which I live, we accept that you can't move from one time to another,' I said, resisting the temptation to tell Richard about airplanes. 'I don't know why it happened to me. But, for what it's worth, if it makes it any easier,' I shrugged, 'pretend I've come here from another town.'

Richard nodded gratefully.

'That's not all, there's more,' I said. 'Janet, the maid? She's like me; only she's been stuck here for nearly two years. She nearly got back once. You remember when Perkins found her in your parlour? He pulled her back. To be fair to him, it must have given him quite a shock to see her begin to disappear. I think he was being honest, for once, when he says he thought she had to be a witch. I know you don't believe in witches; neither do I, and neither does your father – but, if you can't explain something you've still got to give it a name. A nicer person than Perkins might have thought she was an angel.'

'Yes,' he said thoughtfully. 'What is it like, this phenomenon?'

'It's rather like sacks of flour falling down a chute into a cart – only she and I fell down this sort-of time hole.'

'Where is it?'

'In your parlour, that's why it was so difficult for Janet to get in there, because your family are always about. We tried this afternoon, we saw you all going out to visit someone. That's how Perkins found us.'

'I don't understand. If you were there, why didn't go back to this place – wherever it is?'

'Because there was no sun. We didn't know that before, but it has to be sunny.'

'But why, why didn't you tell me? I could have helped.'

I disguised a groan. He would only think I was in pain and be concerned. And I did hurt – the pain sharp and penetrating – despairing. So … so…tragic and yet so futile. I kept my voice light. 'Oh, come on, Richard. Let's be fair, I was like you. I kept trying to find ways to tell you. But who would believe something so weird, you'd have locked me up.'

To my surprise he laughed, his eyes sparkling with mischief. 'So that's what you meant by, *all this could have been avoided.* As for being weird, you never met Molly. She was obsessed by the strangest of ideas. One day, she told me she dreamed of flying to the moon. On another occasion, she dreamed that she was talking to me from a long distance. This is no more extraordinary.'

I wanted to hug him. 'Then you do believe me.'

He held out his hand, taking mine in his. It felt safe. We sat in silence. I didn't need to ask what he was thinking – instinctively knowing his thoughts were the mirror-image of my own; a desperate search for a way that would allow me to stay, so Richard could make good his promise that we would never be apart … followed by the slow and unbelievably painful realisation that it was impossible. But the thought of saying goodbye … *never seeing him again …* was like a kick in the stomach. I felt my breath flutter painfully before stopping altogether.

'What do you want me to do?'

What did I want him to do? Make my dream come true – wave a magic wand so we could live happily every after.

'Get us into your parlour.' The words dragged their way out of my mouth as I closed the door on my dreams. 'But you'll have to get Janet, I can't leave her; and pray for sun.'

Richard nodded. 'Is your life very different?'

'Y – es … absolutely … totally,' I replied without thinking.

'In what way?'

I scrunched down on one arm, the emotions of the last half-hour making me sleepy. I opened my mouth to say, *well you don't have gangs of men roaming the streets tormenting innocent people, for starters*, and hastily shut it again. Women can work, parents don't beat their kids; people don't get persecuted for their religious beliefs; everyone can read and writ*e* – that was crap too. I frowned, searching for something to explain exactly how really different we are in the twenty-first century.

'Everyone goes to school and can vote for their government,' I finally said, rather lamely. 'And children have more freedom and opportunities to learn different things, like sport and dancing and swimming. Oh yes, and children can speak at the dinner table and there's always hot water.'

'We speak at the dinner table and we have hot water,' Richard replied in an amused voice. 'Do you still have good and bad people, and rich and poor people?'

'Well, yes, we do,' I said, staring at him. I'd never really thought about it like that; it's the surroundings that change, not people or their nature.

'So it is not so very different.'

'No, I suppose not.'

'Then you are welcome to your life, Molly, I'll stick to mine. Are you warm?'

I nodded.

'Get some sleep. I'll stay and watch. As soon as it's light, I will find a way to fetch Janet.'

I was suddenly wide-awake. '*But Ann Hampton?* I can't go without seeing her; whatever will she think?' I said wildly. 'I have to tell her.'

'Tell her *what*, Molly; *that you're drowned?* She knows that you are drowned. You cannot walk in there as if nothing has happened.'

'I have to tell her the truth,' I shouted desperately, once again feeling the ready tears push their way to the surface.

He wrapped his arms tightly round me. '*You can't*, it's far too dangerous. The villagers think you dead.' He held me away from him and stared into my eyes 'If you are seen ...'

'But I haven't said goodbye,' I argued. 'I've got to see Agnes and Edward. They'll be so sad. I have to tell them ...' The tears streamed down my face, words heedlessly flying from my mouth. 'If I go now, it's still dark and no one will see me ...'

'*Molly, for once in your life listen to me.*' Richard grabbed my shoulders, shaking me until I felt my teeth rattle. In despair, I flung myself down on the straw. '*You can't go back. You have to see that.*'

I did see it; that was the trouble. It was like being dead. I would never see any of them again – not Richard, not anyone, ever again.

'Molly, if you love them don't make it worse.'

'OK,' I sighed.

'Promise?'

'I just have.'

'You won't move from this room?'

'No, I won't move, but if you ever get the chance, Richard ...'

'I'll say goodbye for you.'

Suddenly, I'd had enough. I had to sleep, my eyelids

closing, leaving me with a picture of children running up and down a wooden staircase and fathomless blue eyes, with a hint of dark in them.

NINETEEN

I opened my eyes and gazed around slowly, unsure of where I was. Then I remembered. The room was light, the lantern still lit and swinging from the beam above my head; but now its colour had changed, no longer deep gold but a yellow so pale it was almost white. I guessed it was daylight outside.

Richard was gone but I could hear movement in the stables, as if the animals had woken up. I felt awful. My throat grated like porcupine quills and I theorised about suffering from tetanus or the plague, until I remembered that Dad had got mad when I suggested the river water would give the villagers typhoid.

There was some milk left in the jug. I sipped it but it tasted gross, slightly warm and beginning to go off. I added *feeling sick* to my other list of woes; a colossal headache, bad eyes, and feet and legs which kept going into spasm because they'd been scrunched up under my chin to keep me warm. I needed a shower and some good food and if it meant going back to my century to get them, I'd go – and the sooner the better.

There was a noise at the door. I froze and tucked myself behind the bales of hay.

'Richard?' I whispered.

The door opened. It was Ann Hampton. I stared at her, unbelieving.

'Richard has always been a bad liar,' she said, answering my unspoken question. She came in, closing the door behind her.

'He told you?' I asked nervously glancing at her face, expecting to see disappointment – my own mum's favourite expression – looming there.

Instead, she smiled gently at me and, sitting down on one of the bales, took my hand. 'Can you imagine Richard trying to get Janet away from the house, without my knowing?'

I felt deliriously happy. I clutched her hands between mine hardly able to believe I had got my wish to see her again.

'Does any one else know?'

'Edward does. He asks unceasingly when the stranger Molly is coming back, but he is only five and will soon forget.'

'Dear, dear Edward. I'm so sorry.'

She smiled at me sadly. 'Oh, my dear child, this is not your fault. It has been such a bad night for us all and a very frightening one for you. You must hate us, for rewarding your bravery with persecution.'

'I couldn't hate any of you,' I interrupted. 'I love you all as if you were my own family. I don't even hate the villagers; they didn't know any better.'

'I am glad to hear that, Molly. Perkins, the steward, was the real troublemaker; the rest simply followed … like sheep.' She patted my hand. 'Last week when Molly failed to return for her dinner, I had a premonition that something terrible had happened to her. But when you appeared I thought I had to be mistaken.'

'Did Richard tell you how I got here?'

She nodded. 'About the time-chute, yes.'

'Do you believe him?'

'That you came from another time? Yes, Molly, I do

believe him. Whilst I was walking here, I was remembering my father. He always told me to approach things we cannot understand with an open mind. He said there were instances where people appeared to be living in the wrong time. He might have been speaking of you.'

'But you didn't guess?'

She smiled – such a sorrowful smile. I remembered Molly was the second child she had lost. 'I am as surprised as you. I cannot believe that a mother does not know her own daughter. I wish you had known her, for she used to be the happiest of children. Her father and I had encouraged her to become an independent person. Had he lived, things would have been so different. If you remember, I told you how things changed after we came here ...'

I nodded, concentrating on the feel of her hands, the skin rough with constant work.

'With the change in my husband, her life changed too, becoming very restricted, very narrow. And, from that moment, she became such an unhappy child. She was determined to break free and, if that meant running counter to her stepfather's wishes, she ran. Even his punishments failed to break her, serving only to make her more obstinate. I tried my best but I was helpless against religious bigotry, and Molly blamed me so bitterly for all her troubles that she and I became estranged. She had no time for the children either, except strangely enough, Agnes. It seems they each recognised a boat tossing around in a storm and clung together. Agnes had lost a mother and found her own father intimidating and little interested in her. I did my best, but it was Molly she really loved. Surprisingly, despite Molly's wild behaviour, which they knew made their father so angry, the children rallied together to protect her from punishment.

'But you, my dear Molly, were so different. You played football with Edward. When the nurse told me I could not believe it and began to think that my prayers had, at long last, been answered and you were growing up. Edward told me about, *"it raining cats and dogs"*, and still I had no clue. When we went to Blandford Forum, you frittered your money on presents for them. The old Molly would never have done that; she hoarded her money, because money represented freedom.'

I tried to imagine what it must have been like growing-up, hemmed in on all sides, even her bed like a box with walls and a top, restricted to domestic chores, having to ask permission to go for a walk; aware it would never change even after she was married off and living in another home. Would I have been strong enough to continue my rebellion? I stared down at my hands, still clutching Ann Hampton's, and knew that I wouldn't.

'Richard told me,' she continued, 'that you believe you came here for a purpose?'

'Yes, but I don't know what,' I said.

'Perhaps, something in your own life? Do you remember in the churchyard, when I said I prayed for something to happen that would change my husband back into the man I once knew?'

'I remember.'

'It was he who found Molly's body. The shock of that discovery, together with the knowledge that the church had failed him, that it was his brothers in religion who had tried to hunt down his daughter, has made him question his life. He believes now that he was much to blame.'

'He was,' I said angrily, remembering my hands. 'Molly wouldn't have died if he'd been kinder.'

'Last night he didn't sleep at all. We talked, as we have not done since we came here. And this morning he has gone to Blandford, to make arrangements for us to move back to our old house. We will start again.'

'Oh, how wonderful!' I remembered my dream. It was

all going to come true, only without me. 'Please let Margaret and Agnes go to school.'

She nodded, a gentle smile on her face. 'And Edward, too, when he grows a little older.'

She got to her feet and I reluctantly let go her hands; her fingers slipping through mine as she made her way to the door. 'It is customary when a child dies to name the next born after it. If my child is a girl, she will be called Molly. And I can wish for nothing better than she resembles you, my dear – brave and fearless, with a loving heart. I have loved you, like a daughter, and I hope you will find the answer as to why you came to us here. We must go. Richard and Janet are waiting at the house.'

I got up then and stood looking at her, her grey eyes almost on a level with my own. She'd been more of a mother to me in one week than my mum had in fifteen years. Any second now, I was going to lose her and I couldn't bear it.

'Come, my dear, I will escort this most handsome youth into the house. You make a most personable boy, Molly, no one would possibly suspect.'

Cheerfully, not giving me any time to make a fuss, she tucked her arm in mine opening the door. The sun was shining.

'There's some money by my bed, will you give it to Agnes? Tell her I love her. And, dear Edward and ...'

She squeezed my arm. 'I will make it right.'

The gravel crunched under our feet, as she and I walked together for the last time under the archway of the stable, into the house by the side door and along the passageway towards the parlour.

I knew the term, "*Dead man walking*". That's exactly what it felt like. Nothing I might do or say could possibly influence or alter what was going to happen. My head whirled. *But how could I leave?* Far too many questions still remained unanswered. I tried to think of them. But all that came into my head were silly trivial things like, *who would own the ship now? Where was Molly to be buried? If Ann Hampton was here, who was milking the cow?*

She kissed me goodbye at the door to the parlour, pushing me in. I found myself somehow on the inside of the door, with the door closing behind me.

Richard was waiting. 'I'm sorry, Molly, she insisted on coming.'

I looked round the room. It was empty. 'Where's Janet?' I asked, my mind still not functioning.

'She's gone.'

'Gone,' I said stupidly.

Richard grinned. 'She said she couldn't risk being stuck here for another two years and bet me a sovereign you would change your mind at the last moment, and refuse to go. Are you going to win her bet for her?'

I heard myself say quite calmly, 'You are right, I have my own life to lead.' Someone else held out their hand to Richard and said, 'Goodbye, Richard. Thank you for being my friend.'

The sun was warm, the circular stone beckoning. I crossed the floor.

'Molly?'

Still in a daze, I gazed back at him. Taller than me and older, with deep blue eyes you wanted to drown in.

'It doesn't make any sense, Molly, but I want you to know that I do love you and probably always will.'

It was too much. I stepped into the sunlight shining warmly through the windows, the circular stone beneath my feet.

In a flash, my head cleared. How could I leave? There were too many people here that I loved and, more importantly, who loved me. Everything I wanted from life was here. How could I even begin to think of turning my back on it?

Already the room was fading and, at the end of a tunnel the parlour began to appear, the parlour as I had last seen it with religious pamphlets on the small table. I heard a voice shout wildly, '*No, I don't want to go! I belong here with you!*'

Someone pushed me and then I was standing in front of the fireplace, tears pouring down my face. Richard had told me he loved me and I'd not said anything. And my family – the mother, Agnes, Margaret and Edward? How could I possibly live my life without them?

TWENTY

I sniffed, wiping my eyes with the back of my hand. A girl stood watching me.

'JANET!' I screeched, so loudly it's a wonder that miserable git, the manager, didn't come rushing in with his *silence at all times* notice. 'You made it.' I rushed to hug her, promptly bursting into tears again. 'I hope I'm not becoming a permanent watering pot,' I said half-laughing. 'But why are you here? Why haven't you returned to your time?'

'I don't know, I don't know,' she replied, frantically shaking her head. 'What about you?'

'Oh help! I don't know that either.' I glanced despairing at the stone – desperately wanting to take that single step, my feet cemented to the floor.

Dad appeared at the door. 'Molly, where on earth have you been, I was just about to call the police?'

I jumped. 'Sorry, Dad, I got carried away and lost track of time.' I gave him a hug.

'Er …' He stepped back a pace, giving me a weird look as if I never hugged him. I stopped in my tracks – astonished – *but I never did, did I?*

'Who's this?'

'That's why I was late. I came across Janet – she's lost, says her parents should be here.' I fabricated the lie, hoping it would hold water. 'She was just going to phone home.'

'Let me know if they aren't there.'

Janet nodded, and in my mind I read tomorrow's headlines. *Girl feared dead, miraculously reappears.*

'If it's okay with you, Dad, we'll go over to my room and phone.'

He nodded, not much interested, and wandered off again, but he would be in a few minutes when the police blasted their way up the gravel drive.

I glanced down at the stone; the temptation overpowering. The sun was still shining on it, the fire screen back in its place before the large grate. I only had to step back onto it and I would see Richard – feel his hand in mine, his gaze gentle and concerned. I took a step forward. I could go back and make it right. *Tell him I loved him right back ...* it would only take a moment. I looked at it longingly, wringing my hands.

'Molly ... you can't. You're dead, remember.'

The bright pictures flew out of sight like motes of dust; too small and fragile to keep hold of, however much I wanted to.

'I'm sorry.'

I stared at her; the sympathy in her eyes plain to read.

I nodded, suddenly feeling very old. 'I know. Do you think there are loads of people, you know like us, stuck in the wrong century?'

I ran to the edge of the heavy rug battling to drag it across the flag-stone floor. 'Give me a hand, Janet, it'll be safer this way. We can't let this happen to anyone else. It's not fair.' The words spun out of me. It didn't matter what I said, how hollow or insincere, if only they would close up that yawning crevice in my heart.

'I don't know and *I don't care*. I'm home. That's all that matters.'

Together, we pulled the carpet over the stone moving the fire screen to one side.

'Yes, but ...' I stopped. I gazed at the sunlight streaming through the neat diamond-shaped panes. My dreams knocked loudly – wanting to take possession again. I turned away, locking the door firmly. 'Come on, let's go and sort you out.'

I looked down. My watch was back on my wrist – it said three thirty. I'd been away nearly five hours. No wonder Dad had been in a strop, I'd missed lunch.

'Well, what *are* you going to do?' We left the parlour, strolling out into the afternoon sunshine and made our way towards the stable block.

It was like coming home by plane after a holiday spent somewhere nice. You say to yourself, this time two hours ago I was chatting up that cool guy on the surfboard, and the sun was hot and there were flowers everywhere. Only for me it was – half an hour ago, I was walking along this path with Ann Hampton, and Richard was there waiting for me. I switched my mind off. I had to think of Janet and what she was going to do. There was plenty of time to remember when I got to bed that night.

'How the hell-long have you been missing?' I said, as we reached the safety of my room.

'What's the date?'

'It's April 10, 2006.'

Frightened eyes stared at me. 'Oh, my God! That means I've been missing since ... the tenth of April ... two years ago. *So why were you only away a few hours?* Why has time only changed for me? It doesn't make sense.'

I didn't have an explanation either. I might be good at maths but besides the April 10 link, I couldn't find the connection, unless ... 'Do you think it's got something to do with you trying to get back?' I guessed, but Janet wasn't listening. Still, it could work. There was a time chute, so why not a time clock? Time passed slowly if you were visiting – like me – but if you went back like Janet had, time speeded up to normal. It was a fantastic idea but since I couldn't go back and Janet didn't care, I had no way of proving it. And, if it could only happen on April 10 when the sun was shining on that particular stone, that might account for there not being dozens of time-travellers cluttering up the parlour in the manor, like a railway station waiting room.

'*But two years!*' Janet groaned, her arms clutching her middle. 'Oh help, what can I say?'

'Well, for starters, you can't just ring up and say, hi Mum, what's for tea?'

'But what if they call the police?'

She began rocking backwards and forwards.

'Then they call the police. Anyway, you have to deal with them sooner or later. They'll want to interview you, to find out where you've been all this time. Tell your mum not to call them until they've picked you up. And if I were you, I'd tell them you ran away.'

'But I'd never run away, they know that. I love my mum and dad.'

'So tell them the truth.'

Janet shot me a look of pure horror.

'OK! Say, you dreamed you were working in a big house as a servant and couldn't escape. If you say that you won't get picked up in a lie, and the cops'll search every house in the area looking for a paedophile ring,' I said. I purposely kept my tone airy in the hope my flippant remarks would stop Janet's hand shaking. All we needed now was for her to hit the wrong button on my mobile, and tell some stranger she'd returned from the dead.

'Here, let me.' I grabbed the phone, swiftly keying in the number.

It rang. I sat with my arm round her, our heads stuck to the earpiece.

'Hello, Mum, it's Janet. Where are you? Why did you leave me here at the manor on my own?'

There was a scream, someone began to sob loudly, and then a man's voice took over.

'Yes, yes, of course it's really me, Dad. Why? My Birthday? It's March 26. I have a sister, Cheryl, who's twenty-one. Yes, honestly. I don't know, Dad. I thought you'd gone without me. I don't understand, what's the matter? Why is Mum crying? Yes, just a minute.' She handed me the phone. 'He wants to talk to you.'

'Molly speaking.'

A voice said, 'I'm Janet's father. Can you describe her to me and what she is wearing?'

I did. I heard him talking to someone in the background and I could hear sobbing.

'Hallo,' I shouted.

Her dad's voice sounded again. 'I'm so sorry, young lady, what did you say your name was?'

'Molly.'

'Well, Molly, this is a bit of a shock, you know; I still can't believe it.' I didn't say anything, but I guessed Janet was going to get a stack of grief for the next year or so, her parents never letting her out of their sight. 'Is she all right?' he asked.

'She's fine, but why are you asking? And what did you say to her, she looks ever so confused?'

He ignored my question. 'Where did you find her?'

'I didn't. She came up to me in the garden,' I lied.

'What was she doing?'

'Looking for you; she said you were on the way to Burnham for a holiday.'

'*But that was two years ago*! She's been missing ever since. We'd given her up for dead!'

'No wonder she looks confused,' I replied innocently. Janet glared ferociously at me and it was all I could do not to giggle, despite feeling that the world had come to an end.

'Look, we're coming to get her, but I'll speak to the police first.'

'No!' I almost shouted it. '*Don't call the police*. Just come and get her and then speak to the police. If Janet really has been missing two years, the last thing she wants is the police bursting in and harassing her.'

There was a pause.

'You're quite right, I never thought. Questions can wait. We should be with you in about three hours. Will you stay with her till then?'

'No problem. We're staying overnight anyway.'

'Please put Janet on the phone again. *Are you sure it's her?* I won't believe it, neither will her mother, until we see her. I'll apologise in advance, but I think we're going to be phoning her every few minutes during the journey to make sure we're not dreaming. Please, *please* stay with her and don't let her out of your sight.'

I let Janet talk then. Strange, when I first saw her in the house, I thought she looked ordinary. Now, the longer she chatted to her parents the better she looked, as if she'd had a makeover; her face pink and her eyes sparkling with life as if someone had put drops in them.

***

The sun was warm. I sat with my back against the hot brick of the church wall, the narrow ribbon-like scar on the knuckles of my right hand just visible through my half-closed eyes. Surprisingly, there'd been no other scars, my legs and feet showing no sign of the trauma they'd suffered in the river – nothing, except this faint scar and the feeling of being tired to death, to remind me that it wasn't a dream.

Janet's parents had arrived as we finished eating and the first five minutes were pretty gross; there was so much wailing and crying, they even managed to upstage Mum. Then that miserable old sod, the manager bloke, who had apparently been interviewed by the police on numerous occasions after Janet disappeared, obligingly – I don't think – phoned them, so they came storming up the drive after all.

We listened to Janet telling her story a dozen times, exactly the way she and I had planned. She couldn't remember anything except this dream that she was in another century, working as a servant girl. No, she hadn't been harmed or raped. No, she hadn't been working in a brothel. No, she didn't do drugs. They had to believe her, what else could they do, except conclude she'd suffered temporary amnesia. Although, I had this sneaky feeling that they weren't as dumb as they looked and, by the time they'd finished interviewing everyone – including her cat – they would have decided Janet was lying and had really run away from home. Then she'd be sent to a psychiatrist to find out why. Still, whatever they really believed, her parents didn't care; they clutched a hand each, still dazed and trembling, hardly able to believe their luck in getting her back.

I don't know how Mum and Dad would have reacted if it had been me. Would they even have missed me?

They stayed the night, the police leaving at last, threatening more questions. Once they'd gone, the sneak of a manager became quite cheerful, actually offering to make tea and coffee *and* he provided biscuits. I guess living under a cloud of being chief suspect in a murder could make you a tad miserable.

'Dad, can we go to Blandford?' I asked after Janet's dad's car had disappeared out of the drive. I would see her again, and we planned to chat often once her new mobile was up and running. I knew we would stay friends and, when we could talk about the past, we would.

He looked surprised.

I shrugged. 'Well, I seen everything here and we've got to do something till dinner. You know Mum; she'll work all day just to spite us.'

Right on cue he frowned. This really bugs me. He knows I'm right, but he won't admit it – but we went to Blandford anyway.

The church wasn't where I remembered it. Tragically, there was nothing in the town I remotely recognised, except street names and the hill down into the market place.

'It was burned down in the late seventeenth century,' Dad explained, seeing my face crumple. 'There was nothing left. What were you looking for?'

'The church.'

We found it, but even that wasn't the same. I hurried to where I thought the grave would be but there was nothing there – all the tombs dating from the twentieth century.

There was a wooden seat by the church entrance. Disappointed, I flopped down on it. It wasn't fair, there had to be something. In the far corner of the neatly arranged lines of granite tombs, a woman bent over a mound of earth a bunch of flowers in her hands. She appeared to be praying. Dad, of course, being Dad, immediately disappeared to look round inside.

'Did you find what you wanted, Molly?' he said, when he eventually reappeared.

I shook my head. 'There's nothing really old here, Dad. Was the church burned as well?'

He nodded, and it was all I could do not to cry.

'I was chatting to the sexton. He says there's still an old graveyard. Will that do?'

I was so excited I had to stop myself hugging him again. I leapt to my feet. 'Do you know where?'

'No, but we can find it, we have tongues in our heads.'

It took us half an hour, most of that trying to park, coaches and cars whizzing non-stop up and down the High Street. Dad said it was a fine example of a Georgian town. Only I wasn't interested in Georgian I wanted Charles-ian.

We found the lane, narrower than when I last saw it a

219

couple of days ago. Now a tarmac road ran between garden walls that created a backdrop for flower borders, filled with hyacinths and daffodils; flowering shrubs on the verge of bursting into life under the warm April skies. Neatly edged front lawns enclosed elegant detached houses with sparkling windows, their original wooden frames replaced with modern double-glazing. But the hillside was as I remembered; windswept and unkempt, overlooking the valley. In the town, the unbroken façade of shops and offices had restricted any wind to a gentle breeze, except where it gusted round corners catching you unawares.

None of the gravestones were still standing, blown over by the gales of centuries and overgrown with grass and moss. I stared about me; there weren't many left, anyway.

'Why did you want to come here, Molly?'

I shrugged. 'I guess looking over the manor yesterday got me to wondering about them.'

'Who?'

'Sir Richard Blaisdale. Don't you remember, you told me about the Civil War.'

'But that family wouldn't have been buried here, Molly; they would have been buried in the family crypt, on one of their estates. That was the custom in those days.'

I knew that – but someone else was buried here. We strolled along the paths. My heart raced, beating so wildly I could hardly breathe. I was surprised Dad didn't notice. And I was muttering non-stop prayers under my breath, so fast and furious, it was a wonder the sheer weight of them didn't blast him off his feet. *If you let me find them, I promise I won't ever argue again.* But then Dad notices very little.

He stopped to peer down at a grave, scraping away the delicate brown seeds of the moss clinging to its stone surface, so he could read the faded inscription.

I kept going, heading for the topmost part of the hill;

the force of the wind whisking my hair into the snake-like strands of Medusa. Huddled behind a tree, I fished in my pocket for a hair-band, twisting my newly washed hair round and round into a knot and ramming my woollen hat on top. Richard had been right. At home, I used my hair as a shield to hide my thoughts from my parents but in the puritan world, every vestige of hair was tidied away, leaving each thought and expression exposed for judgement. No wonder faces from that era seem so wooden.

Still unable to bear the pain of memory, I lifted my face defiantly into the wind, which was roaring across the side of the hill, blustery in that infuriating way it has, and unable to make up its mind which way it should be travelling. I hunched my shoulders, my fists scrunched in my pockets for warmth. Up here, it still felt like winter. I swung round. Lower down the hill it was spring, with daffodils and dandelions glowing bright yellow.

It was there; I knew it would be … I just knew it. The stone had fallen and now lay at an angle on the ground, and the stone seat was cracked and broken. But it was there … three hundred and fifty years later. I sat down in a hurry, unable to catch my breath.

In loving memory of James Henry Blaisdale.
1606 – 1638
Beloved husband to Ann and father to Molly
He gave his life to save another.
Perished at sea April 1638
Also
Molly, beloved daughter
1633 – April 1648

Holding in her hands the gift of love, she came to us a stranger, belonging in our lives for a brief and precious moment: never to be forgotten.

The dirt of the centuries had almost obliterated the letters but I could still read them. I rubbed at the stone, slowly tracing each letter with my finger. It was the only clue I had that I was loved and I knew, without any doubt, that the mother had chosen the words, hoping one day I would see them.

I stared round at the daffodils, their delicate yellow shape a piercing reminder of the canopy above the box bed.

Then I began to cry, this great pool of misery welling up inside me; fifteen years' worth – no longer able to hold it back – painfully aware of an empty space in my life where love had dwelt for that brief, but precious moment. I had never cried in front of my parents. I had screamed and sworn, and banged doors, but never cried. Now, silent tears slid down my face and dripped onto my mobile, as I fumbled about trying to capture evidence of my happier life – a piercing pain in my chest as I thought of what I had lost.

'Molly?'

I rubbed my hand across my face, replacing my mobile in my pocket, but still the tears fell.

He came up the hill. 'I have never seen you cry. What is it? Is it about your swimming?'

I shook my head. In the distance I caught sight of a family of figures, while blue eyes full of love and concern pierced my heart. 'Why don't you love me, Dad?'

He sat down beside me on the stone seat and gave me his handkerchief. He didn't touch me. He didn't put his arms round me and rock my tears to silence as Ann Hampton had done, because he couldn't, he never had. But he did look a tad white around the gills, as though he'd just had a bad shock.

He was silent a few more minutes and I wondered if he had even heard what I said.

That's so typical of my dad. I ask something of earth-shattering importance and he ignores it. It's always been like that. Whatever you ask him, he takes ages to reply and, when he does, it's not a yes, no, possibly, or a maybe – it's a lecture about something quite different. Two days later, a bolt of lightning stuns you with the realisation that he did, after all, answer your question. But it makes me real mad that he can't be like other grown-ups and give you kiss and a straightforward answer.

'We do love you, Molly, indeed we do and it surprises me to think we have failed you so badly, as to leave you with the impression that you are unloved. We have fed and clothed you, provided you with a comfortable home, taken you on holidays – surely sufficient proof of caring parents.'

No dad, it isn't, I wanted to shout out. *Real parents sit their kids on their knees and read them a story, and play games, and wipe their tears when they fall down. And they don't find it impossible to say a kind word, without adding a criticism or showing disappointment.*

I kept silent, the words stuck in my throat, because something important was happening here. Dad and I were having a conversation. He was actually talking to me – and not about history. I kept my mouth shut.

'I have sometimes wondered whether your mother and I should not have had a family. We were both so very much involved in our careers. Unfortunately, a successful career almost always demands a sacrifice of some sort. Possibly a family has to be one of them. And, certainly, we have found raising a family very bewildering.' Dad continued.

'Bewildering?'

'Yes, bewildering. As small children you conformed to what we expected of you, but as teenagers …'

He stopped and I knew he was chewing on the word *teenager* because he simply hates modern slang, pompously clinging to outmoded speech where you never abbreviate anything.

'Your affect on our ordered world, as young people, has been nothing short of catastrophic. Order has descended into chaos.'

'Do you mean just me or Meg too?'

'Meg, too. Indeed, as the first child we suffered even more from this overwhelming sense of confusion. She certainly did not conform to an acceptable stereotype. The only difference between you is that she was silent, whereas you are noisy. That is why your mother retreats into the safety of her work.'

'Oh!' What else was there to say! And all this time I'd thought Meg a paragon of virtue. *Well done, Dad, for the first time in my life, I'm speechless.* I didn't agree with his little speech about Mum, though. He and Mum had always, "retreated into work", even when I was a baby; they just never remember it.

We sat silently, while I thought about things. You know – really thought – and gradually I began to close doors in my mind and, like a small child, take my first tentative step towards my future. Ann Hampton's words rang through my head. "Life is not made of daydreams, and we must deal with it as it comes."

I swung round somehow expecting her to be sitting there. She was right. Like it or not I was stuck with what I'd got, and it wasn't about to change because Dad had seen me crying. Still, it wasn't that long before I could get away and go to uni. I thought of school, my friends – the misfits – and Blue, who meant more to me than my own sister. And my swimming, beginning to understand that it was a substitute for the love I never had … and now, the love I had found and lost.

Poor Molly, she must have felt so desperately alone battling against things she couldn't change. If I was going to be different, I had to accept my life – especially the bits I couldn't change, like my family, for instance. Dad was okay, most of the time – except when Mum got at him, goading him into some unpleasant action. He meant well even if he was stuffy. Still, I'd survived so far surely I could put up with it a bit longer. Meg, well, perhaps one day she might be my friend, once she'd got over my spoiling her fun as a child, and having to stop home and look after me all the time. But Mum – I doubt I could ever like her. Hypercritical, she actually enjoys finding fault. In her eyes, I can't do anything right – ever. Grandma says, you don't choose your parents so you don't have to like them.

But I was lucky I'd been given a chance to choose my family. I closed my eyes, watching a parade of figures file past. A young man with fair hair fishing on a bridge; a chubby boy with sandy eyelashes, and a girl in a white cap who ran everywhere. Agnes, who could bandage hands quicker than lightning, and a tall woman with grey eyes full of love. They stared at me across three centuries of time. I ached inside, missing them so much it hurt.

But at least I now knew what I had to do. And, if I was going to change, I might as well make a start while I felt like it.

'Da-ad, you know that stuff we were talking about before?'

He frowned and I just knew what he was going to say. 'Stuff, Molly, what sort of word is stuff?'

He opened his mouth to say it – he really did – then closed it again. 'Yes, Molly, what?' he replied after a moment. *Way to go, Dad.*

'If it's okay with you, I thought I might study maths, biology, and I've got a choice between history and sociology at A-level.' Okay, so I had to change, but not the bit of me that delights in stirring Dad up a bit.

His face was a picture.

'And your swimming?' he said quietly.

'That hasn't changed, Dad, I still want to swim. You

will let me, won't you?'

Dad sighed. 'I suppose that means you will want to apply to Bath instead of one of the red-brick universities.'

'How do you know about Bath?' I asked gob-smacked.

'I did some research on the best facilities for swimmers, Bath came out top.'

That blew me apart – pieces scattered all over the graveyard – until I remembered that Dad never uttered a word unless he'd researched it first and made sure it was in the right tense.

'I discussed it with your mother. I believe that someone who undoubtedly has a gift should be allowed to pursue it, to discover if they have what it takes – if you will excuse the slang expression ...'

I'll excuse anything. Just keep talking, Dad.

'To reach the top – although I'd prefer to say, achieve your goal.'

DAD!

I began to pick up the bits and pieces of my body from the ground, wondering if Dad had been whisked off to a different point in time – like me. Dad as a cavalier, how cool would that be? I giggled, hastily changing it into a cough, remembering in time how huffy he gets when I laugh at him.

'I won't let you down, Dad.'

'I know you won't, Molly. I will tell your mother about our talk. She will be pleased.'

Oh no, she won't – but I didn't say it aloud. Despite this little talk, it wouldn't be long before she had a go at me. But I had to keep on trying, however much she goaded me; I owed it to Molly.

***

I got to swim in the finals after all, scraping through the

freestyle and one-hundred breaststroke by the skin of my teeth. But *was I tired*, and my times showed it. Coach didn't say anything; she couldn't despite my bad times, because it was me – no one else – standing on that podium to receive the gold medal.

I still had the two hundred to do, which was the last race but one in the afternoon – the Open Free, by tradition, taking the honours as the final race. I sat there feeling lost, miserable and exhausted. I was beginning to ask myself whether I could withdraw, rather than make a fool of myself and come last, when Ben appeared.

'Congrats and all that.' He hugged me and pushing his way in, sat down beside me.

'What are you doing here?' I stared at him in amazement.

'Watching you. You look awful, you sick or something?'

'*Thanks!* It's good to know who your friends are.'

He grinned and thumped me on the back. 'So?'

I shrugged. 'A bit tired, that's all. It's hot in here.'

I heard my race being called and, wearily, got up to go, stuffing my hair into my cap.

'Look Molly, I wondered if we could meet up in the hols?'

'Meet up? I thought you and Jan …'

'Jan – no way – that was first week nerves.'

What did Gran say about boys? *They're like buses; you wait for ages and ages and then two or three come along at once.* I smiled. He wasn't Richard – he never could be. No one could. But he might become a good friend. 'Don't get your hopes up. You'll change your mind when I come in last.'

'Even if you do, there's always another race. By the way, I've already met your Mum – she's great.'

Yuck!

I made my way towards the blocks and took my place in lane number three. The way the system works, if swimmers swim to their entry time, the result should be an arrowhead with lane number four leading.

But that wasn't going to happen, today. I might have lost everything else, but I'd still got my swimming and I was bloody-well going to be the best. I felt the surge of adrenaline. Quickly, I adjusted my goggles and took my stance, glancing out of the corner of my eye towards the girl in lane four who I was going to beat. Four lengths – *nothing to it!* The buzzer sounded and I dived in.

Excerpt from

Melt Down

The long-awaited sequel to Running
Available 2012

Scott's heart thumped uncontrollably, his breath suspended; the words emerging through his headset burned a hole in his brain. The destruction of Europe – what did they mean? And why would anyone say such things unless they were joking – except, the voices didn't sound like they were joking.

Puzzled, he stared through the wall of heavy plate glass seeking the speaker. Somehow wires had become crossed with him a reluctant witness to murder and mayhem, for that's what was being planned. The view was staggering. The vast auditorium formed a crater-like semi-circle extending upwards over three floors, with delegates seated in rows behind curved swathes of polished wood, liberally sprinkled with white-printed name boards, microphones and plastic water bottles. No pecking-order in the seating other than the obvious; Afghanistan at one end, Zimbabwe the other.

Peering down on them from the second floor, like over-anxious parents, was a galaxy of glass-fronted booths. Soundproof, these were the realm of the translator, an army of worker bees, whose job it was to provide a fluent and accurate account of what was being said on the ground floor, no matter what language it was said in. Wired for sound, the little rooms were viewing posts of the most powerful place on earth – the General Assembly of the United Nations.

Scott stared at the set of ear-phones, plugged into the armrest on his seat, as if they were about to explode. Yet, there was nothing odd about them. A neatly packaged set, identical to those handed out by a cheerful stewardess, whenever you embarked on a long-haul flight, although Scott had not yet undergone this particular experience. He'd only ever been on one commercial flight in his life and there had been no head-set on that, the flight from Exeter to Geneva too short. He peered down at the armrest, the keypad offering a bewildering array of options.

The third floor, from where Scott was watching events, had been delegated for private meetings and, automatically, Scott had plugged in the headset in the hope of listening to the debate. It had to be something serious; the woman-speaker very heated and her body-language that of someone determined to win the argument.

Except, it wasn't a translation of the debate he was listening to. It was someone plotting a revolution. Scott clamped the headphones back on determined not to miss a word of the illicit conversation.

'I tire of these prancing lunatics in Europe; their devotion to democracy I find frustrating. How long?'

The language was English. Had it been any other it would have passed straight over Scott's head, for languages were definitely his worst subject at school.

'Lotil Oil continues to resist but they will concede – there is no alternative.'

The voices were clear, distinct, their intention unmistakeable – especially their opening sentence. That was the stuff of nightmares.

'The timetable for Europe's descent into chaos must be moved up.'

And the reply. 'Remember, Europe is not the Middle East; you cannot expect civil unrest to take place in a day, with regime change following in a week. But it *will* happen – and within a year – that I promise you.'

The words sounded theatrical; the voices accented as if English was not their first language, rather one they had adopted. And while one came over the airwaves as a menacing growl, the terse style of someone in authority used to being obeyed, the other seemed more hesitant, almost gentle – patient sounding. And very scary.

It had to be a joke, didn't it? Scot's eyes flicked round the semi-circle of glass. Most rooms were occupied; meetings taking place in full view, people seated around a boardroom table talking among themselves – no one on the phone.

'A small country with an even smaller army. The perfect starting place. If we only achieve a few protesters onto the streets, we will bus in a crowd from Germany. A couple of hundred should be enough to create a little delicate mayhem. A few rounds of live ammunition will do the rest. They're a stupid people, heroic. A mounting death toll will fire even the most cowardly into action.'

Murder and mayhem. *Who was it? And where did it come from?* Scott leaned against the heavy-set window, craning his head to bring all the little booths into view.

'You have obviously warned them of the penalty of delay.'

'Naturally.' The softly-spoken syllables slithered their way into the airwaves. Scott shivered.

'A small explosion might hurry them along.' The words loudly spoken, as if to off-set the cracking on the line, came across as a statement not a request.

'That would prove rather difficult. Security on oil rigs is very tight.'

The conversation had to be taking place within the building, right? Scott stared down at the row of knobs built into the arm rest. They were only for internal use, so where had the hiccup occurred.

Out of the corner of his eye, Scott caught a movement as overhead beam of light picked up an answering sparkle from a watch. A man was seated in the booth on the opposite corner, a phone pressed to his ear. How come? He'd passed at least a dozen notices, on the way up from the underground car park, advising that mobile phones didn't work in the building.

He glanced over his shoulder, catching sight of a telephone receiver tucked away on a narrow shelf next to the boardroom table. So that was it. Each of the viewing stations had access to an outside line. And somewhere it had become connected to the internal system. So how many more people were listening in?

'Naturally, in every ointment there is a fly. Masterson – I understand he's speaking next. How sad that he survived. The Dutch are so unbelievably capable – it's disheartening. We need him out of the way before ...'

Scott gasped and jerked backwards at the sound of his father's name.

As if he had caught the sound, the line was abruptly cut. The man in the booth opposite looked up scouring the room and his razor-sharp glance homed in on Scott.